CAVES
OF
TROLAN

BY JAMES ROLLIN PECK

 FriesenPress

Suite 300 - 990 Fort St
Victoria, BC, V8V 3K2
Canada

www.friesenpress.com

ISBN
978-1-5255-4838-3 (Hardcover)
978-1-5255-4839-0 (Paperback)
978-1-5255-4840-6 (eBook)

1. FICTION, HISTORICAL

Distributed to the trade by The Ingram Book Company

CHAPTER 1

As the light dissipated over the tangerine sky, the moon started to glow. The giant redwood trees swayed in unison, orchestrated by the evening breeze. They were towering, majestic, powerful.

Barook gazed in wonderment at the castle. She was beautiful, and he had designed her. He was proud to be the man who created and built the most awe-inspiring castle in all the known lands. The task had taken ten years; the best ten years of his illustrious career. Now the last of the huge blocks were in place and finely polished, and the final touches were being made. Barook was tingling with excitement.

The castle sat halfway up the mountain, where the cliff had a natural plateau. High above and behind was the snow-covered peak. His favourite part of the castle was the expansive, solid, red doors. Standing fifty-feet high, twenty-feet wide and ten-inches thick, they curved at the top to form a peak. Barook had personally chosen the great redwood the doors were carved from, and they had been polished and hand rubbed until they shone. Ten men had carved the great doors, labouring with love for over a year. The intricate artwork was a depiction of all the village people and the king they loved. It told the history of the inhabitants of Trolan; people who held peace above all and had prospered because no person would harm another. Their king so loved his people that he designed laws to protect every man, woman and child. The people needed nothing; the fields were always filled with a bountiful harvest and the storage bins were full. Every man who had a family also had a home. The story would take hours to read through, but Barook knew it well.

Truly magnificent, Barook thought. It was too bad nobody would see them. Outside the doors was a huge balcony and courtyard. A telescope had been permanently mounted near the edge to improve the view. Past the balcony was a sheer drop to the ocean below. Barook wasn't sure how far down it was, but he knew the bodies of men that had fallen were never retrieved, as the surf pounded the cliffs below. He shuddered at the thought; it was terrible for any man to die. From the edge of the balcony one could see the great ocean and wonder if there was another land on the horizon.

He smiled at the irony of having a front door and no road that led to it. Roads would have been difficult to build on the side of a cliff and weren't needed anyway; the caves that led from the castle to the base of the cliff were perfect roadways. They had been formed thousands of years ago when the now-dormant volcano roared with life. As it erupted and poured lava into the ocean, the steam had left caves when the molten rock cooled, trapping the air and seawater. The mountain was riddled with the caves—so many that most had never been explored.

Barook walked from the balcony back through the giant red doors and into the grand entry. The walls were blocks of lava that had each been cut and polished by hand. The overhead windows let in enough light to make the walls look like they glowed. Although the decor was simple, the style of the artwork and tapestries was impeccable.

Before Barook was the grand stairway. He was still amazed that he had figured out a way to build it. The stairs seemed as if they were standing alone, with no supports to hold them up. Very clever, and quite simple, really. He had also used the giant redwood for his signature stairs, which were curved at the bottom, measuring twelve feet across and rising twenty feet. As they ascended, they drew narrower, to a width of six feet. Each stair had a tread but no riser; therefore, the view of the solarium would not be interrupted as you climbed. From the landing at the top Barook could look back over the garden that was built inside the castle walls.

The king and queen had always loved the trees and fish ponds, so Barook knew they would be pleased. He moved up six more stairs to an open hall, which also appeared to be standing without support. He turned left and took twenty steps, counting as his footsteps echoed on the red oak floors to a shorter hall that overlooked the garden and led to the king's chambers.

All the doors of the castle were glimmering redwood with matching artistic trim, but only the king and queen's quarters had double doors, also richly carved. The king's doors were closed as Barook approached. He hesitated then knocked. He smirked to himself. Why had he knocked? He knew no one would arrive at the castle until the next day at dawn. That was when the people who were unable to help in the construction would be able to serve in maintaining it. Any of the Trolan people would be honoured and feel most fortunate to be able to serve the royal couple. Tomorrow they would prepare to receive the king and queen.

Barook opened the doors and let them swing wide. A king-sized, four-post bed with a tapestry canopy was centered in the room. The gleaming black posts almost disappeared against the black-lava walls surrounding it. Against the far wall a large window overlooked the city far below and the ocean in the distance. He smiled and thought back to when it was just a village. Now it seemed to spread out almost as far as he could see, and although there were many people, they were dispersed enough that the forests had not been damaged. Even from up here he was amazed by the size of the giant trees.

"The king is truly wise," he said aloud. "I'm always impressed with the way he can keep his kingdom beautiful and his subjects happy."

"Barook, Barook!" he heard someone call.

"Is that you, Bastian? I'm up here in the king's chambers."

As Barook re-entered the hall, a stout, barrel-chested man approached. "Barook, old friend. What are you doing here?" The man's face was round and his cheeks were puffy. His lips barely moved when he talked.

"I was just having one more look around before our guests arrive. Just wanted her to myself one more time," Barook explained.

"Yes, sir, know watcha' mean." Bastian's hands were in his pockets and he was rocking on his toes. "I want to check the water and heating, make sure everything works. I don't want to disappoint the king, ya know."

Barook wondered how Bastian made it up the stairs.

"How did you know it was me in here when you called?" Barook queried.

"You always leave the door open." Bastian drawled. "Besides, I knew you couldn't resist one more look at your masterpiece."

"No, no, not my masterpiece, Bastian, but the work of the greatest builders in the land and worthy of a great ruler." Barook raised his arms to shoulder height. "You, Bastian, are the man responsible for bringing my plans to life. You and your men who carved these rocks from the mountain to build the foundations. Who brought the water with your steam-powered pumps and heated the castle with air ducts. Mine was a dream, but yours was a purpose."

He tapped his stout friend on the shoulder and smiled. "Let's go check out the water, shall we?"

Back down the stairs Bastian puffed, waddled and wheezed, but he maintained a steady pace. They walked past the library and down the hall to the kitchen. Bastian leaned heavily on the counter and caught his breath.

"Don't ya hate gettin old? When I was younger, I could carry this body all day. Now I can hardly lift my butt." Bastian laughed long and hard at his own joke.

Barook smiled, somewhat unamused.

Bastian waddled over to the sink and turned a handle beside a faucet. Out of the faucet came cold, clear water. "Best damn idea I've seen, you designing that holding tank for the water. The hot works too. Damn good idea." Bastian grinned.

"Thank you, my friend. Shall we proceed to the basement to check the pumps?" Barook led the way, thinking about the young maidens who would be working in this kitchen tomorrow. It was designed for many people to work in different areas of the room at one time without running into each other. The mountain had provided well for Barook, as she had offered the steam vents that rose from deep within the volcano. The steam made everything work, and people could cook with it. Beside each steam oven was a grill, a work counter and a sink, and these cooking stations surrounded a large round workstation in the middle of the room that was mounted on a swivel base. This made it easier to access the supplies stored inside it from any work station. On the far wall was a large stone warming station with steam pipes running through it; the food could be kept hot for a long time with this. There was another doorway that led to the basement. This was one of five kitchens located throughout the castle and was also the main preparation area.

Bastian grabbed his own butt with both hands and picked himself up on to his toes. He puffed out his cheeks and waddled over to the door. Just before he got there, he slapped his hand down upon his knees and burst into laughter. Barook couldn't help but chuckle over Bastian's hysterical belly laugh.

There was no natural light in the staircase so Barook relied on the handrail until his eyes focussed in the dim light coming from a few small windows in the front wall in the basement. At the bottom of the stairs was the entry chamber from the caves. "Bastian, I think we need more light down here. We wouldn't want the royal family to get hurt before they reach the castle," Barook surmised.

The chamber was large; the ceilings were thirty-feet high and the room was sixty-feet across. There were unlit lanterns on the walls and five doors, each leading to different areas. One led to a big cold room for storing perishable goods. Barook swung the door open and peered inside. Bastian grabbed a lantern and walked inside, ahead of Barook, who walked in and placed his hand on the centre wall.

"The water storage bins on the other side of the wall keep it quite cool in here, don't they?" Bastian smiled.

"Yes, your men did a wonderful job of keeping the water circulating," Barook replied.

Around the three outside walls were three separate storage bins, each set slightly higher than the next. With a series of ducts, the water moved over rough rocks, thus aerating the water. A large steam pump kept fresh water pouring into the first tank, and when full it flowed to the second tank and then to the third. The overflow from the third tank flowed to the tank that held water for the gardens and fish ponds. From here, the water was pumped up to larger tanks above the castle.

The two men looked at each other and smiled, both very proud.

They left the room and Bastian opened the second door and looked up a long, dark stairway that led up into the mountain, to the top of the water storage tanks.

"We don't need to check the storage tanks." He looked back to Barook. "But we should check the pump."

"I agree. Lead the way," Barook replied.

The third door, in the centre of the wall, led to the largest mechanical room in the castle. As Bastian opened the door, he could hear the "hiss, pop, hiss, pop" of the steam-powered pump that brought the water. As a result of the positioning of the storage tanks, the water flowed down to the castle with centrifugal force and fed each floor separately so there would not be a shortage of water.

"It seems incredibly hot in here because of the steam. Perhaps we should have run more venting into this room," Barook mumbled, almost to himself.

Bastian was sweating profusely by now. His chubby face was red, and his dirty-blonde hair was damp. He pulled out a dingy white rag from his pocket and wiped his face. The piston popped back and forth, turning a large wooden wheel connecting to another arm to the pump. The steam was sent to the piston by a long pipe from the Calder that collected the steam. Barook marvelled at the simple steam pump and made a mental note to meet the person who designed and built it. That would mean another long trip to the northern tip of the island to the village of the miners.

Hands clasped in front of them and heads slightly tilted, the men watched the pumps as the sweat beaded on their foreheads.

"Well, I'm out of here," Bastian wheezed. "Gotta get home, gotta feed the fire." He slapped his protruding belly. "All this walking could make a man go skinny." Bastian belly-laughed again, poking his chubby finger into his friend's side.

Barook winced from the sheer weight. He didn't have the padding on his thinner yet taller frame. Although he was twice Bastian's age, he knew he could at least walk up and down the stairs without panting.

"Yes, I too must be going. I have another task to complete before everyone arrives tomorrow," Barook stated. "However, I am planning on spending the night. I will bed down in one of the servant's quarters."

"Not me, gotta get home. I've got a wife and I can't disappoint her, and I can't miss dinner." Half bent over and slapping his knee, Bastian waddled away. Barook followed Bastian to the chamber to the caves. Bastian waved his chubby hand and headed for the stairs, slowly ascending while holding the rail. As Bastian closed the door to the lower chamber, Barook smiled and turned, looking up at the light coming from the kitchen.

He jogged to the top, walked through the kitchen and then down the hall and past the den. He stopped under the great staircase to look over the solarium. In front of him was a path that led to a bridge and onto a gazebo in the center of the garden. It was surrounded by a moat, fed by a waterfall off the far wall. There were paths through the gardens and around the moat that led to the waterfall. Barook noticed the birds were starting to get used to their new surroundings. The men and women had built an place of tropical bliss for the enjoyment of the royal family.

He turned and headed to the servant's quarters. He would return when the moon was overhead.

CHAPTER 2

There was a knock on the open door. "Captain Tragar?"

"Yes, what is it, lieutenant?"

"Captain we've come across an island and it appears to be inhabited." The lieutenant was stiff as he reported.

"I'll come up shortly. Set anchor and wait."

"Yes, sir, very good, sir." The lieutenant turned and walked out, closing the door behind him.

The commander was iron-tough, and his crew knew not to disappoint him. He got up and walked over to the port window. He stared out for a moment and then headed for the bridge.

"Commander on deck." The first officer bellowed.

"Lieutenant, set a course to navigate the island," the captain's baritone voice boomed.

"Yes, sir. Let's go, men, set sail!" the lieutenant shouted as he and the men scrambled to work.

The crew hesitated only briefly, then reset the sails they had taken down only moments earlier. The ship was large; 212 feet in length, with three masts and thirty-five sails, and she could travel at 17 knots with a good wind.

"Slowly, lieutenant, I want to see all of this island," droned the captain.

Lazily, the ship navigated around the island. The captain wondered why he had not seen this island before. He pulled out his telescope and surveyed the land. Had the storm from the previous ten days sent them this far off course? The ship sailed around the first and oldest volcano, which had formed the island thousands of years ago. The dormant peak was no longer the tower it once was. He could tell from here that parts of it had been mined away.

Quietly, the ship cut through the water. Past the volcano in the valley was a heavily treed forest. He was struck by the size of the majestic trees. The shore was lined with a seemingly endless beach, which varied in depth from fifty to a couple-hundred feet. The shoreline was pocked marked with small islands, hundreds of them in varying sizes. The water between the shore and the main island was shallow. There were a few sheltered coves as they went along, but they couldn't see any inhabitants anywhere near the shoreline, which puzzled him. There was an occasional rocky outcrop, and they could see lights in the distance that stretched the entire length of the island. They came across signs of old reef about a hundred feet offshore, but they were sailing at a safe enough distance from the island that the reef presented no danger.

"Lieutenant, check our bearings. I want to know exactly where we are."

Commander's log:

I have come across an island unknown to me. We have been sailing around it for 8 hours now and have completed only half our exploration. The island has the remnants of two volcanos, one at each end, with a heavily wooded valley in between. Although we have not seen any inhabitants, I am convinced they do exist. On our first encounter with the island we have seen evidence of roads and mining activity. We will complete our navigation before we land to explore the interior of the island.

After rounding the northern tip of the island, the topography changed drastically. Replacing the valleys and rolling hills were sheer cliffs that rose thousands of feet into the air, dropping directly into the pounding surf at the base. As far as they could see from here, there were no beaches or openings in the cliff. This side of the island was completely inaccessible and uninhabitable. As darkness closed in, Tragar decided to set anchor where he knew they were safe from being observed. He would wait for the morning so he could see if this side of the island offered a secure landing site. They had travelled for two hours since their course turned them south.

Almost thirty-six hours had past since the crew first spotted the landmass, and the entire route they had taken was up against the cliffs. This side of the island was a large arch that offered only one port that was inhabited, and it was very isolated; almost four hours from the southern tip of the island. The commander returned to the aft deck as the ship rounded the corner of the smaller volcano. Although this volcano did not have the size of the larger volcano, the cliffs were still sheer— straight up out of the ocean to an impressive height. They came across a narrow passage between two islands and could see there were inhabitants. The second small island seemed to be an extension of the main island.

As they sailed around it, they could see the city they had glimpsed on the other side of the island, perched on a cliff about fifty feet above the sandy shoreline. The cliff extended from the city all the way to the base of the cliffs.

"Commander, look!" shouted the first officer, pointing toward the top the mountain. "Look at that castle," he gasped. "It's black"

The commander was stunned. He pulled out his telescope and looked up at the castle. "Continue on. I want to go to the nearest beach, out of sight of the inhabitants. Call me when we get there. I'll be in my quarters."

Tragar turned away from the saluting officer and headed to the rear of the ship. Once the captain had left, the first officer returned to his watch. He sailed about another twenty minutes until he came upon an area meeting the captain's requirements. He turned his watch over to a junior officer and headed for the captain's quarters. The older first officer rapped his knuckles on the solid wooden door and waited for a reply. Captain Tragar opened the door, ready to assume control of the bridge.

"Captain, I believe this landing site is most suitable to your needs, sir."

"Drop anchor, we're going ashore," Tragar ordered, as they walked across the deck.

"It will be dark soon. Should we wait until morning, sir?"

"No, I want to go in under the cover of dark so I can have a look around."

The lieutenant turned and yelled, "Prepare the longboat, party of five going ashore!"

"Lieutenant, take the ship out to deeper water. We have a good moon tonight. We will be able to see alright, but I want to be out of sight from any natives. Return for us here two hours before dawn. If we don't return, leave before you are spotted and return to Lakar. Tell the king what you have seen."

"Aye, sir."

"Let's go, men, move along." The lieutenant cupped both hands around his mouth to emphasize his point. "Good luck, sir, we will see you in nine hours." He stood rigidly.

As darkness dropped over the horizon, the longboat eased into the calm water. The commander sat facing forward at the bow while four oarsmen rowed for shore.

"Lift anchor. We're moving out." The lieutenant's voice echoed in the background.

As the longboat sliced silently through the calm water, the moon was much brighter now. The commander looked up at the great castle and could see no lights. Although they were now quite a distance from the mountain, he couldn't see any sign of activity. Within a few minutes the longboat pierced the sandy shore at the base of a smaller mountain on the other side of the village they had seen earlier. He wondered why he hadn't noticed it on the first pass of the island but thought it was because of the darkness of the castle blending into the background of the mountain. He wanted to land closer to the base of the castle, but the sheer cliffs and treacherous surf made that impossible. No matter, he thought. He had plenty of time to look around.

The four oarsman dragged the longboat ashore and then cut branches to disguise it. Once the boat was well hidden, the commander had the men search up and down the shoreline looking for paths into the forest while he stared up at the castle.

The mirror-black behemoth sat perched on the end of a sheer, walled mountain. He estimated the height at two thousand feet. The mountain itself ran into the distance without any sign of a reprieve from the cliff. He could see only the side of the castle from here, but it looked deserted. He saw no lights, no sign of activity, nothing. This whole island seemed quiet. The trees, even at the shoreline, were huge. There were signs of logging in the area but the trees had been harvested in a very specific way; they were cut down no closer than a hundred feet apart. Even at that, one of these massive trees could surely frame a small ship. Finally, one of the men signalled that he had found a large main roadway leading straight into the middle of the forest.

"Follow in single file, one man every fifteen paces. Stay low and close to the edge of the road. Watch for signals, and if anyone is spotted, I will personally kill them. Is that clear?" Tragar tightened his eyes at the men.

Everyone nodded vigorously.

The road led around the base of the cliff but soon started to head away from the castle. The commander signalled that they were changing to another, smaller road in order to double back and keep the castle in sight. They crept silently along the roadway. Suddenly, the commander heard voices and signalled his men off to the side. They quickly disappeared into the forest behind the large redwoods.

Moments later, a small group of men approached from up the road. They joked and laughed, dancing along like kids. They were led by a short fat man who was not dancing—he was wheezing and panting.

"Bastian, I didn't think we could do it," one man said.

He got no reply, and another man threw in, "What he means is, we didn't think you could do it."

The entire group burst into laughter and passed a flask amongst them.

"You get to meet the Big Guy tomorrow, don't you, old man?" his young apprentice asked.

"I'm not sure he would appreciate being called Big Guy," Bastian wheezed out.

"Your going to piss your pants when you meet him," another joked.

"You'll never know, will ya, rookie?" Bastian grinned.

There was a collective "Oooo" from the group, who then broke into laughter.

When the men had passed, the commander signalled his own men to continue down the road with the same rules. About another twenty minutes along, they came to a clearing. Some quick recognisance of the area revealed four roadways. The commander chose the path that seemed to go toward the castle, although from here he still couldn't see any up to the fortress. The path doubled back toward the cliffs but didn't climb any great altitude.

At this rate, we will end up well below the castle, he thought. He followed the path another twenty-five minutes and it began to narrow. The farther they went, the narrower the path became until they came upon another clearing at the top of a small cliff about a hundred feet above the beach.

The commander sat down on a long log that had been laid down, which offered a stunning view of the sunset. Fortunately, he thought, no one is here tonight. He looked out into the distance. He could only see his ship on the horizon because he knew it was there. He watched her for about three minutes before he turned to the castle on his left.

"How do I get there?" he said, aloud this time. "Where is the road?" He threw up his hands and then sat silently for the next few minutes peering through his telescope. He had been gone for almost four hours. He had another two hours before he had to return. He figured he could reach the shore within two hours of that if they scaled down the cliff they were currently standing on.

"Let's go. The road is here somewhere, and I want to find it."

The men walked cautiously behind the commander. Back down the path, the commander quickened his pace until he reached the field. Three more paths; he couldn't afford to make another mistake. He chose the most beaten path toward the base of the castle. He could not walk for more than a half hour before he would have to return. With a bit less caution, they pushed on up the hill. After another twenty minutes, he had reached the top of the hill that overlooked the base of the cliff. He could see where the path appeared to end at the base of the mountain. At the base of the cliff were huge, cavernous openings. Still, even with a better view of the castle, he could see no roads.

"Alright, men, five minutes' rest, then we will have to return." None of the men said a word and the commander stared at the castle. Without incident, the five weary men returned to the boat still hidden at the beach. They could see the great ship returning for them, and they wanted rest. First they would have to row, and they knew the captain wasn't going to go back slowly.

"Prepare to receive the longboat!" the lieutenant yelled. He was refreshed after having a great sleep in the captain's quarters.

As the boat was raised, the captain bellowed across the deck, "Set sails. I want to be out of sight by dawn."

He approached the lieutenant, who was standing at the helm, "I'm going to rest now. Set sail for home, fastest possible speed. Have the four oarsmen clean that longboat before they rest. Give them one flask of wine then six hours' sleep. I want them ready for the next watch."

"Yes, sir. You heard him, men, get that boat cleaned." He pointed at the longboat and thrust his right fist from his chest in salute. The captain went to his cabin for the rest his body desperately needed.

With him out of sight, the lieutenant assigned four other men to clean the longboat. He took the four that had accompanied the captain, and with the temptation of a flask of wine, he asked to be told everything they had seen.

"I seen the captain was pretty upset about not being able to find a road to that castle," one of the men started.

CHAPTER 3

When Barook awoke, the castle was bubbling with activity. People were running back and forth in the hallway outside his door. He could hear them talking but couldn't make out what they were saying.

"Oh my gosh, I've overslept, oh my gosh." He rose and quickly fumbled for his pants. Boy, I hope nobody comes in here, he thought as he looked at himself in the mirror. He wasn't the best-looking specimen— probably why he wasn't married—but he had the brains, and he was needed. He combed back his longish grey hair and headed for a nice bath.

As he made his entrance into the hallway, he came across Elisiah, the king's best friend and confidant. "Elisiah, welcome to the new home of the royal family. Everything going well, I trust?"

"Wonderfully, Barook. Thank you. You truly have created an incredible palace here. You are a master," the tall, broad-shouldered man replied, bending slightly in respect to his friend.

Barook was a bit embarrassed by the sentiment expressed by the king's most trusted man. "Thank you, Elisiah, you are most kind. But I can only receive a small amount of credit, as it was the people who worked feverishly that should be proud of what they have accomplished here."

"The royal family will arrive at noon; that's about two hours from now, so please make sure the lanterns in the lower hall are bright," Elisiah requested. "They will be accompanied by Marta and Kataan, the village elders."

Barook could only grin.

Elisiah went through his list of events for the day. He stared blankly down over the garden as he recited, "I will receive King Nikodym, Queen

Nateer and Prince Lavar. I will introduce you to them at that point. We will have a short tour and then the feast to open the ceremonies. Then dancing and entertainment." He turned his attention back to Barook. "Please have the musicians play soft music during the feast," he asked.

Although it was not Barooks job to tend to the musicians, he would do it because Elisiah had asked him to.

In the village below, the king was walking amongst the people, led by a procession of men and women singing and dancing. There was a real excitement in the air as they made their way through the city. The royal family was very popular amongst the people because they would not ask a person to do something that they themselves would not do. Many times, against the wishes of his best friend, the king could be found in the fields toiling with the farmers. He had picked iron ore from the ground with the miners and he had cast nets and harvested with the fisherman. He showed pride in every man.

Slowly, the royal family and accompanying guests made their way down the roads to the caves far below the castle, which could be found all around the base of the volcano. Many of them were used to store goods, but the group approached the ones that led to the castle. When they reached the hill that the Lakar commander had stood on earlier that morning, the king also paused and looked up at the great black castle. Perched almost at the top of the mountain, it was perfectly fortified, although the king did not yet know why. The only way to get to the castle was through the caves, as the walls around it were just to steep to build a road.

The party approached the base of the mountain about thirty minutes later. The ocean was calm today near the caves. From here, they would go by oxen-drawn carriage inside the caverns that had been widened by the miners. A cool breeze flowed through the caves, fed by ventilation shafts. Air was also forced in by a large fan in the middle of the journey, run by a small water wheel and piped down from the castle.

Lanterns arranged on each side about fifty feet apart provided adequate lighting. About twenty minutes from the royal families' new home, the cavern widened to twenty-feet wide and twenty-feet high. The king noticed where the cavern had been diverted and joined to another to keep the grade of the climb manageable. King Nikodym was so proud of his people.

Those waiting patiently for the family above were ready. The feast was being prepared and the aroma filled the entire castle, as well as the caverns below.

"Barook, I want you to be with me when we greet the king," Elisiah stated, putting his hand on the man's shoulder. "The king has been very patient in staying away until the castle has been completed. When he sees it, he will want to meet the man responsible for its construction."

"Then he will want to meet Bastian." Barook smiled.

"He will meet Bastian later this evening," replied Elisiah. "The king has only seen the plans, but they do not do justice to this." He held his hand out, panning the area.

Finally, the king's party could be heard approaching. Elisiah was ready but Barook was not so sure. He had only met the king once, when he was consulted to design the castle. His hands shook badly, and his palms were sweaty. He was almost overcome.

The oxen-drawn carriage slowly pulled to a halt. The trip through the caverns had been long. Barook made a mental note to talk to Bastian about a more efficient way to move people up and down the mountain. As he gazed upon the king, Barooks mind slowly emptied.

One of the men opened the carriage door and offered a hand to the queen. The full-figured lady graciously accepted his hand and smiled at the young man as she stepped down. Queen Nateer was lovely; not overly beautiful, but she had a warmness about her smile. Black hair, warm blue eyes and rosy cheeks. Probably from the tight formal dress she was wearing, Barook thought.

The young guard strode beside the queen to make room for Prince Lavar, who was now standing in the carriage waiting his turn to step down. The young prince paused and gazed around the large, open cavern dug deep into the mountain. He took a deep breath before stepping down to stand beside his mother. Although Lavar was still in his teens, he was a tall, strapping young man. Standing six feet, he was a whole head taller than his mother.

Now Barook's attention was solely on the king. Barook started to shake again, and his hands began to sweat. The king looked over to Elisiah and smiled. Placing his hand on the rail of the carriage and pushing down, the king stood. Barook noticed that he too was a big man, much taller than his son. Barook guessed his weight to be over two hundred and fifty pounds. The buggy shook as the king stepped down and with four long strides was at the side of his queen.

Elisiah knelt to the royal couple. Barook hadn't noticed, being transfixed on the king's size. Elisiah discreetly tapped on Barooks pant leg. Barook, now slightly embarrassed and still shaking, bowed awkwardly toward the king and knelt.

The king nodded, and Elisiah and Barook stood. The king looked over at Barook and smiled. Barook was trying to avoid eye contact, which he knew would bring more embarrassment. How could this have happened? he thought.

Elisiah raised both hands to shoulder height and spoke aloud. "Your Majesties, welcome to the great black castle. The people of Trolan have laboured for ten years to build a magnificent home for your family to rule over this land. We have done this with the greatest of love and respect. And now I would like to present to you … Barook, the man who designed the home you will now tour and share."

The king motioned for Barook to step forward, but his feet would not move. Barook was embarrassed again and he could feel his cheeks flush. After a few seconds' hesitation, Barooks feet moved, slowly, step by step, until he was standing in front at the king and looking directly into his chest.

The king was still smiling, which brought a slight smile to Barook when he looked up. The king offered his right hand, and Barooks hand was dwarfed by the giant hand of the king. He shook vigorously to compensate for the size difference.

"So, Barook, I have been told you are the finest architect on the island. I have been looking forward to seeing the inside of this magnificent fortress I have only seen from below. Please be my guide." The king's voice was not what Barook expected; it was deep but not loud.

"King Nikodym, I have so wanted to meet you. I have only been able to admire you from afar, but I hope the castle will reflect how all Trolans feel. I would be honoured to show you around." Barook gazed over at the queen and turned, outstretching his arm to lead to the staircase.

"From here," Barook said, "we go up the stairs to another chamber." Barook led as the king, queen, Prince Lavar and Elisiah started up the long first set of stairs to the room with five doors. The door swung open, and instantly the aroma coming from the kitchen was like a wall.

Barook himself weakened as the enticing smell surrounded him and filled his nostrils.

The king lifted his head and sniffed twice, smiling even wider. The aroma was wonderful, and his palate began to water slightly. Barook waited for the rest of the party to enter and absorb the smells of the kitchen.

"This room," Barook explained, "Was the main artery of the caves under the castle. Each of these doors leads to an essential part of the castle. Shall I explain or would you like the brief tour?"

"How long is the short tour?" the king requested.

"For the entire castle, about an hour, your majesty," Elisiah cut in.

"I don't think I can last that long if the whole place smells like that kitchen." The king chuckled. "Better give us the quick tour now. We'll have plenty of time to explore it."

"Then it's up to the kitchen to start." Barook led again. In the kitchen, the king and queen nodded appreciably as they looked over the young maidens preparing food, who fell measurably quieter when they noticed the royals. There was only the bubbling of the pots and frying food. The staff all bowed and curtseyed.

The king spread out his hand and said, "Welcome, and thank you for preparing what I'm sure will be a grand meal. Please, carry on." He led the parade out of the kitchen and into the hall; he didn't want to distract the young ladies any longer than necessary. Barook was the last one out, and he scurried a bit to get to the king, who was spending considerable time examining the walls and floors. By the time the king was ready to move on, Barook was standing by the large double doors that led to the library.

"Fantastic," the king said. "The walls are beautiful. Look at the fine craftsmanship." He rubbed his hand along the black, glass-like walls. "Nateer, you haven't said a word, my love. Tell me what you think," King Nikodym asked.

The queen walked over and took him by the hand. "I've only seen the kitchen, Hikaru. Ask me later," she replied softly. Only the queen and Elisiah would ever call the king Hikaru, but that was his given name, and he liked it when his friends used to call him that. Now he was always "King Nikodym."

The king entered the library, still holding Nateer's hand, and walked to the centre of the room. As Barook closed the door, the king realized that even the back of the doors had bookcases attached. From the doors, he looked up at the ceiling, which formed a peak over thirty feet high. He turned in a circle and was awed again. The room was perfectly round, with bookcases from floor to ceiling. The only break in the room was the stone fireplace directly across from the doors and two long windows on each side that brought light in. The ceiling also provided luminescence with the ingenious use of light diffraction. Two large, comfortable chairs sat positioned slightly apart, facing the fireplace.

"I will enjoy this room," said the young prince to the delight of his parents.

The king took his queen over to the window, which overlooked the garden. The queen gasped when she saw it. "Oh, Hikaru, let's go have a better look."

"Yes, my dear."

Knowing that the king had noticed his doors with the bookcases, Barook opened them and led the party to the back of the massive stairs where the path to the gardens began. The king and queen headed for the gazebo hand in hand, whispering. Elisiah stopped the group from following. "Let them have the gardens for a few minutes, shall we?"

From down the hall behind him, Barook heard the unmistakable panting and wheezing of Bastian. Before he turned around, he closed his eyes and prayed that Bastian wasn't wearing his work clothes. To his pleasant surprise, Bastian was decked out handsomely. Beside the fact that he was sweating profusely, Bastian looked great. His hair was neat and his fine clothes, although stretched, were very becoming.

Bastian stopped when he realized he was in the midst of royalty. The prince turned to Bastian and looked up and down at the chunky little man in front of him.

"Your majesty, may I present to you the man who actually put together the crews that built the castle. This is Bastian." Barook also bowed in the direction of the prince. "And this is Prince Lavar, son of King Nikodym and Queen Nateer."

Bastian bowed again and offered his hand to the young man. Lavar smiled and shook Bastians fat, sweaty hand. He was surprised at the strength of the stout little man.

"Yer majesty, I'm very honoured to meet ya, and I hope you and your parents will be very happy here for many years," Bastian drawled.

"Thank you, sir, from what I have seen so far, you are truly a craftsman of excellence," the prince replied, wiping his hand discreetly on his pant leg.

Hand in hand, the royal couple walked along a raised boardwalk that was six feet wide, with a handrail. Every twenty feet or so was a spot to get a better view of all the wonderful and aromatic flowers and shrubbery. The water flowed all around them and under the path they were walking on. In the centre of the garden was an eight-sided gazebo surrounded by the tranquil sound of the flowing water.

The king and queen sat and stared into each other's eyes, reliving their youth. It was hard not to feel that way in this enchanting setting. The water fell off the end wall with just enough force to create a fine mist and a mild rumble. The queen only looked away when she heard the birds for the first time. She stood and looked, but she could not see the birds. She strained to scan the trees until she spotted one and then another.

"Oh, Hikaru, this is where I will spend my free time." She whirled to face the king again. "This is all so amazing. How is it that we are so fortunate to be the rulers of all we can see? We must always have people here. I want everyone to share our home with us."

"If that is what you wish, then that is what we will do. Now, we have to get back to Barook and Elisiah. It would be rude to be gone for too long," Hikaru replied. He stood and reached out his hand to Nateer. She smiled and placed her hand in his. Nateer had a bit more bounce in her step as she crossed the bridge, almost dragging the king behind her and laughing.

Barook felt much more relaxed now that he had seen the queen laugh. As the royal pair approached, Bastian prepared himself for his presentation. He wiped his sweaty hand on the buttocks of his pants, then immediately rubbed his hand together again. He tried not to fumble.

The king was openly smiling by now and didn't wait for Barook to introduce the new man. He approached with his right hand already extended. "Who might you be?" King Nikodym asked, shaking the chubby little hand. He tried not to bend down when he did so.

"This is…" Barook started.

"Bastian … Bastian, sir." Bastian was nodding and shaking the large hand.

"Pleased to meet you, Bastian," the king replied.

"Bastian was the man truly responsible for the castle being so beautiful. It was he and his men that built what I had only drawn," Barook added.

The king raised an eyebrow, stepped back and bowed to Bastian. "Then I salute you, sir." The king smiled. "This is my wife, Queen Nateer, and I take it you have already met my son, Prince Lavar."

Barook noticed how calm Bastian seemed around royalty and wondered how he did it. He was still shaking and nervous, trying to keep his voice from cracking.

"Enchanted, Yer Majesty." Bastian bowed to the queen, who bowed her head in return.

Barook cut in, "Your Majesty, would you care to see the balcony out front?"

The king motioned toward the front doors. Barook and Bastian walked side by side ahead of the entourage. Each man grabbed a handle of the two massive front doors and swung them open. The doors moved slowly open, which brought even more light into the entry.

The king ran his hands upon the gleaming, hand-carved doors. He had walked outside of the castle while only looking at the doors. He hadn't even noticed the balcony, as he was transfixed on the magical doors.

The queen was more interested in the breathtaking views the balcony displayed. She quickened her step to the edge and rested her hands on the rail. With her eyes closed, she took a deep breath and then reopened her eyes. The ocean breeze blew up the cliff and lightly salted the air. She looked over to the small island that sat out past the left point of the harbour. Below her was the semi-circular harbour and the city of Kataan against the hill on the right. Beyond the harbour was a great ocean, which disappeared into the horizon. She closed her eyes again and took another deep breath. She didn't hear Hikaru as he approached from behind.

He slowly put his arms around her from behind and gently squeezed. "The doors are magnificent," he attested.

"It's all so magnificent, Hikaru. It's overwhelming, to say the least. It's so large. I don't know what to say." Nateer smiled and sighed. "Please tell me I'm not dreaming, my love."

"It seems like a dream, doesn't it?" he replied as he rested is head on her shoulder. "Soon, all the people who built this dream will be here to share a feast with us. Then we can thank them in person for what they have built."

The couple turned to the group hanging around the front doors waiting patiently. As the two approached, the queen looked directly at Barook. "Take me to the hall where we will be receiving our guests this evening," she requested.

Barook was a bit surprised at the request but eagerly replied, "Please follow me, Your Majesty."

Hikaru turned to Elisiah and put his large maul on his shoulder. "Elisiah," he said sternly, "You have lied to me, old friend."

"How can that be?" Elisiah was shaken.

"You never told me the castle was anything like this," the king mused.

"If I did, I would never have been able to keep you away." Elisiah realized he had been teased. "Besides, what kind of surprise would it have been if you knew?"

Hikaru took one more look back past the balcony and admired the view. He looked up again at the towering doors in front of him. "Why do you suppose Barook put such impressive doors in an area no one will see them?"

"If the doors were where everyone could see them, no one would be able to take the time to appreciate them." Elisiah smiled slightly.

The king shrugged and followed Elisiah into the grand entry. Hikaru walked over to the impressive stairway and stopped at the bottom. He ran his right hand along the redwood handrail and looked up the stairs. He was careful to notice the fine carvings on the spindles as well as the see-through stairs. He climbed four stairs and appreciated the gazebo from here.

Nateer noticed the king lagging behind. "Hikaru, we are going to the grand hall to receive our guests."

"Yes, my dear. I will have time to look over the garden another time."

The group went down the hall to a room parallel to the garden. It was prepared to receive seven hundred and fifty guests, some of which had already arrived.

"The room we are in is only one of two we have prepared," Barook revealed. "The other is next door and is exactly the same. The formal dining room is far too small for such a venue. Each of these rooms is one hundred and fifty feet long and seventy feet wide; however, this one has an impressive view of the gardens from the far end. Your majesties, would you like to see your chambers to freshen up before we continue?"

"Yes, Barook," the queen spoke up. "I would love to freshen up. It's been a long, hot and dusty ride."

"I expect our guests will be arriving for the next several hours. There will be fifteen hundred guests in total," Elisiah added.

"Well then," Barook said. "Please follow me to your quarters upstairs." Barook led a rather quiet pair and the prince up the stairs where he stopped for a few minutes, knowing they would like to see the gardens from up here. To his surprise, it was the queen who spent the most time admiring them again. Barook pointed to the double doors at the end of the hall. "Your majesties, this is your room."

Reluctantly, the queen headed down the hall toward their room, hanging on to the rail and looking over the garden. Hikaru followed. He took Nateer by the hand and led her through the double doors and closed them behind them.

Barook focussed on Prince Lavar. "If you would follow me, I will take you to your room." They walked to the opposite end of the hall, where Barook left the young prince to explore his room. As the royals were no longer in his presence, Barook felt a calm come over him and the tension of the last few hours slowly left his body. He felt as though he could breathe again. He walked quickly back down the stairs.

"Well, Bastian, Elisiah, shall we go welcome the king's guests?" Barook asked.

At the bottom of the stairs, a few of the men who had worked on the castle were discussing various aspects of construction. Bastian stayed behind to talk with his men, leaving Barook and Elisiah to go to the main kitchen. As the two men walked through, they stopped briefly to take in the aroma once again. They headed down to the main chamber where they had received the royal family earlier and a good crowd had been gathering.

From there, the guests would go up a different stairway that led past the kitchen and exited in the library in a secret door hidden in the book-case. The guests knew of this passage, as it was used as a secondary route to the main floor during construction.

Barook was mobbed by congratulatory men who had recognized him. Elisiah simply smiled and waved and went to find Kataan, the village elder, who along with his wife, Marta, would sit with the king and queen during the feast. Kataan was one of the oldest men on the island and was highly regarded as a wise man. Besides Elisiah, Kataan was the king's most trusted advisor. The king always enjoyed talking to Kataan, and now they would have a lot to talk about.

Elisiah had timed his arrival perfectly. As he approached the tunnel, he saw the carriage carrying Kataan and Marta coming slowly into view with an entourage walking behind, most of them from Kataan's city, which was near the base of the small volcano. His village was quite large and was mostly a farming community. The caves under the volcano provided excellent storage areas, especially in the rainy season. They were the main supplier of grain and fresh fruit to the mining towns at the north end of the island at the larger volcano and the valley between the two.

Kataan was always generous with his time and resources and was well respected by all the elders on the island. Each of the villages was named after the elder that governed over it. Many times, when a new elder was necessary, he would take the name of the previous elder, so the names of the towns did not change. Leadership was always handed down from father to son but in the case of Kataan and Marta, there was no son. Their only son had died in a farming accident almost twenty years ago. Kataan had personally supervised the meals of all the men who worked on the castle. He had been up there every day from the start of construction until it was finally finished.

Elisiah greeted Kataan and Marta at their carriage and opened the door for them. Kataan smiled and graciously nodded.

"Kataan, Marta, it is truly a privilege and an honour to welcome you on behalf of the king and queen." Elisiah was humble to the elders even though he had higher status amongst the kingdom. "Marta, you look lovely."

She smiled and bowed respectfully. "Thank you, my dear," was all she said.

"Elisiah, it is good to see you again." Kataan had known Elisiah since he was a child and had great respect for the man who had become the king's friend and confidant. "The last time I saw you, you were smaller than me," he joked.

"Come with me and we will wait for the king in the library. We will toast to the castle and the long life of the king and queen." Elisiah bowed slightly and spread out his hands for his friends to lead.

"When do Anan and Holied and the other elders arrive?" Kataan asked Elisiah.

"All of the elders arrive in half-hour intervals to avoid overcrowding in the lower tunnels. Each must be afforded the dignity they deserve," Elisiah offered. "You were chosen first as your city is the closest."

"I look forward to seeing them all again. It's too bad we don't get together more often," Kataan added.

Elisiah and the first party were intercepted by Bastian as they arrived in the library. Kataan was the first to see him. "Bastian! It's always a pleasure to see you."

"Thank you, yer honour." Bastian bowed to Kataan "And Mrs... yer honour," he added awkwardly, which got a laugh of approval from Marta.

Kataan was very fond of Bastian, although he didn't generally show it. In all the time he had come up here he had not seen a harder-working man than Bastian.

Now thoroughly embarrassed, Bastian asked, "Can I get either of you a refreshment?"

"Thank you, Bastian, but if the three of you will excuse me, I have to tend to the dining room and the rest of the guests." Elisiah bowed away with his hands clasped in front of him.

Kataan and Marta gave a slight bow of their heads.

"Actually, I would like an ale. And you, my dear?" He turned to Marta.

"I would love a white wine, if it's not too much trouble." Marta smiled at the chubby little man.

Kataan rocked on his toes with his hands clasped behind his back, thinking about the last time he had an ale. As Bastian wandered off to fetch the drinks, Kataan remembered it was with Bastian as they toasted the beginning of this project some ten years ago. He took Marta's hand and led her out of the library to the side of the grand staircase that afforded a fantastic view of the gardens. Silently, they gazed over the expansive area teeming with life, from the fish to the birds to the bees that pollinated to the otters, and on and on. It was a surreal moment for the two. The mild rumble of the waterfall was mesmerizing.

Bastian found them, approaching with two one-quart ales and a very generous goblet of white wine for Marta. He handed out the drinks and silently toasted the two.

"My goodness, young man," Marta said to Bastian, "This could make for a tough day tomorrow." She giggled.

As the chuckling settled, Kataan turned to Bastian. "I should have you build us a new home, although we may be dead by the time you get it finished."

"This castle only had one difficult thing…" Bastian was starting a belly laugh. "The stairs." He slapped his knee. "Don't build a house with stairs."

Kataan chuckled as Bastian's belly moved up and down as he laughed.

Barook walked through the door from the lower chamber with Anan, the village elder from the town of the miners in the north which bore his name. Anan was usually more boisterous than the other elders, as his upbringing was a bit harder. When he was a younger man, he worked in the mines and was largely responsible for the treaties that helped this people prosper as the farmers had. He was a large man, well built and powerfully strong. His flaming red hair made him stand out in a crowd. He was not married any longer, as his wife of twenty years had passed away three years ago of an unknown illness. They did have two sons, and he had a maiden that took care of all three of them.

Together with Kataan, they had found ways to make machinery from the minerals the miners had unearthed. As the machinery improved, the farming practises became better and everyone prospered. Now the kingdom had an excess of food and that helped prepare for the unknown of the seasonal storms.

"Anan."

"Kataan!"

Anan hugged Kataan vigorously. Kataan stiffened up as the much stronger and younger man held on tight.

"You look good, old man." Anan released his hold and grabbed Kataan by the shoulders. "Where is your beautiful wife?" he asked.

"She has gone to see the queen," Kataan replied. "I probably won't see her again until dinner."

"Bastian, could you please tend to these gentleman as I have to return to the caverns to greet the next group?" Barook was sympathetic with his plea.

"Yes, yes, of course, Barook. Anan, can I get you an ale?" Bastian asked.

"I would love to see the waterfall from the garden. Would you like to join me, gentlemen?" Kataan asked.

"Bastian, I would love an ale. And Kataan, lead on," Anan replied.

"I'll meet ya at the gazebo," Bastian called out as he waddled away.

The two honoured guests departed for the waterfall at the end of the garden. They walked slowly to take in the amazing views and sat at a bench to the right of the cascading water, which flowed down from a height of fifty feet so. It created a gentle mist but avoided the roar and splash of a sheer drop. The mist was refreshing but did not soak the two. They sat in relative quiet, with their heads tilted back slightly and their eyes closed.

During the next few hours, Barook and Elisiah took turns welcoming the fifteen hundred guests. Many had walked up the cavern trail in large groups, and the two men did their best to do the impossible task of meeting them. Most simply continued on their own to the massive dining halls to leave more time for the two exasperated men to keep up with the flow of dignitaries. Bastian had all the elders gathered in the library, which had filled up quickly. He had the help of fifteen maidens to help entertain the large group, which helped keep him from overheating.

The crowd began to form, and the elders were led from the library to line up at the base of the grand staircase. After the crowd had quieted down, the king and queen appeared from their room and stopped at the top of the stairs, where they were joined by Prince Lavar. They were all adorned in the most elegant traditional accoutrements. They stood hand in hand and waited to be introduced by their friend Elisiah.

Elisiah ascended the mighty stairs until he reached the royal couple. He bowed to them and turned to the anticipating crowd. A hush fell. "Without further ado," Elisiah began, "I want to thank you all for attending this evening's festivities. All of you here today played a pivotal role in creating this masterpiece that will be known from this time forward as Castle Nikodym.."

The crowd erupted spontaneously. Elisiah waited a bit and motioned for them to relent. As they did, he continued.

"I could talk for hours about what you have done here, but I know you are all hungry from the long journey and no one wants to be bored to death waiting for me to stop talking, so please join me in welcoming…" he gestured to the royal couple, "King Nikodym, Queen Nateer and Prince Lavar."

Again, the crowd erupted in jubilant cheer.

Slowly, the king and queen descended the stairs followed by the prince and Elisiah. The king paused a few times on the descent and looked over the growing crowd. Finally, he approached Kataan, the first elder in line.

He nodded to his friend, who was bowing in respect, along with Marta. The queen had a huge smile on her face as she gazed upon her old friend Marta. Everyone was silent as the king and queen progressed down the line of elders until they had personally greeted each person. The precession headed for the meeting rooms where the formal dinner would begin.

King Nikodym could feel his stomach tighten as they entered the great hall and led the elders to the head table. The crowd broke into boisterous cheers and clapping as the royal entourage took their place at the long table prepared for them. The king smiled and waved to the crowd in front of him, revelling in all the attention. The queen and the young prince shared in the festivities but felt a bit embarrassed by all the fuss.

The crowd died down as the king signalled for them to be seated. "Ladies and gentlemen," he started, "I cannot begin to express my gratitude to you; each and every one of you." His voice quivered a bit. "For decades, we have slowly evolved into the people we are today. Although it has not always been easy, we have chosen to make our lands strong and our people generous and kind. As the land has been good to us, we have been vigilant in our efforts to keep the land healthy. In turn, we have become an amazingly tightknit community of people. Although we don't all live in the same village, we do live on one incredible island made so by the people that inhabit it. To honour one man would be a dishonour to so many others therefore. I call upon all men and women to rejoice and sing and dance in you own honour. People…," the king raised his glass again, "I salute you."

The crowd broke into a deafening roar, the musicians struck up a festive tune and the feast began.

CHAPTER 4

"Your Grace." The young sentry waited for Commander Beil to acknowledge him.

The commander was a huge man, standing six foot nine and weighing over three hundred and fifty pounds. He had long salt-and-pepper hair and an equally long beard split in two, coming to two points that looked like upside down horns. He rarely smiled, and his hard features made him even more intimidating. He looked up from behind his desk and motioned the young man forward.

The sentry approached with his right hand crossed over his chest. He stopped, bowed his head and looked up at the commander. "One of your men was found dead, sir."

The commander lowered his head, shaking it slowly. He rose from behind his desk and stared momentarily at the ridged sentry before him. He released a huge sigh. "Where?"

"Davar City, Your Grace."

"How"

"It is believed he was returning to his barracks after a night out drinking. He was found this morning by a routine patrol. It appears he has a fractured skull," the sentry reported, standing firmly, eyes straight ahead.

Beil stood silently for a few minutes, staring blankly ahead and breathing hard with his jaw clenched. "Round up the city counsel and bring them to me. We need answers to this, and I think they might know something about it. Obviously he was killed by one of the peasants." Beil scowled. "I can use this to reinforce my authority. Return to your duties."

The sentry bowed and turned away.

Commander Beil had run this district for thirteen years. He was strict and demanded order. His job was to keep order, but how he did it was his discretion. Beil had learned the power of fear from his many successful campaigns. He had won more land and riches for the king than any man in history. He was rewarded this conquered kingdom as a retirement gift from his king. Although he was relatively young, at only fifty-five, he deserved everything he had achieved. His king, Dolmar, had come to have great respect for Beil who in turn used his influence with the king to further his ambitions and set his place atop the ranks of the other provincial leaders. He felt it was his destiny to become king when Dolmar died, and he waited for that day.

Now a resistance was forming in the Alkar peasants and they were staging stealth attacks against his authority. This incident was another such attack, in his mind, and it would not go unpunished. He paced back and forth with his left hand on his chin. In the fingers of his right hand he rolled a firestone; he squeezed it in his fist and then rolled it in his fingers again, repeating the action.

The firestone was said to help you think when you held it. It was a roundish, opaque stone with a bright-red centre. The red veins through the rock gave the appearance of pulsing as you rolled it. Beil had not believed the stories when he took it from around the neck of one of his enemies. Now he felt it had a calming effect on him when he rolled it in his fingers.

"How many of these peasants am I going to have to kill before they realize I'm not going away?" Biel slammed his left hand down on the table and kicked the chair across the room. He looked down at the firestone in his right hand and put it in its pouch.

Now was not the time to be calm. He turned to the window behind him that looked over the centre of Davar City. He watched as the oppressed society scrambled below him. Beil knew he didn't have enough of an army to control this province, yet he dared not show weakness and knew fear was on his side. He had asked the king for more soldiers but the king had waged another war and would not reassign more forces to an already conquered province. King Dolmar was a man who got what he wanted, but his ambitions left Beil in a dangerous situation.

He watched as down below his soldiers dragged seven old men down the middle of the street, headed toward him. The Lakar soldiers held no respect for the counsel of Alkar. They dragged them by the hair or their robes or whatever they could grab hold of. They would throw the old men to the ground and kick them if they didn't get moving fast enough. Beil smiled to himself and thought back to when he used to round up guests for his commander.

Finally, the loud procession came up the stairs to the second-storey interrogation room. The old men were thrown to the floor at the foot of Beils desk. Beil remained at the window, staring out blankly. He waited a minute for effect.

"Gentlemen, I'm pleased you could join me." This was the only pleasantry Beil would make. He turned to face the cowering counsel. "It has come to my attention that you are no longer performing your duties to my expectations. No indeed, to me or the king."

"Please, Your Grace. We are unsure why you have summoned us," one spoke up.

Beil nodded to the sentry and pointed up. A group of them grabbed the counsel and dragged them to their feet. He smirked at the toothless elders. He pointed at the oldest and then to the ground. The sentry kicked the feet out from under the old man, who winced in pain as he hit the floor. Then he looked at the next elder in line and pointed to the ground. The quivering old man started down when he was slammed down from behind. When Beil looked at the third, all the remaining men fell to the floor and Beil smiled in evil disdain.

Beil walked from the window, past the trembling old men and sat on the corner of his desk. He bent down and grabbed the face of the old man who had spoken up. "You are not talking, you are listening." He pushed the wrinkled old face away from him. He looked up at the sentry. "Go get the soldier you found this morning and bring him in here."

With precision, two Lakar soldiers brought their right hands across their chests and bowed to the commander. They turned in unison and headed out the door.

Beil pivoted on the desk and retrieved a three-foot-long foil from a sheath attached to the side of the cabinet. He looked over the blade as he twisted it in the light. The metal glowed magnificently as he twisted and turned it in his hand. The room was dead silent.

"You." Beil pointed to the eldest again. He glared down the row of wracked faces and back to the first. "For thirteen years…" he hesitated. "Thirteen years we have been here on this land, on these shores. We have defeated you, processed you and enslaved you. I am your master." He looked down the line again. "As long as you obey, I treat you well."

He raised his foil to the cheek of the elder. "And yet some of you refuse to follow the orders I have set out for you." Beil slowly pressed the tip of the foil into the old man's cheek until a trickle of blood formed. The old man howled in pain but could not move away.

"I have shown you and your families mercy so you could control the peasants. For some time, this worked very well. I gave orders and you carried them out. I must admit, you saved a lot of lives." Beil looked at the second victim, still holding the foil in the face of the first. The second man held his right shoulder and looked back weakly. Beil moved his foil against the wounded shoulder.

"It seems to me that you think I am getting weaker. You seem to take for granted what I have given you. Perhaps you feel that because you see few soldiers, I am vulnerable." He pressed the tip of the foil about an inch into the shoulder, and the old man screamed horribly, passing out from the pain. "Let me assure you pathetic little creatures of one thing. I am not weak!" He pulled the blade from the shoulder and wiped it on his victim's clothing.

The sentries returned, carrying the dead body of the soldier discovered the previous night.

"Put him down here." Beil pointed to the desk in front of the fallen elders.

The two sentries carefully placed the lifeless form on his back across the desk and turned his head so he faced the elders.

"This man," Beil started, "was killed last night while returning to his barracks."

He looked down the row of quivering old men who were all looking down at the floor except for the one who was unconscious. Beil slashed his foil across the back of the third man in line, who cowered and winced in pain.

"Look at this man!" he screamed. "You have taken him from me!" He tried to contain his anger. "For each of my men that are killed, I will kill an entire family of you peasants."

Beil pointed his foil at the unconscious elder. "We will start with his family."

The remaining men gasped at the ruthlessness of Beil, as they had done nothing. They cried and cowered on the floor.

"I want something visible that everyone will see." Beil walked over to the window and pointed to the city centre. "There. I want his entire family right, down to the grandchildren, publicly executed right down there. Kill the children first!" He turned and looked back at the old men. "Look at me," he screamed. "Now, kill the woman next. I want all the men to see their families die. I want everyone to know the value of a Lakar life and the worthlessness of their own."

The Lakar sentries glanced at each other, surprised by Beils actions, but none would dare question him. Beil turned his back to the elders.

"You peasants will wash the body of my soldier. Then you will dress him in full uniform. He will attend the execution to see that his death did not go unanswered. Until that day you will stay with the body and care for it, or you can join your friend and his family."

Beil turned from the window and looked at the young soldiers that had brought the body in. "You two accompany the rest of these creatures to the stateroom where they can prepare the body." He turned to the third guard at the doorway. "Throw the other one in a cell. Then I want you to take a battalion of men and round up every member of this peasant's family. They will be executed in two days. I want everyone to know about it and why it is happening."

The soldiers, in unison, crossed their chests, bowed their heads and carried on with their duties.

Beil reached into his right pocket and pulled out his firestone. He rolled it in his fingers and then squeezed it in his fist. Now he could calm down.

The next day, confusion reigned as an army of Lakar soldiers ransacked the houses and properties of the elder's family. Without warning, the Lakar soldiers kicked in the doors. In large raiding parties, they went from room to room. The buildings were torn apart and the furniture was smashed. The women were raped in front of their husbands and children. Everyone was beaten without provocation. The screams of the women and children sent chills up the spines of the people powerless to help. Some of the Alkar were lucky, when they were killed resisting the onslaught. One by one, the men, women and children were gathered up. They were dragged by their hair into the waiting arms of the army of ruthless soldiers. The Lakar soldiers didn't have as much time as they would have liked, and a small handful of the elder's relatives had been spared. The final count was thirty grandchildren, twenty-two women and thirty-six men.

The soldiers separated the children from the women without mercy. Six women had already been killed trying to stop the soldiers from taking their babies. Five of the oldest men had also been killed trying to protect their families. This would still make a good display.

The day had come. After a hearty breakfast, Beil was now ready to commence with today's execution. He stood in the window, overlooking the city center. It was almost noon and the streets were almost empty. Beil's eyes were cold as he stared down into the square.

A grand procession came into view down the street. An impressive number of soldiers marched in unison and with precision. With the prisoners in the middle and another large procession behind, they approached the city centre.

The thirty grandchildren were separated by age and then into two groups, the youngest and oldest. They were tied together and held by soldiers. The fifteen youngest were lined up against a wall first. The women were dragged out into the street and forced to the ground. They were all shackled at the ankles and hands as well as to each other. The men were held back under the heaviest guard.

Thirty Lakar soldiers lined up in front of the crying, hysterical children. They set their arrows in their bows. The lieutenant in charge raised his hand and looked up to Commander Beil in the window.

Beil looked down at the crying, screaming women begging him not to kill their babies. The soldiers drew their bows and waited. Biel looked slowly around the city below him while the lieutenant waited patiently with his hand still raised over his head. Beads of sweat began to form on the brows of the soldiers with bows drawn. Their muscles strained as they struggled to keep their concentration against the pull of the bow. Biel knew the men were straining and revelled in the thought of ultimate power. He looked back at the lieutenant and nodded. Relieved, the lieutenant dropped his hand and the soldiers released their deadly barrage. The arrows whistled to a dull thud as they pierced their targets. The soldiers were expert marksmen, and the children dropped instantly dead.

The woman screamed as the soldiers loaded the bodies onto a large cart used to haul manure to the fields. It was the largest the soldiers could find on short notice. Beil sneered down at the rest of the family, who were now totally hysterical. He motioned for the second group of older children to be arranged against the same wall. Many of the children were screaming and retaliating as best they could, to no avail. They too were forced against the wall in sheer terror, not knowing what they had done, waiting for death. Beil smiled as he watched the spectacle replay. As the soldiers started to retrieve the woman, now totally spent emotionally, Beil stopped them with a loud roar from the window.

"Bring out the racks," Beil hollered.

A renewed sense of terror went through the elder's remaining family.

The rack was a most unpleasant and slow way to die. It was a simple and effective device designed to tear a body apart. The diabolical machine was eight-sided and ten feet across. It had five leather straps strategically placed toward the centre: three from the top for the wrists and neck, and two at the bottom for the ankles. The straps were soaked in saltwater and stretched.

The victim was wrapped in soaked leather sheets very tightly before being strapped to the rack. The head was placed in a full mask that had a loop at the top and secured the chin and back of the neck. With wrist, ankles and head supported, the victim was hoisted upright where he would hang until the beating Sun and the rack had done its job. It could take up to five days to die; most died within two. Either way, it was excruciating.

As the racks were being rolled down the road, Beil decided he wanted a closer view of the festivities. He headed out to the city center where he could be as close as he wanted. Immediately, two of his personal guards retrieved a large, double-armed padded chair and followed. The leather straps and sheets were now being soaked and stretched repeatedly to maximize the shrinking. He watched intently as one by one the women were tied to the wicked device. The screaming and crying continued and the soldiers, who were losing their patience, beat the women in a futile attempt to quiet them.

Beil enjoyed the screams of pain and terror. He felt invigorated by his ability to humiliate and terrorize the peasants under his rule. This display would not go unnoticed by the people of Alkar. He felt secure with this show of force.

The people of Altar were not warriors like the people of Lakar. They were much smaller in stature, averaging five foot eight to six feet at the tallest. The Lakar soldiers averaged almost a foot taller. All the people in this province were intimidated by the much-larger conquering army. The people did not want the Lakar soldiers to return, as they knew that next time the soldiers would not spare anyone. The death of one family was an acceptable loss if it prevented the cruelty and slaughter.

As Beil sat watching, the six remaining elders brought the elaborately dressed body of the dead soldier and held him up beside the commander. "Get him a chair," he ordered. Immediately, one of the elders ran off to the retrieve one. He returned quickly and waited silently for orders.

"Put it here beside me," Beil growled.

The man placed the chair beside Beil and helped the others carefully place the corpse in front of the twenty-one racks lined up in front. They wept as they watched the women struggle against their bindings.

Beil now looked at the lieutenant and signalled for the men to be brought forward to their place of execution. The men had been tied together so they would not try to escape. The Alkar men would not dare move, as they knew it would only cause more death. With heads bowed, they marched up in front of the women before Beil. The men were silent, almost as though they accepted the fate bestowed upon them.

Beil did not care that none of these men had anything to do with the death of his soldier. He did not care that the children were the most innocent of all. All that mattered to him was control— complete control.

The soldiers brought the next means of vengeance down the road; another huge wagon with a large chopping block in the back. A heavy curved blade was leaned up against it.

Even through this slaughter, Beil was preoccupied momentarily with the thought of the depleted size of his army now that King Dolmar had started another campaign and recalled most of his forces.

Beil snapped his stare to the lieutenant, who was standing ridged. The commander raised his right hand and extended his fingers. He hesitated and then brought his hand down in a chopping motion.

The lieutenant in turn looked at a soldier leading a small squad of men accompanying and pulling the next means of death. They removed the block from the wagon and waited for the executioner. A giant, painted-faced man walked to the back of the wagon, looking over the crowd and stopping at Commander Beil. He bowed to Beil and awaited a response. Beil nodded to him and he jumped down from his perch. He picked up his blade and strode over to Beil and bowed his head again. The commander pointed, and the man took his place at the block.

The soldiers grabbed the first man in line and, without compassion, dragged the wide-eyed, screaming man to the block.

The executioner looked over to the commander, who had a smirk on this face. Beil nodded, and the big Lakar soldier mercilessly brought the axe down and ended the life of the first Alkar man.

One by one, the rest were led to the block amidst the hysteria of screaming men and women. Thirty-six times the axe fell, and every time Beil smiled sadistically.

"Put the heads up, lieutenant," the commander finally spoke. He raised his hand and twirled a finger.

The soldiers gathered the heads and put them on fifteen-foot poles, placing them around the city center. They also placed them so the dying women could look into the faces of their men. The screams had now given way to the sobbing of the tortured women. It would be days before the last of them died. The city center would be cleaned up in a couple weeks, but it would be months before the people of Alkar would return to the market. Beil knew the people were sufficiently intimidated and there should not be a need for a repeat performance anytime soon.

CHAPTER 5

It had been three months since Hikaru Nikodym first stood at what had become his favourite window. The sun was rising slowly out of the water, and the king's view of the valley was becoming more splendid. The tops of the giant redwoods glowed magnificently. Slowly, more and more of the island opened up to the sun. The shadows quietly made their way down the mountain and disappeared in the valley. A large white cloud rested against the cliff of the smaller volcano. Quietly, the cloud moved around the peak and lazily released its grip to reveal the snow capped cliffs that rose majestically. Hikaru traced the path of a stream that started at the base of a waterfall careening off the cliff. Down the mountain the stream weaved, picking up momentum as other streams funneled in. Soon the stream was a river, which fed half of the island. It wasn't long before he could no longer see the river through the trees, but still he traced the path he knew the river travelled to the ocean. A light mist lifted from a small lake to his right. The king shifted his weight to his hands as he thought about fishing with Elisiah when they were young.

"Hikaru," Nateer spoke softly. "What are you looking at, my love?"

"The valley, my dear," Hikaru replied. "The cliffs, the streams … everything. I was
thinking of going fishing with Elisiah and Lavar."

"And what of me? Am I to sit here while you boys …"

"And of course I wouldn't go without my good luck charm," Hikaru cut in, "Just promise me you won't catch any bigger than me." He chuckled.

"Oh, Hikaru, I was just teasing." Nateer threw back her head laughing.

"Yes, my love."

"You watch the sun come up every morning," Nateer sighed. "I often wonder what you see." She took Hikaru's hand.

"I see it all, my love. I see the beginning, the end, and everything in between. Every morning brings new life. I enjoy every minute of a new day and my mind feels at ease. I can't quite fathom life being so good, and I can't help thinking something is going to go wrong. We have lived in this castle for three months. It's so large … and so quiet. Even with all our friends we can't fill the halls of this place. I think we should return this castle to the people. Although I love the grandeur, I feel it separates us from our people. I don't want to look down upon them, I want to live among them, share in their struggles and … well, I suppose I just miss having people around me all the time." Hikaru was opening up.

Nateer put her arms around him from behind. "Why don't we invite all the village elders to come and live here with us? I'm sure we have more than enough room for all of them."

Hikaru turned, still in Nateer's arms. "I don't think they would. They are all so proud … so set in their beliefs of the kingdom and so respectful of tradition. However, I could try to persuade them."

Nateer put her head on Hikaru's chest. "I know you can, my love." She hugged the king tightly. "Breakfast in the garden?"

After breakfast, King Nikodym, Elisiah and Lavar went off fishing. Along the way, the king discussed the idea of the elders moving into the castle.

For almost two months, Barook had toiled with the thought of a lift system in order to move the people up to and down from the castle more efficiently. Although the tunnels were well lit and relatively easy to travel, he knew the view from the lift would be well worth the effort on his part. He smirked to himself as he thought about Bastian. His chubby little friend could use a new challenge. First they would have to build a new road to where the lift would dock at the bottom of the cliff. It would indeed be a challenge to build such a structure, but Barook had it all worked out, and now Bastian could do the rest. The road had already been planned for years, and the route had been strategically cleared. This provided building materials, which were processed and distributed to the villages that needed them. Although small trees had sprouted and would have to be removed, the basic structure of the road was in place. Bastian's crews would have the route cleared in four months.

Barook pulled on his overcoat and headed out the door to Bastian's house. They were going on a fourteen-day trip to the foundry at the northern end of the island. He always liked to oversee every aspect of construction, including the winch-and-pulley system. Bastian wanted to make sure he knew everything he could about Barook's design. The trip would also provide time to finalize plans, make out work schedules and define a timeline from start to finish.

As Barook's carriage approached Bastian's bungalow, the chubby man brought out the last of his bags. He carried with him a large portfolio containing the plans for the road and timber salvage as well as three large chests.

Bastian waved vigorously as Barook's driver brought the carriage to a halt. "Good evening, Barook."

"Good evening, Bastian. Do you need a hand with the bags?" Barook's greeting was a bit less enthusiastic than his friend's.

Bastian was straining to reach to coachman with his bags. "Thank you," he said.

Stepping down from the coach, Barook easily reached the driver with the rest of Bastian's luggage.

CHAPTER 6

"Commander Beil, one of King Dolmar's ships is approaching the harbour. It appears to be the long-range cargo ship Exeter, which disappeared six months ago," the first officer reported from the doorway.

Beil sat behind his desk going over treasury logs "Come in," he said and looked up when the man approached. "What condition is she in?" Beil was somewhat surprised at the sudden return of the missing ship.

"She appears to be undamaged from what we can see from here. I can conduct a closer inspection when she docks, if you wish." Lieutenant Kern was Beil's right hand man when it came to controlling the province. His official duties were to collect taxes and implement discipline, but he also oversaw many aspects of Beil's command. Like Beil, he stood almost seven feet tall but was much younger and not as husky. He had risen quickly through the ranks, as he had shown excellent aptitude and practicality when dealing with issues of state.

"That won't be necessary, Lieutenant. Have the captain of the ship report to me as soon as the ship docks."

A moment's silence followed, and Kern stood ridgidly waiting to be dismissed.

"Close the door on the way out."

Beil stood and turned to face the window. The only trace of his last military exercise was on the faces of the market merchant who were slowly returning. The women were long dead and buried in a mass grave beside their men and children. The people were slowly filtering back to the merchants, and life was returning to normal.

"Where has she been for so long?" Beil thought aloud. "The captain of that ship had better have a good reason for disobeying King Dolmar's orders or he will be a dead man. What would be worth risking his life for?"

He walked over to the door and swung it open. "Lieutenant. Have a messenger on standby. I may have information for the king. When the captain of the ship arrives, have him brought to me immediately. We will be entertaining him for dinner tonight, so have the chef prepare something special." Beil went into his office and then poked his head back out the door. "Bring me the manifest and a list of crew from the Exeter."

He walked back to the window and stared down into the market. He hated this place and the weak people he was ordered to control. He wanted more than this babysitting job, which he didn't find fulfilling. He wanted to be back on the front lines, displaying his strategies and cunning. Controlling sheep was not the test of a warrior, and he was a warrior. He could feel his anger starting to burn inside him. Placing his hand on his hip, he felt the pouch containing his firestone. He raised an eyebrow as he lifted the stone from its sheath, raising it to the light. The stone seemed to pulse quickly and brightly. Slowly, as Beil calmed down, the stone also slowed its pulse and started to dim. By the time the captain of the ship arrived, the stone and Beil were calm. The loud knock on the door brought Beil out of his trancelike state.

"Enter!" Beil had recomposed himself by the time the captain walked up to his desk.

"Commander Beil. I am Captain Irid Tragar of the king's ship Exeter."

"Welcome, Captain, to my humble village." Beil looked down at the manifest on his desk and back into Tragar's eyes. "You are a very brave man, captain. Tell me why you have returned before completing your mission."

Tragar smiled. "You are direct. I like that in a man. Tell me ... Where is our king, that I might report to him?"

Biel kept his eyes on Tragar. "Captain, when you dock your vessel in my port before you complete your mission, you must expect a few questions."

Tragar was stoic, not wanting to show weakness. "Commander, fix us a drink and I shall tell you a tale."

Beil stared at Tragar. "Kern," he yelled to the lieutenant.

Within seconds, Kern appeared in the doorway. "Yes, Commander."

"Lieutenant, bring me a flask of wine and two glasses. Captain Tragar has a story he wishes to share with me." Beil continued sating at Tragar, who was starting to feel uncomfortable but did not waver. Moments later, Kern returned with two glasses of wine and handed one to each of the men. He gave the flask to the commander. Beil motioned for Tragar to retrieve a chair from the far wall.

"That will be all, Lieutenant, close the door on the way out," Beil told Kern.

Tragar retrieved the chair and sat across from the commander, raising his glass to Beil, who was still watching him closely.

"I'm waiting, Captain."

Tragar shook his head slightly at Beil's disrespect. "After we left port, we sailed west under calm skies. The first month was uneventful, the seas were calm, and the wind was at our backs. On the eve of the second month, I could see a storm brewing behind us. We altered our course to try to avoid the brunt of the storm, but it moved on us quickly. The ship wallowed under the weight of her full cargo holds and strained to turn in the increasingly rough seas. Then, with all the furry of hell, the storm smashed into the side of the ship. Eight men were lost when the initial wave rolled across the deck, washing them away. My men fought bravely against an enemy they could not defeat. I ordered every man on deck to attach themselves to safety lines to prevent losing any more to the sea. The winds were so strong it took hours to take all the sails down to ride her out."

Tragar stopped to take a drink. Biel was listening intently.

"The skies were so black we could not see fifty feet in front of us. For nine days the sun did not return, and the storm carried us with it. At times the wind would die down and the black skies would pour down rain. It rained so hard the drops bounced off the water-soaked deck eight inches into the air. At one point we were forced to lighten our load. We emptied the perishable goods into the ocean and pumped out the water-laden holds. Violently, the winds returned and hammered the waves into the ship. We had lost control of the ship on the third day when the rudder broke. For seven more days we drifted aimlessly and defenceless. On the tenth day of the storm, the winds calmed as quickly as they had risen. The black skies cleared, and the sun broke through. Suddenly, everything was quiet, and the creaking of the ship was all we could hear."

Tragar stopped for another drink of his wine and noticed Beil had not touched his.

"I immediately dispatched repair crews to tend to the rudder and fix the torn sails. Fortunately, the Exeter is a worthy vessel, and the other damage was minimal considering our ordeal. Two more days passed before we had regained control of both the rudder and sails. We set a course to return to port to finish repairs and replace the missing crew. The rudder would not make it to the destined port, so we had to head back. The first two days of the return trip were slow, as the winds had not favoured us. I changed our direction to the southeast to take advantage of the winds we did have. Our rations were low, as we had to toss most of them overboard to save the vessel. I decided to return to the nearest navigable port— this one."

Tragar lifted his glass to the light and swirled the blood-red wine, peering into it. He lowered the glass and swallowed the contents.

Beil, still looking at Tragar, opened his throat and swallowed his full glass in one gulp. He slowly lowered the glass to the table as he stood up and then waved a finger to motion Tragar over to the window.

"Look at the village." Beil spread out his hand.

Tragar approached the window and looked over the village. The people below moved slowly with their heads down. They rarely looked up except to make a purchase from a merchant. There were less than half the people he remembered from the last time he was here.

"The people of this city depend on those shipments to get through. I depend on the goods that are being returned to me. I'm not interested in why you failed to complete your mission. I'm only concerned that you did fail," Beil continued, stone faced.

Tragar raised his left hand to chest height and cut off Beil. "Commander, there's more, much more. While we followed the wind, on the third day we came across an island. It was never on any of our charts until now. As we approached, I realized I had never seen anything like this. I plotted a course around and completed a survey of the island." He turned from the window and sat back down in his chair. "Come and refill our glasses, as what I have to say will amaze you." He motioned for Beil to return.

Beil was intrigued but did not show it to Tragar. He topped up both glasses and returned to his chair, which was much more comfortable than the one afforded the other man. Tragar continued.

. "As we circled the island, we noticed signs of inhabitants through strip mining and farming and so on. The island was basically two dormant volcanos at each end, the larger of the two at the northern tip. We circled from the southwest of the island up north and then south again around the other side. As we rounded the southern tip, way up high on the cliff we beheld an incredible sight. A miraculous black castle on a sheer rock cliff. I could see no roads leading up to it. It appears to be carved into the side of the mountain and glowed black in the evening sun. I looked for a secluded port to set anchor. With a few men, I stopped to explore a bit of the island by moonlight. I ordered the ship to clear the horizon and returned for me in the predawn. We travelled several roads in an attempt to find a way up but were unsuccessful. We did observe some natives of the island but remained hidden. Just before dawn, we returned to the ship and continued our voyage home." Tragar stopped to sip his wine.

"What kind of people inhabit the island?" was Beil's initial retort.

"We only came across a few of them walking on a road. We were not sure where they came from. When we followed the road back the direction they had come, we came to a place that overlooked a clearing at the base of the sheer cliffs. I could only see them from a short distance, but they carried no weapons."

"You obviously feel King Dolmar would be interested in this island," Beil concluded.

"I think he would be very interested in this castle. It was incredible, from what I saw, and in the hands of the right man, impenetrable. We made absolutely sure we were not detected so the next contact with them will come as a complete surprise." Tragar felt shrewd in his assessment.

"I will send a messenger to the king," Beil replied. "Send a copy of your ship's logs and include a complete list of goods that were disposed of. While we await a reply, you should have your repairs completed and replace any men you lost. I will arrange to replace the lost goods. Inform me when you are ready to set sail. Perhaps the king will overlook this inconvenience, but I need the goods you were supposed to return with. You will set sail at your earliest convenience."

Tragar was a bit stunned at Beil's reply. "Don't you think I should be here when the messenger returns?"

"I think you will be fortunate if the king lets you live after your display of incompetence. If you wish to wait for the messenger, then resign your commission and wait." Beil stared deep into Tragar's eyes.

"Of course you are right, Commander." Tragar suddenly realized who was in command here. "Excuse me while I leave to make repairs and gather new recruits." Tragar crossed his chest with his right hand and bowed his head, waiting to be dismissed.

Beil nodded. "Close the door on the way out," was all he said.

After Tragar left the room, Beil carried on as though he had never been there.

Tragar walked back to harbour steaming inside, but he dared not show emotion to his superiors. He realized that the word of a cargo ship's captain was not as respected as a man like Beil's, who controlled an entire province. Now Beil would take his information and expand his own power. He thought about sending his own messenger but decided not to push his luck with a man obviously as ruthless as Beil. When he reached his ship, he prepared the information Beil had requested and got ready to dry dock the immense ship.

When Beil received the copies of the ship's logs, he studied them carefully. After spending the better part of two days going over and over the details, he sent for a messenger. He was impressed with how detail-oriented Tragar was. He also noticed the island's location was very vague. He edited some of the details and produced a plan for the king. He was sure that by undermining Tragar, the king would allow him to get out of this situation he was in and mount a glorious campaign against this new island. He had neglected to mention the black castle so the king would not be too curious about the new land. After all, he was usually only interested in how a new land would expand his empire.

"Take these papers to the king," he told the messenger. "Be sure no one else sees them." Beil handed him a sealed leather pouch and then pulled a separate envelope from the top drawer of his desk. "This letter contains my personal seal to ensure safe passage. I want you to wait for the king's reply before you return."

The messenger bowed to Commander Beil, and after saluting, he turned to leave.

"Send in Lieutenant Kern on your way through," Beil added.

"Yes, Commander," the messenger acknowledged as he closed the door behind him.

Almost immediately there was a knock at the door.

"Enter."

"You called, Commander." Lieutenant Kern was at attention.

"Yes, Lieutenant, I have need of a few items to be delivered here as quickly as possible. I need a large table and maps of all the oceans to the west and south of us. And send for Captain Batris on the ship Revenge. Tell him I have a mission for him."

"Yes, Commander. Would you like a new table constructed or should I confiscate one from one of the carpenters?" the soldier inquired.

"Confiscate one. I don't have time to wait for a new one. Make sure it is large enough to lay out many maps at once. Bring a couple more lanterns as well. Go now." He pointed at the door.

Kern bowed, crossed his right hand over his chest and turned to leave.

Beil walked over to the window and peered out. His eyes fixed on the spot where Batris's ship would dock if he could see it past the city walls. He reached into the pouch on his right hip and pulled out his firestone. He glanced at it and rolled it in the fingers of his right hand. Beil often paced back and forth between his desk and the window, but today he just stared in the direction of the ship and thought about the tale he had been told.

For the next few days, Beil went over the maps upon an immense table that had been constructed in the middle of the room. It was twenty-four feet long, six feet wide and four-and-a-half feet high. It rested on fourteen sturdy legs. Finally, Beil decided he knew where the island was located and drew it in according to Tragar's description. He marked the location on two maps, which he placed in a secure box built into his desk and rolled up the remaining maps.

With a sharp rap on the door, Beil stood upright. "Enter."

A man standing six foot eight, with a large barrel chest and large arms, poked his body through the door.

"Beil, my good friend, how have you been?" The man seemed to be in good spirits.

"Batris, you old dog, you look great." The two men embraced in a hearty hug.

"I haven't seen you since we blasted these little peasants and took over this country." Batris laughed.

"Yes, it was glorious back then, wasn't it? Tell me, what have you been up to all these years?" Beil inquired.

"Oh, just a bunch of routine missions, going from port to port wherever there may be trouble. I usually only travel with ten ships in my armada, rarely needing more. When my ships pour into port at once and unload a thousand men, well, the trouble doesn't usually last too long. Speaking of ships, why is the Exeter in dry dock?"

"That, my friend," Beil put his hand on Batris's shoulder, "Is why I called you here. Sit on down. Would you like a drink?"

"I would prefer a large ale," Batris decided. "I haven't had a good ale in some time."

"I'll have the guard fetch us some," Beil replied as he walked to the door and called out, "Fetch us a cooler full of ale and get a more comfortable chair for my guest."

He motioned for Batris to join him at the table as he retrieved the maps from his desk. Batris ran his hand along the wooden structure, impressed with the craftsmanship.

Beil rolled out the map with the probable location of the island drawn in.

Beil started the tale. "The captain of the Exeter, an Irid Tragar, returned to port a week ago. It seems the ship encountered a severe storm. They suffered a broken rudder that allowed them to drift off course, far off course. When the storm passed and temporary repairs had been made, they returned to the nearest port to make proper repairs and re-crew."

"So he came here," Batris interceded. "Before completing his assignment?"

"Yes, that was my initial reaction as well. However, it seems he came across an island that was previously unknown to us. Here." Beil pointed down to the hand-drawn island on the map.

Batris was surprised. Although they were not explorers, they thought they knew of all the lands from reading the maps of the countries they had conquered.

"There is something on the island that intrigues me. Tragar says that when they rounded the southern tip of the island, there was an immense black castle perched very high up on a sheer cliff." Beil waited for a reaction. "I have studied Tragar's logs and determined that this is the location of the island."

"And what of Tragar?" Batris asked.

"Yes, Tragar." Beil smiled. "Tragar has gone back to his ship. He values his job and he knows his place. I don't think there will be any trouble from him; however, it may be prudent to stop his crew from about talking about what they have seen. We don't need rumours."

"I'll take care of that, Commander." Batris smiled. "So, you want me to go and investigate the island?"

"I've sent a messenger to the king, but I don't want to waste his time. I've seen what happens to people who waste his time. However, if this castle is what Tragar says it is, it would make an excellent gift to the king. I'm sure you are well aware of how gracious the king can be to those who show such extravagance toward him." Beil raised an eyebrow.

"Yes, I see your point." Batris looked down at the map. "I'm sure you have a plan on how we should proceed?"

"Yes, my friend, I do, but first, what would you say to an excellent meal and a good wench for the evening?" Beil countered.

Before Batris could answer, there was a loud knock at the door.

"Come in," Beil yelled.

The door swung open and Kern walked in carrying a large cooler. He walked over and placed it on the chair formerly used by Tragar. He opened the cooler and pulled out two large, frosted mugs and followed with two quart-sized bottles of ale. He slowly poured the golden elixir into the frosted glasses while both commanders stood silently. He handed one to each of the men.

"Beil, I would like a black-haired girl with olive skin, not too old."

"A good choice, Batris. I will have a red-haired wench with green eyes." Beil looked at Lieutenant Kern. "Make sure they are pretty girls," he added.

"Yes sir, I will make sure they are ready after dinner. Do you have a preference for dinner, sir?" Kern asked.

Beil looked over at his guest. "Do you have any idea what you would like?"

"I don't want fish!" Batris laughed. "How about veal? Does your chef prepare a good veal?"

"Have the chef prepare veal," Beil added. "You'll love the veal."

While Kern carried on with his duties, the two men raised their glasses in a toast to their renewed friendship and the start of a mission that could bring wealth and glory to both of them.

Beil went over his plan carefully. It was not complicated; he wanted Batris to verify Tragar's claims, evaluate their defensive potential and bring back a detailed reconnaissance of the island. Once Beil had this information, he could devise a plan to conquer the island. He felt if Batris left now, he would be back around the same time as his messenger with his reply from the king.

"It would be good to fight at your side again, Commander," Batris said. "Although I see some action, it is not like the feeling of a good war. I find my blade is rusty from inactivity. We will restock the ship tomorrow, with your help, of course, and set sail the following dawn."

"I will make sure you have everything you need. If by chance there is something you can not find, take it from the Exeter. I'm sure Captain Tragar wouldn't mind." Beil let out an evil little laugh and raised his glass to Batris.

Irid Tragar stood on the bridge of the Exeter and looked down the dock at the warship Revenge anchored nearby. He looked down at Beil, who was there to see the Revenge off on her next mission. He had noticed the ship's arrival three days earlier and knew the captain had met with Beil. Now that Beil was here on the dock it meant he was up to something. Tragar didn't have to guess what that was. He was seething mad that he was going to be cheated out of a commission that should be his. He ground his teeth together and clenched his fist. Somehow he would get even, and he knew his reward would come from patience. He watched as Beil shook the hand of the large man in front of him. Although he had not met him, Tragar knew he must be the captain of the Revenge.

His ship, Exeter, was also now ready to leave dry dock. The rudder was replaced and the lost crew was replaced in the local taverns. As soon as the Revenge left port, the Exeter would be returned to the water. He waited until Beil had left the docks before he sent him an update. He spent the rest of the evening watching the Revenge as she was being loaded with supplies and readied for departure at dawn.

The next morning it was raining hard and a cold wind blew up from the south.

"Lieutenant," Tragar yelled, "Send a message to Commander Beil. Tell him we will be ready to sail tomorrow at dawn if the ship can be loaded today. Bring me his reply."

"Yes, sir."

Tragar was spending his spare time planning his revenge against Beil. First, he knew, he would need to be in a position of power in order to challenge Beil on any level. In order to do this, he wrote a letter to the king with all his credentials and asked for a transfer to a warship. He would rather be first officer on a warship than the captain of a merchant freighter, if it would serve him later. His fear was Beil, who could override his transfer if he found out about it. Right now, he didn't want Beil to suspect anything. He was also counting on the fact that Beil would be too busy planning an attack on the island to be bothered with a transfer.

The next morning, the Exeter left port to complete her mission. It would be at least four months under full speed before she would be back with a return load.

CHAPTER 7

For the past two months, King Nikodym had been meeting with the village elders in an effort to have them move into the castle. Initially, each of the elders respectfully declined, citing tradition. They had always believed the king must rule from above, as his authority was always highest. Nikodym had finally convinced them that they also deserved to be there, as their authority was highest in each of their respective cities. By being closer to the king, each would have a hand in planning and development. Finally, they had conceded to the king's wishes and agreed to join the royal family in occupying the fortress. The elders' final request of the king had to do with accommodations. The royal family would be on the floor above the elders, and that would satisfy tradition.

Finally, the day had arrived, and the first of the elders' families were moving into their new accommodations. King Nikodym had put the idea of the lift system on hold so the renovations to the new accommodations could be completed and made ready for the new occupants.

Barook had placed all the working parts of the lift into storage in one of the caves at the top of the mountain, near the place where it would be installed. He knew he would be wanting it before long, but for now he had the alterations to the castle to take care of. Bastian was put in charge of carrying out the renovations. Each unit had particular challenges to overcome depending on the elders' family needs. However, the road was now complete to the base of the cliff. With the alterations nearly complete and the elders moving in, Barook and Bastian could soon consider returning to the lift.

King Nikodym and Elisiah met with each of the elders as they and their families moved their belongings in. The king had sixteen suites built in the meeting halls that held the grand-opening party, and another two meeting halls in the front of the castle across from the ballroom. Each room had been decorated to the elders' tastes.

Nikodym and Elisiah helped Kataan from the carriage that held his wife and adopted daughter. Marta had been at Kataan's side for sixty years. She was easily the most respected woman on the island, except for the queen, who also looked up to Marta. Their daughter was eighteen years old and sprouting into a beautiful girl. Although Chalna was not their natural child, they had raised her as their own since her mother died during birth. Chalna was her mother's name, and Marta thought it was right to honour her. Chalna was a well-educated and well-mannered young lady. Her long, wavy black hair and olive complexion were a wonderful contrast to her light-green eyes.

As Elisiah helped Marta from the carriage, Lavar arrived and stood beside his father.

"Lavar, you know Kataan and Marta," the king offered.

"Yes, sir. Kataan, welcome. Marta, it's always a pleasure to see you," Lavar said graciously.

"This is my daughter, Chalna," Kataan said.

Lavar was speechless as the young lady smiled in his direction. She stood in the doorway and waited for a hand. King Nikodym gave his son a little nudge and Lavar offered his hand to help Chalna down. He realized she was nearly as tall as he was. Chalna smiled again at the prince, which brought a blush to his cheeks.

"It seems my son has an interest in your daughter." Nikodym smiled.

Kataan bowed. "I'm too old to think about things like that, your majesty." "Hikaru, call me Hikaru," the king said.

"It would not be proper etiquette to call you by your first name," Kataan returned respectfully.

"Hikaru, where is your wife?" Marta asked. Kataan cast a look of disdain at Marta, who simply shrugged it off.

"She is in the main kitchen overlooking dinner. She wants everything to be perfect tonight," replied the king. "If you would care to join her, I could have Elisiah escort you."

"I think I should help organize the move into our new home." She sighed. "I'm too old to be moving, although I may put a rocker outside the front door on the balcony."

Hikaru made a mental note to have rocking chairs placed out on the balcony for his guests.

"Please excuse us, Your Majesty, we would like to see our new accommodations and prepare for dinner." Kataan bowed graciously again and took Marta's hand.

Marta also bowed to the king, who returned the gesture to the woman he had known all his life. Hikaru thought back for a moment to when he was much younger and Marta had taught him the sciences. He knew Marta well. He smiled.

Lavar overcame his initial bout of shyness and proceeded to unload Chalna's personal luggage. "I would be honoured if you allowed me to pack your bags to your room," the young prince offered.

Chalna now showed signs of shyness, which wasn't her nature. Her olive cheeks reddened slightly as she lowered her eyes. "I am honoured you would share your time catering to my needs." Her soft voice was barely audible.

"I could think of nothing that would please me more." Lavar smiled at her, which brought a smile to her face as well.

Two of the king's personal valets gathered as many of Chalna's bags as they could carry, leaving one for the prince. Lavar winked at the young valets, who smiled and nodded in return. Lavar returned his attention to Chalna, and he offered the young lady his right arm as he raised the lone bag under his left arm.

Chalna was gracious yet slightly embarrassed by the attention bestowed upon her by the young prince. She accepted Lavar's arm with a delicate curtsy.

Lavar bowed to his father and left arm in arm with Chalna to the passage and stairwell that led to the library.

"I've never been to the castle before. I would be honoured if you had time to show me around. I must say, the caves under the castle are intriguing," Chalna said, her courage returning. Lavar led the way up the passage with Chalna now hand in hand and the young valets slightly behind. The stairway was wide but dimly lit as it wound around and up to the library.

"This particular corridor was used by the tradesman to transport the building supplies up to the castle. I think you will be impressed with the craftsmanship displayed by the many men and women," Lavar started as the group approached a large redwood panel at the top of the stairs.

"A secret stairway?" Chalna asked.

"I suppose it is now, but I don't think it was meant to be that way," Lavar replied. "Barook, the man who designed the castle, needed a good construction route, but wanted the room behind this door to be a quiet place as opposed to a high-traffic area." Lavar stopped in front of the panel and released a catch that allowed it to open.

Chalna was stunned at the beauty of the library as she walked through the door and into the room. She turned around in the centre of the room. "This is magnificent," she finally said.

"Could you please take the bags to Kataan's suite and inform Marta that I will return Chalna to her care after a brief tour," Lavar instructed the valets.

"Look at all the books," Chalna was impressed.

"Compiled here are the works of the greatest writers in the history of the island. Do you like to read?" Lavar asked.

"Oh yes, I love the poetry of Corrigan," Chalna revealed. "Many nights I would sit under the moonlight and close my eyes as I played the poems in my mind. My mother has an extensive library as well. I'm pretty sure a lot of the books here were donated by her."

Lavar walked over to the immense fireplace and selected a book from a shelf. "I think you might like this, if you like Corrigan. If you would permit me." Lavar returned with book in hand to gave to Chalna. "These are poems by a lesser-known author who passed away at the early age of twenty-seven. His name was Bandi, and he is one of my favorites." Lavar stood in front of Chalna and looked into her eyes as he handed her the book. As she reached for it, he held onto it.

"One moonlit night I would be happy to recite some to you, if you wish." He smiled.

Chalna smiled back somewhat devilishly, "Your majesty, I think you will have to know me better if you are to recite poetry to me."

"Lavar," the prince asked, "Please call me Lavar. I want friends, not followers. If it pleases you, I will call you Chalna."

"Lavar…" Chalna tried the young man's name, tilting her head. "If my father hears me call you by your first name, he will surely not see the light of day for some time."

Lavar chuckled. "Okay, how about when we are alone then?"

"Agreed." Her devilish grin returned. "Are you planning on being alone with me a lot?"

Lavar blushed, which made Chalna blush as well.

"Come and let me show you the garden." Lavar offered his arm to the young lady. Chalna gently placed her hand on his arm, more out of respect than affection, but she was more than a little interested in the handsome young prince.

Outside the library, Chalna's wonderment grew. She looked up at the great staircase and marvelled at its beauty. Slowly, the pair walked to the steps of the garden. "This is amazing." She was in awe. "Please walk me through the garden, Lavar."

The prince smiled, as Chalna had called him by his given name. "It would be my pleasure."

CHAPTER 8

For three weeks, the Revenge had sailed according to Beil's maps. Commander Batris searched patiently for the island described by Tragar, and finally its peaks could be seen on the horizon.

Batris was on deck as the ships drew near. He reached out his massive hand and grabbed one of the passing guards. "Prepare a longboat and inform the other ships to drop anchor and stand down. They are to wait until our return."

"Yes, Commander." The guard turned and ordered, "You there, prepare to launch a longboat."

Once the boat had been prepared, Batris ordered his ship to approach the southern harbour of the island.

One of the valets approached the king. "Your Majesty, there is a fleet of ships approaching from the southeast. One ship is coming in and nine others are sitting on the horizon."

"Ten ships? Are you sure?" The king was surprised.

"Yes, yes. Come quickly, you can see them from the balcony." The valet was anxious.

Nikodym hastily apologized to his guests and hurried to the great redwood doors that led to the balcony. He watched through the telescope momentarily as the lone ship approached.

"Send for Elisiah. Have him meet me where the ship docks. We must see who these people are." Nikodym headed for his chambers and dressed appropriately to receive guests. He hurriedly headed down to the garden to relay the news of the arrival to the queen. Nateer was in the gazebo reading quietly, enjoying the songs of the birds. He sat down beside her and waited for her to acknowledge him. Nateer finished the paragraph she was reading and closed the book.

"I thought you were entertaining your friends?" she asked coyly. "Why are you here disrupting my reading?"

"Yes, about that…" Hikaru started. "It seems we have guests."

"We always have guests, my dear."

"Not like this. The guests have arrived from the ocean itself," he replied.

"What? What do you mean?"

"Ten ships have arrived on the horizon and one is approaching the harbour. I must go down and greet them, but I had to let you know first," Hikaru informed her.

"So that is why you're all dressed up. And I thought it was for me." She smiled.

"I'll be back after I see who these people are and where they came from." He held her hand and gently kissed her cheek.

"Shouldn't Elisiah be the person in charge here? We know nothing about them. What if they are hostile? I don't like the idea of you going down there."

"I promise I will be careful, my love," Hikaru tried to reassure the queen.

Batris ordered the ship drop anchor about two hundred yards off shore and watched as the curious people gathered on the beach.

"Lieutenant, bring up a keg of wine and an array of our finest weapons. We will need gifts to carry out our reconnaissance." Batris was ready to appear friendly.

The men on the Revenge worked quickly to prepare the longboat that would carry Batris to the new shores. Two additional boats would complete the shore party, with a total of thirty men. "Have the shore party on deck in five minutes. I want to clarify our position on the subject of reconnaissance," was his parting order.

"Yes, Commander. Shall I have the men with or without weapons, sir?" the second-in- command asked.

"No weapons; not yet, anyway. I want this to be a friendly and productive meeting. We don't want to raise any alarms just yet."

As the lieutenant carried out his orders, Commander Batris retired to his cabin to prepare the ceremonial uniform in which he would attend the inaugural meeting. He made the final adjustments.

Caves of Trolan

The crowd on the beach was patiently waiting for the appearance of the strangers. They were curiously quiet, whispering to each other as if they were afraid to speak up. There was a lot of talk about the size of the ship, as they had not seen anything like it. Many were in awe of not only this ship but the ones on the horizon.

Batris arrived on deck to find all the men in formation and awaiting his orders to depart. He walked past and inspected each man individually, staring silently into their eyes. He walked to the stern of the ship and looked over the now-crowded beach.

"Gentlemen," Batris said, practicing his congeniality. "This reconnaissance must be carried out without incident. Our objectives are simple. We are under the pretence of setting up trade. Keep your eyes sharp and don't cause any trouble. I want to know everything I can about this island. Today, you are not soldiers. Remember that." With that, Batris ordered the longboats over the side. "Commander Colig, you're with me."

"Elisiah. Just in time. What do you make of these strangers?" the king asked as he came across his friend on the road to the city of Kataan.

"Your Majesty, please return to the castle. We don't know who they are or what they want. You must allow me to assess these people first." Elisiah was a bit frantic.

The king stopped and thought about Elisiah's request. He watched as the boats were unloaded over the side of the larger ship and the men, one by one, filled the longboats.

"Perhaps you are right, Elisiah," the king considered. "Take them to Kataan's city and have them put up in Kataan's old house. Don't allow them access to the caves or castle just yet. I will await your evaluation and we will make our decisions from there."

"Thank you, Your Majesty. I was afraid you would go against me on this one." Elisiah was relieved.

"Offer them every hospitality and send a messenger for me when and if you feel comfortable," the king instructed. "Watch them carefully, Elisiah. Find out why they are here."

"Yes, Your Majesty. You can count on me," Elisiah reassured the king.

With the men in the boats and rowing for shore, King Nikodym made a hasty retreat to the caves at the base of the cliff.

"Put your hearts into it, men. I don't have all day," Batris yelled across the three boats.

"They don't appear armed, Commander." Lieutenant Commander Colig, the first officer aboard the Revenge, had a keen eye and a sharp mind. He had sailed with Commander Batris for three years and was an astute listener as well as a strategic planner. Batris often used his negotiating skills prior to invasion.

"They come forward without any apprehension. Look up at that castle, Colig. Magnificent. It truly is a marvel, perched on the cliff so high up. I think I would like to have a look inside," Batris said matter-of-factly.

"It really is a sight, isn't it, sir?" Colig was equally as monotone.

"I think it shall soon be mine." Batris smiled.

"Elisiah." Prince Lavar joined Elisiah as the longboat drew near.

"Lavar, you shouldn't be here right now." Elisiah was a bit nervous and excited but was trying hard not to show it.

"Someone from the ruling family should be here to greet the strangers." Lavar was also excited.

"Really, Your Majesty. I just had this conversation with your father. He had the good sense to return to the castle and let me see what we're dealing with. I urge you to do the same. If the king knew you were here, he would not be happy." Elisiah tried to sound stern with the young prince.

Before he could send the prince away, the longboats pierced the beach. For the first time, both Lavar and Elisiah saw the size of the visitors.

Batris and Colig were the first out of the boats and together they approached the crowd on the beach. The group parted as the men continued to walk up the beach until they reached Lavar and Elisiah, who didn't move. The two giants stopped and stood silently, sizing up the inhabitants of the island and the two representatives sent to greet them.

"Gentlemen, I am Commander Batris. This is Lieutenant Commander Colig, my second in command. My authority is the Lakar first fleet," Batris stated. "As you can see, I command the nine ships on the horizon as well as my ship in your harbour. I control over a thousand men. Commander Colig is my chief negotiator and personal assistant. We require food and water." He looked over his right shoulder and nodded. With that, two men from the longboats brought forward the weapons and wine, placing the bounty at the feet of Batris. "Please accept these gifts as a token of respect for your people."

Elisiah looked down at the cache of weapons, cringing inside. Weapons were foreign to the islanders, but he was curious about what the cask contained.

Elisiah was just getting over the size of the men in front of him. "My name is Elisiah, and I am the chief negotiator for the people of Trolan." He spread out his arms in welcome. "Please allow me to provide you with any needs you may have."

Colig looked down at the prince. "And you are?"

"I am Prince Lavar. My father, King Nikodym, is the ruler of this island." The young prince stuck out his chest and tried to stand as tall as possible.

"Please, join us, we have set up accommodations for you in the city. You can have the use of it for as long as you need," Elisiah added and showed the way.

The two soldiers gathered up the wine and weapons and followed behind. Batris and Colig walked behind Elisiah and Lavar, and the Lakar soldiers followed silently behind in perfect unison. The entourage was followed by hundreds of curious islanders who were keeping a safe distance between them. When they arrived, Batris stopped, turned to his soldiers and then back to Elisiah.

"May I have your permission to set my men at ease?" Batris asked.

"Yes, of course. How many men will be staying ashore so I can arrange adequate accommodations?" Elisiah replied.

"Just these thirty." Batris pointed them out as Colig dismissed the men.

The men dispersed and systematically began to question the villagers who showed less intimidation. They looked around the city, assessing the peaceful inhabitants.

"Shall we go inside, gentlemen?" Elisiah offered. Batris approached the front door of the house formerly inhabited by Kataan, Marta and Chalna. He waited for Lavar to enter before he proceeded.

The interior of the house was moderately adorned with simple furnishings, as it had not yet been allocated to a new family. Two of the Lakar soldiers brought in the cask and cache of weapons, placing them on the table in the dining room.

"This is a quaint little city you have here ... Elisiah, was it?" Colig surveyed the room and walked to the living room window.

Elisiah overlooked Colig's comments and asked one of the housekeepers to bring food and glasses in order to share the contents of the cask.

Prince Lavar joined the Lieutenant Commander at the window. "The view from here is wonderful, isn't it, Commander Colig?"

"Yes, it is." Colig's monotone voice sent chills down the spine of the young prince. "Tell me about the castle on the cliff."

The prince looked momentarily at Elisiah, who tilted his head slightly but only looked back for a second.

"The king rules the people from the castle. It is forbidden to go there unless personally invited by the king." Lavar stretched the truth a bit.

"Or from the prince?" Colig inquired.

"Actually, you would find I am a prince more by name than stature. I work the fields and man the fish boats and share in many other trades. My father calls it a king's apprenticeship," Lavar added.

"Please be sure to ask the king if we could have an audience. I'm sure I would enjoy a tour of the castle. Interesting … there appear to be no roads." Colig was testing the prince.

"No, it doesn't appear that way," Lavar said with a smirk.

"Surely the king would welcome friends seeking trade with his people?" Batris said with little emotion.

"Lavar, why don't you go and help organize the meals for Commander Batris's men while I try to answer their questions." Elisiah wanted Lavar at a safe distance until he knew more about the motives of these men. The young prince was wise enough to know what Elisiah wanted and volunteered readily.

"Commander Batris, the king has sent me to establish trade with you and your King. What did you say his name was?" Elisiah continued.

"I didn't." Batris looked directly into Elisiah's eyes. "No matter. His name is King Dolmar … and he is the greatest ruler known to man." He puffed up his chest as he watched Lavar leave through the front door.

Colig also watch Lavar as he left to carry out Elisiah's wishes. Barely noticeable, Colig looked down to a soldier outside the house and then in the direction of Lavar. The soldier nodded and stealthily followed the prince.

"Tell me, Elisiah, do you have a good supply of water?" Batris tried to distract Elisiah so he wouldn't notice Colig.

"Why, yes, and food as well," Elisiah said. "Our farmers have excellent irrigation channels fed by several main rivers that lead from the mountains. I'm sure you will find we have many items for trade with your people. Tell me, Commander, why have we never heard of your people before?"

"It would seem we never knew you were here." Batris sat in the chair that looked the most comfortable. "Only a few months ago we were made aware of your location by a merchant ship lost in a storm. It seems you are not on the maps of any of our trading partners. Ordinarily, I would not travel this far out. I mostly travel from port to port and help negotiate ... trade agreements."

"What kinds of goods do you offer for trade?" Elisiah tried to pry.

"We have access to many goods and materials. We supply many kingdoms with food and raw materials. We are always looking for new supplies as old routes die off or become unproductive. We are merchants, if you will, for many kingdoms. We merely act as distributors for their wares. We find it advantageous for everyone if we always have the needed items," Colig interjected.

"Yes, I can see the logic in having a greater range of supply and demand," Elisiah reasoned. "Am I to believe it is your intention to market our goods in several different kingdoms?"

"That way the fruit is always fresh." Colig smiled for the first time.

"Gentleman, I don't think I know of any great need that our people have. We are very self sufficient as a people. You have to understand, until a few hours ago, we were not even sure there were other kingdoms." Elisiah wanted more information.

Batris played along. "How about advances in education?"

"How about advances in ship building and fishing and forest removal?" Colig also played along as he continued to survey the castle from the window.

"We grow what we eat and only take what we need. If we take too much, we would ruin the balance of nature," Elisiah returned. He was also aware of Colig's interest in the castle.

A loud rap on the door brought forth a small woman with a basket of fruit and another of bread. Behind followed a slightly taller girl with glasses for the contents of the flask and a platter full of meats and cheeses.

Elisiah noticed Batris eyeing the young woman. "Please, gentleman, enjoy a snack while we talk."

Batris looked at Elisiah and smiled. "Thank you." The word was uncomfortable to the Lakar commander.

Colig returned to the table and picked up one of the long, shiny weapons. "Tell me, Elisiah, do your blacksmiths make weapons as fine as these?"

"Commander, I don't think you understand. We have no need for weapons; the people of the island have not fought for many generations." Elisiah was unsure where the conversation was headed.

"No matter," Colig conceded. "With our advice and help, your black-smiths can be taught to produce many valuable items."

"Our blacksmiths are excellent at producing machinery to work the fields or pumps to carry the water; however, instruments of destruction are forbidden, except for hunting," Elisiah retorted.

Colig took the sword and pierced an apple from the bowl and brought it to his mouth. "Fresh fruit is something we see little of."

"We have plenty on the island, and you are welcome to as much as you want while you are here." Elisiah was still being gracious.

"Does that go for everything on the island?" Colig asked.

"Feel free to ask for whatever you need and if we can provide it, we would be happy too do so." Elisiah replied.

"Perhaps it is time to restock our water supply and perhaps you would be generous enough to help us with some of your perishables. Fruit and vegetables, maybe. I should also send a message to the king about our newfound friends." Batris smiled again at Elisiah.

"Yes, of course. Please follow me, and I will have some of the men help you." Elisiah gestured toward the door.

"Have these gifts sent to your king and ask him for an audience." Batris's request was more of an order.

"Certainly," Elisiah replied.

For the next several hours, the villagers help fill the requirements of the strangers and then helped load the huge vessel. They brought large casks of water and baskets of fresh fruit for the men on the ships.

Elisiah was very careful, backtracking several times, to be sure he was not followed to the caves leading to the castle.

King Nikodym sat near the ledge of the balcony and gazed at the ships on the horizon. Elisiah announced his presence to the king but received no response. As he approached the king he paused and spoke again. "Your Majesty, I've returned from meeting with our … guests."

"You don't sound very pleased, Elisiah," the king commented, still looking at the ships.

"It would seem these people are here to trade with us," Elisiah offered with a tone of sarcasm.

"Elisiah." King Nikodym was a bit surprised. "It's not like you to frown upon someone so quickly. Tell me what they have done to earn your disrespect."

"They are very large, intimidating men. They look down upon us like we were savages. They say they want to talk trade, yet they offer to educate us in weapon-making. They seemed insulted that you were not there to greet them personally. I don't think it would be wise to trust them. They say they are merchants, but why would merchants travel in such a large circle of ships? Why are the rest of the ships sitting on the horizon if they are here to trade? I don't like it."

"Don't you think you are overreacting, my old friend?" Nikodym smiled, trying to ease Elisiah's frustration.

"These people are very different from what we are used to," Elisiah continued calmly. "They are very disciplined in the way they analyse their surroundings and in their behaviour. They seem to have a single-mindedness in their purpose. The question is, what is their real purpose? They certainly are not merchants."

"You've met them. How do you feel we should handle them?" Nikodym quizzed his old friend.

"Your Majesty, please be careful. Don't allow them access to our resources, or I fear they will only want more. They openly display their weapons, which makes me think they are used to using them. If they are the people I think they are, they could be very dangerous." Elisiah looked into the eyes of the man he had grown up with. "You are wise, Hikaru, you will do the right thing."

"Well, Colig, what do you think of our hosts?" Batris and Colig joked about the defensive capabilities of the Trolan.

"Once King Dolmar gives the word, we will be going to war with people who think weapons are for farming," Colig sneered.

"Send this message to Dolmar." Batris handed a sealed envelope to Colig, who flipped it a couple times to check the seal.

"I'll dispatch a ship immediately, Commander." Colig knew when to show respect. "Would you like me to send a messenger to Beil, or do you want this sent directly to the king?"

"Commander Beil has control of Alkar. It's a large province, which I helped him acquire. I believe this island will be mine. I shall offer the newly conquered land to the king, and I shall control this island. It will become another province under the king's flag." Batris looked over at

Colig. "I don't want any mention of the castle to the king. No use arousing curiosity unnecessarily, Commander. It's how we go up the ladder, eh, lieutenant?"

Colig thought about Beil's reaction at Batris's defiance but only smiled.

"You realize that you would then become the man that controlled the fleet," Batris stated.

"Thank you for your support, Commander." Colig thought about how Beil would react when he realized his friend was now going behind his back in competition for the island. "You know what Beil will do when he finds out," he warned.

"I have thought about Beil for many years, Lieutenant." Batris sneered. "Before you joined this vessel, I was second in command under Beil. It was my expertise that secured Alkar for him, and now it is time for me to share in the spoils of war. I think this island will do nicely, and I do not intend to lose it."

"But what of the king?" Colig protested.

"No, Commander, the king is too far away to be bothered with an island, hundreds of miles from the nearest trading route. You can't control a kingdom from out here. As long as this island can produce a profit, no one will investigate further," Batris surmised.

"I am only concerned that Beil can be a most dangerous opponent if he feels he has been wronged," Colig reminded his commander.

"Let me worry about Beil." Batris was confident in his ability to deal with Beil and the king.

"With your permission, I will take a boat out to rendezvous with the fleet and dispatch a ship to the king." Colig wanted to return before dark.

"The king is on the northern tip of Lakar," Batris informed Colig. "Send Captain Sordain and tell him best speed. I want him back here with the king's response as soon as possible."

The morning brought torrential rains, which bounced off the hardened roadways. Although visibility was poor, Hikaru Nikodym could see only eight ships on the horizon where nine had been the night before. He knew the strangers had been mingling with his people and asking questions. He decided it was time to meet with the strangers and try to evaluate what their real purpose was on his island. He closed his eyes and took a deep breath of the fresh, salty air. Somehow, he felt that his peaceful island was about to change drastically. Opening his eyes, he headed for Elisiah's quarters. As he closed the large redwood doors to the castle, Elisiah emerged from the garden.

"Elisiah, I've decided to meet with the visitors. However," Nikodym raised his hand to avert Elisiah's protest, "I think you are correct in limiting their movements until we have more information about them."

"Thank you for your support in this matter, Your Majesty."

"Send a messenger to Commander Batris and arrange to meet in Kataan's city house," Nikodym requested. "Arrange a time that is convenient for the commander."

"Yes, Your Majesty. I will deliver the message personally, as he already knows me," Elisiah returned. "With your permission, I would also like to attend the meeting."

"Yes, of course. I'll await your reply."

With that, Elisiah turned and headed for the library to the passage down the mountain.

Commander Batris was relaxed, with his feet up on the rail and his fingers clasped behind his head. He watched closely for any guards or soldiers who might protect the king. Occasionally one of his own soldiers would approach with updates on the surveillance. Batris was now convinced more than ever of the outcome of any conflict. All he needed was an answer from King Dolmar, and the island would be his. He showed little emotion as Elisiah approached.

"Elisiah," he said, "I'm sure you have an answer for me."

"Yes, Commander. King Nikodym would like to meet with you here at your earliest convenience," Elisiah replied.

"Here?" Batris queried. "What do you mean here? It seems your king has little respect for the emissaries of the great King Dolmar."

"Not at all, Commander," Elisiah started diplomatically. "The journey to the castle is perilous, and King Nikodym is only concerned with your safety."

"My safety?" Batris went on the offensive and raised his voice slightly. "Do I look like I need to be cared for? Tell me, Elisiah, what gifts does your king have to bestow upon the great King Dolmar?"

"I'm sure when King Nikodym meets with you, he will bestow the gifts you desire." Elisiah was calm on the outside but seething inside.

"Let us speak frankly, shall we?" Batris lowered his tone slightly. "I have already dispatched a ship with my report to the king, the only true king here. In a few weeks, that ship will return with a message from him.

I will meet with your ruler then. Be warned, Elisiah, my king will not tolerate disrespect."

"Your king won't tolerate disrespect?" Elisiah's tone was now raised slightly. "You ask for an audience with the great King Nikodym and now you refuse to see him for weeks, perhaps longer."

"Elisiah." Batris smiled widely. "I will meet with your ruler only in the castle. Only that action will show the respect that is our due. Leave now, and only return when you have arranged a meeting up there." He pointed at the black fortress.

Elisiah glared at Batris for a moment and turned to leave.

"Elisiah," Batris warned "I think I am going to like it here."

As Elisiah walked away, he could hear Batris's roaring laughter, and he could feel his face redden with rage.

"So peaceful trading will not work with these people?" King Nikodym walked alongside an obviously shaken Elisiah.

"They are barbarians. I've been watching them closely, Your Majesty," Elisiah replied. "They are not interested in trading. They haven't even approached one merchant with the prospect of trade. So far, they have visited the foundry in search of only weapons. They seem obsessed with our defensive capabilities and this castle."

"And Commander Batris made it clear that he would only meet me here in the castle?" Nikodym asked.

"Commander Batris insists it is the only way to show the respect they feel they deserve," Elisiah revealed.

"And what do you recommend we do?" Nikodym asked.

Elisiah looked apologetically toward the king, paused for a moment, and methodically spoke the unthinkable. "Hikaru, I think we have to prepare for the worst. I think they plan to take this land as their own. They have come in force and have now completed their reconnaissance. There are over a thousand men sitting on those ships on the horizon. Batris said the ship he sent to their king would return in a few weeks. I feel we have that long to prepare ourselves."

"Prepare ourselves? We haven't had even a skirmish in generations. We know nothing about war. We have no military and no weapons. If you are correct, we will be sheep at a slaughter," the king said.

"We do have several advantages over them, Your Majesty," Elisiah stated calmly. "They depend on fear, intimidation and military might. I've noticed they react with emotion rather than calculation. I don't think they have had to use much strategy in their conquests, and we can use that against them. We also know the island, and they have yet to discover the caves. We must block off all the entrances to the castle and defend from here."

"Are you saying we should barricade ourselves up here? What of the people who cannot defend themselves? I'm sorry, my friend, but I cannot leave my people when they need me the most. Go out and warn the people of our fears and bring as many woman and children as possible. Be extremely careful not to arouse the suspicions of Batris or his men. Let's move as many as possible by night so we have a better chance of not being detected. We will need a distraction to keep their attention away from what we are doing." Hikaru put his hand on Elisiah's shoulder. "If you are correct about them, we must be ready."

"Let's hope the messenger they sent has a long journey ahead of them. I will take care of the distraction."

CHAPTER 9

"Behold the most powerful man in the world." King Dolmar admired his rugged, once-handsome features in a mirror of polished gold. Grey had taken his previously black beard, which was showing only traces of its former colour. His long hair was pulled back in a ponytail as he had always worn it. He looked up and down at his reflection in admiration. He was still a fine specimen, kept fit by his many battles. Then he looked back to the eyes; the eyes that struck fear into every man. He spread an evil smile as he looked into the coal-black eyes of a ruthless dictator.

His favourite colour was red. He always wore a red vest and topcoat over a white shirt. His black trousers were tucked into knee-high, glistening black boots and a black cape draped from his shoulders to his knees. On the back of the cape was the king's family crest, a shield with a red-and-white checker pattern on the left, cutting diagonally down to the bottom right. On the upper right was a gold lion, standing up and facing left with a gold crown upon its head. The king stepped back from the image in front of him and turned away.

Finally, the third messenger had arrived. Dolmar was duly impressed with the first two. Now he wanted to hear what Commander Batris had to say. He walked over to a set of white marble stairs, which rose to a magnificent throne from which he conducted his affairs. The throne was older than anyone could remember and was in his family from the beginning of the empire. The framework was a beautiful red wood, the origin of which was unknown. The legs and arms were adorned with gold and embedded with precious stones. The seat was padded and tufted in black leather with the backrest padded and adorned with the same crest as his cape. Down each armrest to the floor weaved a root system of the same polished wood. Above the crest to the top of the throne and down the back was a carved history of Dolmar's ancestors. Somehow, the wars and time had taken the meaning of the carvings and left only the splendour and beauty.

Dolmar ascended the three stairs to the throne and took his place among the gods. The great king slowly lowered himself onto his pedestal and looked down to the lone guard at the other end of the chamber.

"Send in Captain Sordain," he ordered.

The guard pulled open the two golden doors behind him. Captain Sordain, properly cleaned and dressed, approached the king and stopped at the foot of a blood-red carpet that stretched twenty feet to the base of the marble stairs. The carpet was trimmed in gold bands that held it in place. He placed his right hand on his forehead and knelt down before the mighty king.

"Stand," the king's voice boomed.

Sordain rose, placed his hand over his heart and thrust it out toward Dolmar. Bringing his hand back down to his side, he waited.

"Approach me now."

Looking down and taking a deep breath, Sordain walked down the red carpet toward the king.

"Stop and drop your cape."

Without hesitation, Sordain stopped and bowed. He untied his cape and let it drop to the floor. Dolmar rose from his throne and stood above his subordinate, as if to prove his stature. He looked back at the guard and pointed to the doors. The guard turned and left the great hall, closing the doors behind him. Dolmar slowly descended the stairs one by one with a click and tap as he walked down to the servant of Batris, stopping on the final stair.

"Come closer."

The messenger approached Dolmar and stopped at the foot of the king.

"Look up into my eyes." The king spoke with no emotion.

Slowly, the man looked up from the floor, taking in the black boots and trousers, then up to the red vest and overcoat, past the grey beard to the coal-black eyes.

"What do you have for me, Captain Sordain?" the king asked.

"I have an envelope in my vest from Commander Batris, Your Grace." Sordain was surprised the king knew his name, as they had never met. His commission had been instituted at sea when his commander was killed in action. He opened his vest slowly and pulled out a large envelope, which he handed to the king, bowing his head again.

"Before I open this envelope, do you have any statement you wish to make?" Dolmar offered.

"Your grace, only Commander Batris's ship approached the island. The other nine ships approached no closer than the horizon," Captain Sordain replied.

"Why do you think that is important, Captain?"

"Only Commanders Batris and Colig know what is on the island. I only know they have interacted with the islanders, but no other information was made available to the other ship captains," Sordain offered.

"Very well, return to your ship and await my reply."

Captain Sordain took two steps back, bowed to the king then stepped backwards to his cape, which he retrieved and placed around his shoulders. Looking into Dolmar's eyes one last time, he turned and walked to the doors, pulling them open without losing stride. The guard then returned to the room, closing the doors behind him.

"Send for... Irid Tragar," the king ordered. "He is the captain of a merchant ship, Exeter. Find him and have him brought to me. His first officer will temporarily assume command."

The guard nodded and left the room.

Dolmar returned to his throne to get comfortable before opening the envelope.

"Chalna?" the young prince called out.

"I'm in the garden," came a faint response.

Lavar jumped down the four stairs leading to the garden and walked the path to the gazebo where he was sure to find Chalna. Much to his dismay, she was nowhere to be found when he arrived. He looked out each side until he found her crouched in a flower bed on the other side of the moat, by the library.

"There you are," he called out, barely audible over the waterfall nearby. "I'll be right over."

Chalna stood and brushed herself off. She teased her hair and adjusted her dress at the shoulders. As Lavar approached, she curtsied and bowed her head. Lavar dropped to one knee and tenderly kissed the olive hand of the beautiful young lady.

Chalna blushed as he rose and took her other hand as well. His warm smile made her feel comfortable around him.

"I've been waiting for you." She smiled.

"I've been wanting for you." The prince chuckled as Chalna half-heartedly slapped at him.

"If your mother could hear you, I'm sure she would douse you with cold water." Chalna laughed too.

"Well, I'll have to keep a close eye out for her then," Lavar shot back, still chuckling.

Chalna looked deep into Lavar's eyes and passionately embraced the young prince as they had done many times in the past few weeks.

"Please come and sit with me, I have something to tell you," Lavar said as he pulled Chalna down the path toward the entrance of the garden.

"What is so important that you have to drag me down the path?" She was laughing again.

"Keep running, you'll see," the prince returned.

Around the corner and down the path to the gazebo they ran until they reached the bridge over the moat. The prince stopped and turned to look at Chalna.

She put her arms around his neck and looked into his eyes. As she was about to kiss him, he smiled and scooped her up in his arms. He carried the astonished young lady and to the centre of the gazebo. Even here he was reluctant to put her down, and he stole the kiss she had offered at the bridge. As she embraced him, he slowly put her feet back upon the ground.

"Now," she said. "What is so important?"

Lavar motioned for Chalna to sit, and he sat with her. "Many years ago, while you were a child, Kataan and Marta entrusted my father to give you the only item your mother valued. Now that you are seventeen, my father feels you are old enough to have it and asked me to give it to you."

The prince reached into his pocket and pulled out a small case. Holding it toward her, he opened it to reveal a splendid, shiny disc with the inscription, "To my beloved Chalna, love Irid."

Chalna was genuinely stunned at the sight of the beautiful object. She flipped it over to reveal a heart imprinted in the centre and clear stones around the outside. As she moved it around in the light, she was dazzled by the sparkling stones the likes of which she had never seen before.

"What exactly is it?" she finally said, still twisting it in the light.

"My father doesn't really know but thinks they must be precious stones and metal from the land your mother came from," Lavar replied also in awe of the sparkling stones.

Chalna lifted the disc from the box and saw it was attached to a long, delicate chain. Lavar spread the chain in his hands and placed it around her neck.

"It was your mother's last wish that you wear this," he said.

"Your Grace, I present to you Irid Tragar, captain of the supply ship Exeter," the guard broadcast loudly from the golden double doors.

Irid entered the doorway confidently and approached the edge of the blood-red carpet where he stopped, bowed, and awaited the king's instructions.

The king looked down from the throne, unimpressed with the man at the end of the carpet. "Come forward," he said solemnly.

Tragar raised his head and walked confidently down the carpet. The king noticed he wore no cape, and allowed him to approach to the bottom of the stairs. Dolmar looked deep into Tragar's eyes for a moment before he spoke.

"There seems to be a great deal of interest in this island you claim to have discovered." The king tapped his fingers on the arm of his throne as he spoke. "Commander Beil of Alkar province has sent me some very detailed information. It seems he wants this island very badly. Probably a bit bored with the Alkar, a bunch of passive peasants. You undoubtedly think you deserve some commission for your discovery." Dolmar didn't wait for a response.

"Very well, you will travel with me," he decided. "I have received a message from Commander Batris with his reconnaissance report. There is a glaring difference between the two accounts. You have mentioned a massive black castle high up on a cliff on the southern tip of the island, yet Batris, who has also landed on the island, failed to mention this castle."

Dolmar stared at Tragar. "Apparently, this will be a swift victory for my troops, so I will have little time to decide the fate of the people of Trolan, as Batris called it. If this island brings me a usable extension to my empire, you will be rewarded. If this is a waste of my time, you will find the price of my time is very high."

Dolmar continued to stare down at Tragar, looking for weakness or fear in the man who had yet to speak. "What reward do you feel you deserve for discovering this island?" Dolmar asked, wanting to understand Tragar's motives.

"Your Majesty," Tragar began graciously. "I wish only to serve my king. This island I give you with my open heart that it expands your glory. I would like to add, there is a great castle on the island as I have described. I also landed on the island when we were lost in a storm with a damaged ship. We were undetected, I assure you. I do not know why Commander Batris does not mention the castle, as I do not know his intentions." Tragar bowed to the king. "If it suits your Grace, I would appreciate the opportunity to serve your empire in a more meaningful role, say as first officer on one of your warships."

King Dolmar smiled, something he rarely did. "You know well the chain of command. We will see what this adventure brings, then I will decide. As for now, you are relieved of your duties as captain of the Exeter. We will leave tomorrow at noon."

"Yes, Your Majesty." Tragar could feel the excitement building within him. "I shall be ready to go, and I promise you, you will not be disappointed." He bowed to the king.

"Your life depends on it," were the king's final words.

CHAPTER 10

The exodus to the castle by the woman and children was going well. Commander Batris was spending more and more of his time on his ship, finalizing his invasion plans. His men visited the island less, as Batris was now confident in his ability to destroy the inhabitants. The islanders were setting minor distractions to him, which annoyed him but did not prove to be a problem. The most bothersome were the fires the inhabitants had set that brought thick, billowing smoke that impaired his vision of the land mass and the castle. Let it burn, he thought. There would be a lot more burning before he was through.

King Nikodym was busy with Elisiah and Lavar, going over defensive strategies and preparing supplies. He was stressed over the idea of these people threatening the Islands lifestyle of peace and contentment. He felt his only hope was with King Dolmar. Surely a great king would know the value of peace. Perhaps he could arrange a truce to maintain the peace, but judging by the people Elisiah had described, this seemed fruitless.

"We will need alternative water supplies," Elisiah surmised. "I'll have Bastian and Barook devise something. Are you listening, Your Majesty?"

"Hum, oh yes, Elisiah, I'm sorry, I'm having trouble concentrating. We have packed the castle with woman and children, but we are running out of room," he thought aloud. "Send some men deeper into the caves. We must find some kind of advantage in our own home."

Elisiah thought for a moment. "Your Majesty," he started, as he relived the island's history in his mind. "In the ancient texts, there are stories of our people coming down to the valley from the highest peaks on the mountains. What if this is true ... and there is a part of this island which has long been forgotten?"

Hikaru also remembered these stories once Elisiah mentioned it.

"Perhaps I could lead the men on the expedition," Prince Lavar spoke up. "It would raise the spirits of the men and help keep their minds off the woman and children."

"Perhaps the prince is right, Your Majesty. It would help the men to know they are being led by the future king," Elisiah didn't realize how prophetic his words would be.

King Nikodym walked over to Lavar and put his arms around his son. "Please be careful, son, the caves can be unstable. Good luck," was all he said.

Irid Tragar walked the deck of the Exeter for the last time. He took his time to look up at the height of the towering masts and thought about the thrill of climbing them for the first time. This ship had been the love of his life since he lost his wife and daughter some sixteen years ago. He had made several successful voyages to many ports and always returned with a bounty for his king. He ran his hand along the rails and looked over the side to the water below. Then he looked forward another hundred feet or so to the bow. Sitting just off the bow another two hundred yards sat the king's ship Royal Descent, one of the most beautiful ships to ever sail the seas. It was over fifty years old and built by Dolmar's father, King Elbrin.

It was originally started by the Paramien ship builders as a vessel for their king to enter the afterlife. Once King Elbrin saw the ship, he confiscated it for back taxes. It was taken apart piece by piece and brought to the Mayak shipyards, where it was reassembled. King Elbrin made sure it was the most lavish and extravagant vessel ever constructed. Gold, ivory and exotic woods were imported and integrated into the design. Massive marble columns provided ballast, which took two years to acquire from the farthest lands. Although she was not the largest vessel, half the size of the Exeter, she stole the horizon with her glow.

Transfixed on the Royal Descent for a few minutes, Tragar returned his attention to the old friend he was leaving behind. Walking slowly to the bow, he looked in the port window of the crews' quarters. He smiled, thinking how rarely he had been in that room considering how long he had been on the vessel. When he was younger, he had a bunk in there but since he took command, he rarely fraternized with the crew.

Now it was eleven o'clock and time to hand the ship over to his first officer. In a little over an hour, he would be embarking on an adventure with the king that could very well change his life. He was about to give up a great deal in a huge gamble in a new land.

From his cabin, Batris had a clear view of the great black castle perched on the cliff overlooking the pounding surf. The smoke had finally cleared after he ordered his men to put out the fires the inhabitants kept lighting. No matter how hard he tried, none of his men had been successful in finding a way up to the castle. He figured there must be a trail up the back side of the mountain.

He was incensed the king had not invited him up there. Soon enough, he would be able to exact his revenge. He surveyed the sheer rock cliff that surrounded the castle on three sides. Straight up a thousand feet on a four-thousand foot sheer rock wall; the odds of climbing up the outside seemed insurmountable. Somehow, he must find a way up if he had to go through every Trolan male on the island, a prospect that only seemed to elate the commander. Batris walked over and opened his cabin door.

"Colig," he called out. "Come into my cabin."

Colig was standing at the wheelhouse, also admiring and despising the magnificent black fortress. He walked down the stairs that led to the cabin of Commander Batris and rapped firmly on the door.

"Enter." Batris's booming baritone voice echoed through the door.

Colig opened the small door, hunched over to go through, and closed it behind him.

"Drink?" Batris offered the sweating, thirsty giant.

"Thank you, Commander." Colig graciously accepted a large mug of ale, which was reserved for the commanding officers.

Batris nodded in the direction of the castle. "What do you think about that?" he spat out with contempt.

"There must be a tunnel up to the castle," Colig surmised. "My men have been around the mountain as far as possible and have found no roads or pathways. We know they get up there somehow, so it must be a tunnel."

"I've been thinking the same thing." Batris smiled. "You show intuition in your analysis, my friend. I want you to break your men into groups of three and follow the peasants that head in the direction of the castle. They are getting in somehow, and large groups of men are too easy for them to spot. Try hiding men in the forest where they can't be seen. They have to slip up sometime, and I want to exploit that."

"I agree, Commander." Colig was showing the confidence he would need if he was to take the place of Batris. "I will dispatch the men immediately and have messengers provide updates every few hours."

"Have the men be discreet. The peasants won't give up any secrets easily, and we can't be too aggressive without permission from the king," Batris warned.

"Commander, can I have your permission to send a couple of ships around the island and scout out landing locations? Perhaps we can see something from the water that we can't see from land."

Batris walked over to the port window and viewed the eight ships still on the horizon, just within eyesight. "Very well. Bring the remaining ships in a bit closer. I would like to set up a little display when Captain Sordain returns with the king's orders. Send four ships, two from each direction. Have them stay two hundred yards apart, one closer to the island to give different views as they patrol. Hopefully we can find something the previous ship missed."

Lavar had already said his goodbyes to his mother and Chalna, and now he prepared to lead the six men in his group to the inner depths of the volcano. King Nikodym had decided on ten groups of seven men to explore the ten largest unexplored caves that led deep into the volcano. Unsure of what they would find, each man had the courage to sacrifice himself for the good of the people. Elisiah was the first to hug the prince and shake the hand of each man who had volunteered. They silently entered the caves, marking their route with a nearly invisible symbols that the hunters had used for eons. Hopefully, if the caves were discovered, they would not leave any clues to be followed, unless it was by a skilled hunter.

"Lavar." Elisiah put one hand on Lavar's shoulder and shook the prince's hand. "Good luck. Make your father proud and save your people from these savages."

Lavar looked into Elisiah's eyes and smiled. "Don't worry, Elisiah. Take care of Mom and Dad while I'm gone and keep the boys away from Chalna." The prince chuckled and disappeared into the tunnel that led up into an old shaft. Elisiah again wished Lavar luck under his breath.

As the king's ship Royal Descent sailed strongly down the straight to the Bay of Alkar, she was accompanied by four of the king's personal warships. They followed the Royal Descent on every voyage to protect the king from the possibility of looters. Even without these ships, no one would have the audacity to provoke the king. The four ships were small and fast, although heavily armed. They could surround and pummel a ship with lightning speed and ferocity. Following a good distance back was Captain Sordain's ship Infamy with her orders to break off at Alkar and deliver a message to Commander Beil.

Captain Sordain was not looking forward to talking to Commander Beil, who had been captain on the Revenge when Sordain was a junior officer aboard the ship, and he was well aware of Beil's temper. He also knew how much power a man like Beil could wield, considering he controlled an entire province, the largest in the kingdom. Beil was feared by all the other provincial commanders, and they always tried to stay out of his way. However, when it came to war, Beil was generally regarded as the master, as he had been the man to secure the largest land mass. His ruthless efficiency was well known by all.

As the Royal Descent passed Alkar City, Irid Tragar was standing behind the wheelhouse and leaning on the rail looking back to the Infamy, which was starting to make her turn for port. He smiled as he thought about Beil's reaction to the king's orders. Generally, not a sympathetic man, he felt a bit sorry for Captain Sordain, thinking about his own dressing down at the hands of Beil. The smile slowly left his face as his lips tightened. He knew the king was his only hope of achieving the credit for finding the island. If he had not sent a message to the king, Beil would probably have control of the island, and he would probably have disappeared somehow. Tragar was confident the king would be impressed with the black palace once he saw it. The smile returned to his face as he pondered the possibilities of the king's reward.

Finally, the Infamy was out of sight and Alkar City slowly disappeared on the horizon. Irid slapped his hand down on the rail and turned to head back to his cabin, a simple room compared to the splendour of the rest of the ship. Another couple of weeks and he would be a happy man, but a little trickle of anxiousness started to build within him.

As the other six men woke one morning, Lavar was already up and staring into the tunnel they were exploring. Now on their fifth day, the troop was breathing the same fresh air. Although the tunnels were pitch black without the torches, they burned bright with the brisk tunnel breeze. Along with Lavar was Barin, one of the prince's oldest friends, along with Jessard, one of the brightest young scientific minds on the island. Jessard was born in a village near the northern tip of the island

and had come to study under Marta, which was a great honour. The other four men were chosen for their different skills, such as Jonas, the mountain climber, and Kaleb, the biologist. Randal was a zoologist and Bodie was one of the general labourers and was big and strong.

Barin approached Lavar and sat on the rock beside him. "What are you thinking about?" he asked brashly.

"I'm thinking about where this tunnel is headed," the prince replied quietly. "I see it's getting narrower, and I wonder what's around the corner. And I'm wondering if we should send a man back to let Elisiah know what's happening." The prince kept his eyes on the tunnel.

"Perhaps we should wait until we have something to tell him," Barin said, a bit more quietly this time.

"Perhaps you're right, Barin. Perhaps you're right." The young prince sighed. "Today we will find something, I can feel it. Listen closely and you can hear a trickle of water. And smell the air, still fresh this far into the mountain. That means there must be another large opening somewhere else in the volcano. With a little luck, we may find something today. I only hope we don't end up hanging over a cliff." He chuckled. "After breakfast we will head out."

"Right then, what's for breakfast?" Barin blurted out.

"Heat up a pot of water with a torch and we'll make some grain meal," Lavar replied.

"Oh yeah, my favourite," Barin said sarcastically. The men chuckled and set about making breakfast.

The young prince had noticed how quiet Jessard had been throughout the trip and decided to ask the young man his opinion on what they had seen so far.

"With the consistency of the tunnel, I would suspect the eruption of the volcano must have been massive and involved a lot of water to leave so many caves and air passages," Jessard said, soft-spoken. Although Jessard was a well-respected young man, he never felt comfortable around people he considered his superiors. Lavar, however, had a way of making people feel comfortable.

"You're right about the tunnels. There must be an exit to the surface nearby," Jessard continued.

"Well, let's go see if we can find it, shall we?" The young prince stood, torch in hand, and led the way. Each man carrying a torch had about twenty feet of visibility and walking fifteen feet apart lit the tunnel quite well. As Lavar led, the wind in the tunnel started to pick up as the cavern started to narrow and the ceiling began to expand upwards. The pace slowed as the footing became a bit more treacherous. Suddenly and without warning, the trail ended. The men stood at the bottom of a sheer cliff extending past the limit of the light. They could still feel the rush of fresh air flowing down upon them.

The prince looked over to Barin and Jessard and back to the cliff. Silently, he decided to try to ascend the cliff. Jonas approached with rope in hand and smiled at the prince.

"Allow me, Your Majesty. This is why you brought me, and I don't think your father would be too happy with me if I let you endanger yourself."

Lavar thought about it for a second and realized he wasn't being insulted, but protected. "Very well, Jonas, the honor is yours." Lavar held the torch up high above his head.

Jonas was nimble and climbed the rock face with expertise. Within a few moments, his feet disappeared from sight.

"Can you see anything?" Barin yelled up the cliff. Seconds later a handful of sand hit the ground beside his feet.

"Did you see that coming?" a faint voice chuckled from above. The sand was followed by another handful and more laughter, this time from everyone but Barin. "I can see enough. There is a faint light ahead over a ridge. Hang on..." There was a strain in his voice. "I'm almost at the top … just a couple more feet and … wow.…"

"What is it, what do you see?" the prince yelled up enthusiastically.

"I think you better see for yourself," Jonas replied from the darkness above as a rope dropped within eight feet of the ground.

"Lower the rope a bit farther," Barin hollered up at Jonas.

"That's all there is," was the reply from above.

"Crap," Barin said under his breath as he looked up at the dangling rope. He climbed the rock face a few feet and reached out to grab the rope. He applied all his weight as he kicked off the wall as he climbed. Hand over hand, Barin struggled to reach the top. Down below he could hear riotous laughter as the rope lowered to the floor. The rest of the group laughed as they realized Jonas had pulled one over on Barin.

The laughter made the climb that much easier for the rest of the men as the ascended into the darkness. Once at the top of the cliff, Lavar had to let his eyes adjust to the natural light. He blinked a few times before shielding his eyes with one hand.

"Oh my…" the prince started.

"Well, how do we get out of this one?" Barin added.

Before the men was clearly the centre of the volcano. The ledge they were standing on was really a sheer rock wall about fifteen feet thick and about two hundred feet straight down.

They all stood in awe at the massive cavern that shot up around them.

"How far would you say the cavern is across?" Lavar asked Jessard.

"At least a thousand feet, I'd say, maybe more. The question is, are there any more caverns leading out of here," Jessard replied.

"Well, we're going to have to go down there if we are going to find out," Barin threw in.

Jonas sighed with a smile and pulled up the rope from the tunnel floor behind them. Before he tossed the rope to the floor of the volcano, he tied two more ropes together and secured them to the first, tossing them over the edge.

"See you soon," Jonas said as he lowered himself over the edge and out of sight of the men above.

Barin resisted the temptation to drop a handful of sand over the side and focussed his attention on the opening several hundred feet above him. The pockmarked cavern walls glowed eerily in the overhead light. He could feel a slight pressure in his ears as he thought about the quietness, the click of Jonas's boots against the rock wall and the slight trickle of water. He couldn't see the water, but he knew it was below them somewhere.

After about fifteen minutes, Jonas voice echoed up the cliff. "Okay, come on down."

"That's me," Barin spoke up as he grabbed hold of the rope and started making his descent.

The prince sat down beside Jessard quietly in the dim light as they waited for their turn.

Commander Batris was spending the evening as he had spent many evenings, staring at the immense black fortress. Tonight was cooler than it had been for the last couple of weeks, and the wind made the seas choppy. The ship bobbed up and down gently as the waves splashed against the wooden hull. The moon glistened off the cresting waves. Batris watched as the longboat struggled against the forces of nature.

He knew it was Colig returning after meeting with his scouting parties. Slowly, the boat made its way through on the backs of six large soldiers. Finally reaching their destination, the exhausted men held the drop lines taunt so Commander Colig could disembark. Before the men could rest, they would first have to raise and clean the longboat.

"Commander." Colig, soaked from the return trip, approached Batris. "Sir, we have found the entrance to the castle."

Batris stood motionless for a moment, absorbing Colig's comment. He raised an eyebrow as he looked at his first officer. "Where?"

"At the base of the cliff there is a series of caverns. We have watched as people have discreetly entered and exited the caves."

"How can you be sure this is the entrance to the castle?" Batris said calmly.

Colig approached Batris slowly and stood beside him, staring up at the castle as well. "We saw Elisiah going in and coming out several hours later."

Batris smiled, now confident of Colig's assessment of the situation. "Continue to search for more openings; there may be more than one-way in."

"Yes, Commander. If you don't mind me asking, sir, have you heard anything from the king?" Colig asked.

"No," was the quiet reply. "Dismissed."

King Nikodym was spending the morning with Elisiah and Queen Nateer on the balcony outside the front doors. The warm breeze that filtered up the cliffs was refreshing after the cool evening before. He sat back and closed his eyes for a few minutes as the warm sun beamed down upon his face.

"Hikaru, what is that on the horizon?" Queen Nateer pointed to the small objects slowly coming into view.

Elisiah was standing as the king opened his eyes and strained to make out the objects on the horizon.

"I believe it is the return message from their king." Elisiah was solemn.

"Only one ship left, old friend. It looks like four or five ships have returned," Leer said.

As the ships approached the island, both Hikaru and Elisiah realized that none of these ships was the one that left. King Leer could see the scrambling below on the ship that had been in the harbour for some time. He was mesmerized by the sheer beauty of the magnificent vessel that just dropped anchor off his shores.

"Whoever is on the ship is a lot more important than Commander Batris," Elisiah observed almost under his breath.

"Perhaps you should go and talk to Batris again," King Nikodym said softly. "I think they will want to talk now."

The three watched as a longboat lowered over the side of Commander Batris's ship and two men joined the six oarsmen. The men seemed panicky from the king's vantage point, and he realized Batris was not expecting these ships to return.

"That must be their king. Look at how panicked Commander Batris is," Nikodym concluded.

"I never thought I would see Batris react like this," Elisiah added.

"Why would their king come here?" Nateer asked.

"The island must be very important to them," Elisiah said.

"What is so important about the island? We don't have anything of value," the king wondered.

"We have this castle," the queen said.

"Your Majesty." The burly guard opened the door to King Dolmar's quarters. "I present to you Commander Batris and his first officer, Commander Colig."

The king waved his hand half-heartedly and the two men entered the room, stopping just inside the door. Dolmar was now looking up through his telescope at the castle perched high on the cliff.

"I can't say as I've seen anything quite like that," he spoke quietly. "I wonder why you didn't mention it in your report. Is there so much more here that it became inconsequential?" The king turned to face the two men standing at the doorway. "Drop your capes."

Quietly, the two warriors dropped their capes and draped them over the chair by the door.

The king extended his hand to the two men. "Come closer, over to the window."

Batris led the two men over and stood beside the king, looking up at the castle.

"Tell me what you have discovered about this island, Commander Batris," Dolmar started.

"Commander Colig assures me we have found the entrance which leads up to the castle, your Majesty. May I say it is a pleasant surprise that you would honour us with your visit." Batris was trying to be cordial in the presence of the great king.

"You mean to tell me you haven't been in there?" Dolmar asked.

"No, your Majesty. Their ruler has offered to meet me but only in the city. I told them it was an insult to you, our great King Dolmar, that they try to belittle us so. Since that time, we have been doing reconnaissance work and awaiting your orders," Batris responded.

Dolmar looked at Batris, unsure of his dedication to his duties since he had not mentioned the castle in his report. "Very well, Commander, what did you find with your reconnaissance?"

"Commander Colig is in charge of the reconnaissance teams, your Majesty. He will offer the report," Batris stated.

Colig began. "This island is lush with farmland and the peasants grow a variety of grains and vegetables. They also grow a variety of fruit and have a prosperous fishing industry. There is an open mine on the northern tip of the island and a foundry that makes mostly farming implements. You can see the forest … the trees are massive. There is enough wood here to build an incredible fleet. And the castle. As Commander Batris stated, we have found a cave that draws a lot of traffic, and we believe it leads to the castle through an underground passage."

The king looked at the guard standing at attention inside the door. "Bring him in." Dolmar looked into the eyes of Colig and Batris as his guest entered the room. "Gentlemen, I would like you to meet Irid Tragar." Tragar entered the room and stopped ten feet away. "Irid Tragar was formerly the captain of the merchant ship Exeter. He claims to have found the island at the tail end of a fierce storm about four months ago."

Batris's eyes widened slightly at the second surprise of the day. He was shrewd and knew how to hold his emotions, and now every fibre of his body was straining to hold his composure.

"Tragar feels he should be rewarded for his find, and that you and Commander Biel are trying to keep him from receiving his due. How do you feel, Commander?" the king asked.

"Your Majesty," Batris began, "My only wish is to serve you and your empire. I sent a message directly to you in order to more quickly secure this new land. It was not my intention to undermine anyone's plans." Batris strained to sound sincere in his backtracking. "If Commander Beil had other plans, I was not aware of them," he lied.

"Very well, Commander, send a message to the ruler of this island of Trolan. I want to meet him in order to discuss terms of surrender."

"Do you wish me to express your message in those terms, Your Majesty?" Batris requested.

"Tell their ruler I wish to meet him alone in the city. We don't want to alarm anyone just yet. Make it for noon, the hottest time of the day." The king smiled.

CHAPTER 11

Elisiah was at the beach awaiting Colig as his longboat raced for shore. The small craft pierced the sandy shoreline and ground to a halt.

"You're not wasting any time, are you, Elisiah?" Colig called out as he stepped from the longboat.

"You seem a little shaken, Commander," Elisiah speculated. "It seems you weren't expecting the visitor who arrived this morning."

"The inevitable only happened a little sooner than anticipated," Colig shot back.

"I take it your visitor is the king of your empire," Elisiah continued.

"He is the king of his empire," Colig corrected. "And now he wants to meet with your ruler," he added coldly.

"When would you like to have this meeting?" Elisiah was cautious.

"At noon in the city," Colig answered.

"All right, I'll inform the king of your ruler's intention to meet," Elisiah replied as he backed away from his large adversary.

Colig smirked at Elisiah's use of the term "ruler."

Unsure of what to expect, Elisiah travelled as quickly as possible to the caves to relay the message to the king. With fear in his heart, Elisiah did not take the usual precautions he had earlier to ensure the secret of the entrance. Although he did not know it, every step he made was being carefully monitored.

After descending the two-hundred-foot cliff, Lavar had the men fan out in all directions, searching for any other openings in the cavern walls. Jessard stayed behind to more closely survey the plant life on the floor of the dimly lit cavern. Now that their eyes had adjusted to the light, the men extinguished the torches to save them for the return trip.

Jessard was on his hands and knees as he looked over the floor. The soil was thick and fertile, and the plants grew hardily despite the low light. Closer inspection of the walls revealed open piles of coal, as well as veins running along and into the steep walls. Totally consumed in what he had discovered, Jessard hadn't heard Barin as he called for the men to meet him at the base of the far wall.

As the rest of the men gathered, Jonas started toward a large split in the face of the rock, about thirty feet off the ground.

"Barin, I want you to go with Jonas and explore the tunnel while I return with Bodie. We can start bringing supplies into the cavern while you continue to explore. There is plenty of fresh water and we will leave all the rations we can spare," the prince informed his friend.

"Don't worry, Lavar, if there is a way out of here, we will find it." Barin put his hand on Lavar's shoulder.

"Prince Lavar." Jessard approached the two, holding a piece of coal. "If you don't mind, I would like to see you and Randall on the other side of the cavern."

"Go ahead, my friend," the prince said to Barin. He followed Jessard to the other side of the cavern.

"Your Majesty, look at this." Jessard pointed to the ground in front of him. Embedded in the mud beside the creek that ran through were the unmistakable impressions of small animals. "Obviously animals have been visiting this area, and fairly recently," Jessard observed.

Randall got down to investigate the footprints in the mud.

"That means we must be close to another exit." The prince looked around.

"That also means food," Jessard surmised.

"They are probably coming in to eat the vegetation as well as drink the water," Randall added. "I don't see any large predator tracks yet, so they may also be coming in for safety."

Jessard turned to the large veins of coal. "Look here, raw coal, veins of it. With your permission, I would like to stay and continue my studies."

"Of course," the young prince agreed. "I will travel back with Bodie. We will return with a crew of men to do something about these walls. We are going to need a better way to get up and down that two-hundred-foot wall."

"Your Majesty, I could use the help of Randall, but the others will be of little use to me. Take them back with you and bring Barook and Bastian to solve the engineering problems," Jessard suggested.

Lavar smiled at Jessard. "You know, what they say about you is true."

Jessard blushed a bit but now felt as though he had known Lavar for years.

"I am going to leave you in charge, but I am going to leave the men. There is plenty to explore outside of your expertise, and the more men looking, the better. There is everything you need here, and enough for everyone."

"As you wish, Your Majesty."

Lavar took only the food rations he and Bodie would need and headed off toward the two-hundred-foot return trip up the cliff.

The time had arrived for King Nikodym to leave for his meeting with King Dolmar. He was dressed as richly as possible by the island's resources. As he descended the stairs of the castle, Queen Nateer was waiting for him, along with Elisiah. He held out his large hand and smiled at his beautiful queen. Nateer took Hikaru's hand and squeezed hard. He picked her up and hugged her tightly. He looked past Nateer to Chalna, who was sitting in the garden.

"Please be careful, Hikaru." The queen spoke the obvious.

"Be strong, Nateer, this won't take long," Hikaru spoke softly. "Look at Chalna over there in the garden."

"She's waiting for your son." The queen tried to smile.

"Well, you go and wait with her," Hikaru said. "I'll be back soon."

He hugged her again and kissed her deeply. Setting her back down on the floor, he slowly walked away. Elisiah accompanied the king to the library and the passage to the depths of the castle. Hikaru walked quickly, which barely gave Elisiah time to talk; he could hardly keep up.

"Your Majesty," Elisiah called out. "Hikaru," he tried again. "What's your hurry?"

The king stopped. "I don't know," he said, looking down. "I don't know." He started back down the stairs. They reached the bottom and went into the lower chamber, but the king walked past the carriage prepared for him and continued on foot.

"Your Majesty." Elisiah was stern.

Hikaru stopped again and paused with his hands on his hips. Elisiah walked over and opened the door to the coach.

"You must arrive in the style befitting a king."

Hikaru returned to the carriage and stopped at the door, looking sternly at Elisiah, who didn't flinch as he returned the look. The carriage rocked as King Nikodym stepped up and took his seat, crossing his hands on his lap. Elisiah took his seat across from the king.

"Your Majesty," Elisiah began slowly. "You're so quiet today. Is there something I can help you with?"

The king sat solemnly and motioned for the driver to begin the trip down the mountain. He looked back into Elisiah's eyes. "I'm a bit scared," he said quietly. Elisiah sat back in his seat and digested the comment.

"My stomach is all tied up in knots and my pulse is racing," the king continued. "I haven't felt like this since the day I got married." He smiled, thinking back to the day.

"Perhaps you are just a bit nervous," Elisiah said, trying to comfort his old friend in some way. "After all, it's been a hectic few months."

"I only hope you are wrong about these people." The king sighed.

"So do I," Elisiah replied. "So do I."

The remaining trip down the tunnel was quiet as the king relived his wedding day in his mind. He had never been as nervous as he was that day. Even Elisiah had been visibly shaking and sweating then, the memory of which brought a smile. Hikaru hadn't thought much about his wedding until now, and he wondered why. Everyone was invited to the royal wedding as the then- young prince married the woman who had been raised to stand by his side. Although the marriage had been arranged by Hikaru's father, the king could not have chosen better himself. It was his good fortune that his father had chosen the woman he was deeply in love with.

The king looked back at Elisiah, who had given up his own happiness to help provide for the royal couple. Perhaps he had been selfish for wanting a friend like Elisiah. "Elisiah, why didn't you ever marry?" the king asked.

"Marry? What brought that up?" Elisiah asked.

"I don't know. I was just thinking of Nateer and wondered why you never married," the king wondered.

"After you got married, there was no one left." Elisiah tried to lighten the mood.

As the carriage approached the entrance to the caves, the driver stopped.

"We'll have to walk from here." Elisiah stood and opened the door to the carriage. "We have been blocking up the tunnel, leaving only enough room to walk through."

Hikaru stepped down from the carriage and walked with Elisiah down a path that had been narrowed to under three feet and almost fifty feet long. Once at the end of the pathway, the men had to stop and let their eyes adjust to the bright sunlight. Just outside the cave, another carriage was waiting to complete the trip to the city of Kataan.

King Nikodym stood beside the carriage for a moment and surveyed the landscape. The scent of flowers filled the air, and he heard the birds singing. He noticed a rabbit dart across the path and disappear into the forest. He bent down and picked a handful of flowers, choosing the brightest colours and the sweetest scents. He handed them to one of the men standing guard over the entrance of the cave.

"Please take these to the man driving the carriage inside the tunnel. Ask him to take these to Queen Nateer and tell her … I love her. And I will be back soon." Hikaru smiled.

The man was understandably shaken but did as the king asked. Nikodym returned to the carriage and got in. He thought about the simple things in life that were about to change. Another twenty minutes and they would be in the city.

"Did you send a carriage to transport the Lakar king to the city?" Hikaru asked Elisiah.

"Yes, Your Majesty," he replied "I sent Kataan's carriage shortly after meeting with Colig. It should be at his disposal whenever he needs it."

"Thank you, Elisiah, you think of everything," the king spoke quietly.

As the carriage approached the city, Hikaru noticed how quiet it had become. The market was almost empty, as the people had been warned about the pending danger. The carriage stopped just outside Kataan's door about ten minutes before the scheduled meeting.

"We will wait here for their king," Hikaru decided.

Elisiah could feel the sweat beading on his brow, but King Nikodym seemed curiously unaffected by the heat.

A few minutes later, a grand entourage headed up the roadway from the beach. Thirty or forty men, Elisiah estimated, leading a procession of fifty or sixty more behind the king's carriage. He noticed the oxen he had provided no longer pulled the carriage. Instead, it was pulled by eight of the king's own men.

As the party approached, the soldiers leading split down the middle and moved to the roadside to allow the carriage through. The men pulling the carriage stopped about twenty feet in front of King Nikodym.

Commander Colig opened the carriage door and Commander Batris stepped down, followed by another man Elisiah was not familiar with. The third man in the carriage was obviously the king. He stood slowly and gazed around from his vantage point, looking over at King Nikodym, who was still sitting.

King Nikodym realised that King Dolmar was waiting for him and slowly stood, facing the Lakar king. Unsure of how to proceed, King Nikodym bowed slightly as a sign of respect. The Lakar king held his eyes firmly and did not return the gesture. The two men stood facing each other, and everyone was silent.

King Nikodym took the initiative and stepped down from the coach. With Elisiah at his side and under the watchful eye of King Dolmar, Nikodym walked up the stairs and through the doors of Kataan's house, which was more like a small castle. It was constructed almost a hundred years ago for the first king of the island. Two other castles had been built since then, for each of the succeeding kings. The family of Kataan was given the home when the original king took up his new residence. Elisiah stopped at the bottom of the stairs and waited for the Lakar king. Dolmar's eyes were firmly planted on him. Two or three minutes passed before Dolmar decided to step down and slowly walk over to the foot of the stairs, stopping only long enough to take a better look at Elisiah. He ascended the stairs, pushed the door wide open and looked in.

He turned and nodded back at Commander Batris before walking into the house, closing the door behind him.

Commander Colig walked up to Elisiah and stood beside him with his hands clasped behind his back.

"Where are the oxen we provided to pull the carriage?" Elisiah asked the big man.

"We killed them and hung them. Should be good eating," Colig answered with a smile.

Elisiah was stunned at the response, which effectively crushed any thought of conversation. Colig continued to smile as he rocked back and forth on his toes.

As Dolmar closed the door behind him, he turned his attention to King Nikodym, who was standing across the room. Beside Dolmar and extending to Nikodym was a long table carefully prepared with meats, vegetables and fresh fruit.

"King Dolmar," King Nikodym graciously started. "Welcome to the island kingdom of Trolan."

Dolmar said nothing. He walked over to the table and picked up an apple. He looked at it curiously and replaced it. "We don't see much fresh fruit."

"Although we do not have much, we are willing to share with our friends." King Nikodym gestured at the table. "Please, join me for a bite to eat." Nikodym was trying to ease the tension in the room.

"Where did you get this table?" Dolmar asked, running his hand along the smooth surface.

"It was made by one of our craftsmen. The wood is from the redwood which grow abundantly on the island. If you like it, consider it a gift from my people."

"And what can I give you?" Dolmar asked, still admiring the construction.

"We require very little," Nikodym responded.

Dolmar scanned the rest of the room and walked over to the door. He called out to Commander Batris, who immediately approached the king and bowed in his presence.

"Stand." Dolmar was stern. Commander Batris looked up to the king, who whispered in his ear. Elisiah was standing nearby but could not make out what the king had said.

Batris backed away from the king, raised his right hand to his chest and thrust it out. He returned to the carriage and brought out a large oval object covered with a cloth. Batris struggled with the big yet thin object, which must have been very heavy. He returned to the house, looked down at Elisiah and smiled. Elisiah was always nervous when these men smiled.

"King Nikodym." Dolmar was now trying to be gracious. "Please except this gift from me and my people."

Leaning the package against the wall, Dolmar removed the cloth. Hikaru gasped at the beauty of the object, which cast his reflection.

"It's a mirror," Dolmar revealed. "Made from solid gold and polished by the tradesmen of Mayak, a province in my kingdom."

"I've never seen anything like it." Hikaru was genuinely impressed as he stared at himself in the mirror.

"Tell me of your land," Dolmar asked, finished with the formalities.

"Well, my family has ruled this land for as long as anyone can remember. We have been at peace for a hundred years, since we worked out guidelines for peace amongst all the villages. Until Commander Batris arrived on our shores, we were unsure of the existence of other people. The land provides everything we need, and we are careful in how we manage our resources," King Nikodym confided.

"Sounds quaint." Dolmar sneered.

"And what of your people?" Nikodym asked.

Dolmar walked over slowly, and stopped three feet away from Nikodym. He towered over the king by a full four inches and outweighed him by thirty or forty pounds. He crossed his arms over his chest and sighed.

"My kingdom is the largest in the world. We trade with those we have to and take from those we don't." He glared down at Nikodym, looking for a reaction. "Your island would seem to have a lot to offer. Do you think we could … trade?" Dolmar was blunt and showed no emotion on his bearded face. He stepped back and turned away from Nikodym.

"I suppose we could engage in a limited trade agreement." King Nikodym said, his voice low and his eyes tightening.

"Limited trade." Dolmar turned back with a sarcastic tone. "What would you consider limited trade?" He raised his voice a bit. "Would you consider your forests, your tradesman? Are you prepared to pay taxes?" He stared into Nikodym's eyes coldly, distracting him as he slowly pulled a four-inch knife from a sheath concealed in his cape at his crossed arms and cuffed it in his hand.

"No, sir, we are not!" Nikodym sternly replied, raising his voice to the same level as Dolmar's.

"Now, now, now." Dolmar lowered his voice to taunt Nikodym. "Consider your people before you make so hasty a decision and consider what could happen to them if you refuse."

"My forests and my people are not for sale, and we will pay no taxes for the privilege of trade." Nikodym ignored the taunts and stood his ground.

"That's a pity and a mistake. Consider one more thing, King Nikodym … consider this." Dolmar thrust the blade of the knife deep into Nikodym's chest. "You can watch yourself die."

Nikodym's face stretched in agony and shock, and his arms spasmed straight out and his knees buckled as he fell to the floor at Dolmar's feet, gasping for air.

Dolmar stepped back from the fallen king and looked into his widened eyes. He left the knife in Nikodym's chest and turned and walked to the door. He looked back at Nikodym, who was holding the handle of the knife and still gasping for air. Dolmar then opened the door and motioned for Batris and his soldiers to approach.

"Take the table." He looked over at Elisiah and smiled. "A gift from the people of Trolan," he said sarcastically. Four of the soldiers entered the home and retrieved the table. Elisiah could hear the crashing of plates as the soldiers cleared the hundred-year-old table. Carefully, they eased the table out the door. Dolmar went straight for the shore and motioned for his soldiers to follow, not slowing down to take the carriage. Colig smirked as he left Elisiah's side to join the parade.

Elisiah tensed up as he waited for King Nikodym to appear. He looked at the soldiers walking away and then looked back at the door. He bolted and flung it open as terror started to build inside him. Across the room he saw the king, who had both hands on the handle of the knife and was gasping openly.

"Get some help over here!" he screamed. "Hikaru!" He lowered his voice as he ran over to hold the king. "Hang on, Hikaru." The tears welled up in his eyes as he realized what had happened.

Immediately, four men scrambled into the room and also saw the horror. Elisiah quickly looked around the room. "Grab that tablecloth and bring it over here." He pointed to the heap of smashed dishes left by Dolmar's men.

Immediately, two men broke for the pile and shook loose the tablecloth.

"I never should have let this happen." Elisiah said as he looked into the eyes of his wounded friend.

The men quickly made a sling from the tablecloth to carry the king. Easing him into it, Elisiah steadied his wounded friend as the men gently lifted the king and rushed for the door. Hikaru weakly raised his right hand to Elisiah's shoulder.

"Take me to Marta," he whispered, "And bring Nateer to me." He smiled slightly to try to ease his friend.

Straining to hold back his tears, Elisiah smiled at Hikaru. "Of course, Your Majesty. You just hang on, and we will be there shortly."

Carefully, the men eased the king into his carriage and rested him in Elisiah's arms.

"Send someone ahead to inform Marta of the king's condition. Make sure she is ready to receive him." Elisiah tried not to show the panic he felt. "Try not to inform the queen. That is something I must do." He tapped the driver on the shoulder. "Let's go."

As the carriage sped for the castle, a young man ran as fast as he could to inform Marta and Kataan. "Gather everyone you can; we have to fill in the cave. These people are going to attack." Elisiah pointed to one of the young men running beside the carriage. "Tell as many people as you can. Tell them to get away anywhere they can to hide from the predators." The men in the surrounding crowd scrambled to spread the word.

The return trip to the cave, which had taken twenty minutes earlier, took five. A group of twenty men had gathered at the entrance, having already heard the news. As the carriage pulled to a halt, the men sprang into action. As four of them attended to the king and Elisiah, two others ripped the back cushion off the carriage to complete a makeshift gurney to transport the king. One of the men would have travel through the tunnel on his hands and knees in order to stabilize the king through the narrow tunnel.

While they hurried to ready the king, Elisiah took the rest of the men to prepare a defense. "Hikaru," Elisiah started, trying to hold his composure. "I must leave you in the hands of your people. I have to prepare for the imminent attack, and time is of the essence. Please forgive me, old friend, but this is something I must do."

Nikodym smiled slightly and tried to speak but could not. He squeezed Elisiah's hand and tried to smile. Elisiah watched as the men disappeared into the tunnel, and with his eyes watering, turned to begin his task.

As the longboats approached the Royal Descent, the crew had just finished loading the large redwood table. Throughout the return trip, Dolmar had said nothing. His men paid close attention to every wave of his hand and nod of his head. Over the side of the ship, a large padded throne was lowered to retrieve the king. The men on the longboat steadied the chair as Dolmar took his time sitting down. With the wave of his left hand, the crew raised the throne up over the edge and lowered it onto the deck. The deck was glowing in the bright sun as the king stood slowly and looked over the men awaiting his orders.

Dolmar was in no hurry as he walked over to inspect the first of many prizes to come. The table was even more beautiful now that it was uncovered. Rolling his fingers over the rounded edges, he couldn't help but notice the similarities to the magnificent throne that graced his castle at home. The colour of the wood was unmistakable and the craftsmanship unsurpassed. As Dolmar continued to caress the table in admiration, Commander Batris and Colig had arrived on deck and were awaiting the king's acknowledgment of their presence.

King Dolmar looked at Commander Batris and then over to Commander Colig before waving his hand to allow them to approach.

"Commander Batris," the king finally said, "Tonight we will dine on my ship with the rest of the ships' captains. A small celebration to commemorate our new friendship with the Trolan." He smiled openly, obviously impressed with what he had seen. "Tomorrow we will take control, and you, Commander, will lead the assimilation of their culture."

"Your Worship, nothing would give me greater pleasure than presenting you with that beautiful castle." Batris then felt he could speak freely. "Once we have control of the island, the castle will fall, and looking at these people, I think you can plan to move in right away."

"I have done half your job for you … I have eliminated their king. Now I will sit back and watch you work," Dolmar replied, still with a sinister smile. "Have Commander Colig go and inform the other captains to arrive at seven o'clock. You can come to my cabin to tell me your plans."

When the men carrying the king arrived, Marta and Kataan were waiting with medical attention. Marta was the first to inspect the wounds of the now-unconscious king. Although his breathing was irregular, his pulse was weak but steady.

"I have no choice. I have to remove his shirt to see how to best remove the knife. Bring water and cloths." Marta was incredibly calm and composed. "How did this happen?" she asked.

The men looked at each other, remembering what Elisiah had said. One finally spoke. "It was their king; he did this. They are cowards, attacking an unarmed man." He spat out with overwhelming contempt.

"Bring him over here and lay him down," she barked out as she stepped back from the king so the men could move him.

Looking at the open wound as she opened the shirt and vest, Marta realized the knife had punctured the lung. Removing the blade, she plugged the hole with her finger and applied steady pressure to control the bleeding.

Tears welled up in Kataan's eyes as his wife worked feverishly to save the king's life. His old body grew cold as the reality of the situation began to set in.

"I can heal the wound and make him comfortable," Marta spoke softly. "But now we can only wait. The chest has filled with air, and the air has no way to escape. The hole created by the knife acts as a one-way valve, letting the air in but not out. With each breath, more air collects in the chest. Now the lung has completely collapsed, and it is putting pressure on his heart. I've put a tube in his chest to drain the air, but I don't have the expertise to seal the wound in the lung. We will have to wait and see if his body can repair the rupture. I fear the long journey back may have been too long and done too much damage. Let's get him to his own bed; the queen will want to see him."

As two men carried the king up the stairs, Marta picked up the knife that had been in the king's chest and put it in the medical bag she carried.

Under the watchful eyes of the Lakar soldiers, Elisiah and the gathering crowds began to disappear into the caves. For more than two hours they filed through the narrow tunnel until the last man was in. Altogether, the Lakar soldiers had watched over three hundred men enter the cave.

There was a dead silence when the Lakar soldier arrived with his reconnaissance report. As the soldier wrote up his report, the background started to echo with the sounds of rocks and dirt being poured into the caves from the inside. Immediately, the messenger ran for the shore to deliver his report to the king.

Elisiah had now entered the second phase of his plan to defend the castle. As a large group of men filled in the cave below, he was preparing to defend it from above. He had over two hundred men cutting and transporting rock to bombard the cave entrance. During the construction of the castle, large sections had been cut into the cliffs as building material to extend the balcony in front of the great fortress. These terraces provided ample working room around the cliffs for all the men involved.

Now he had other matters to attend to. He knew the queen would not be in any condition to organize the kingdom, and until Hikaru recovered or Prince Lavar returned, he would have to hold that responsibility.

Returning to the castle, Elisiah met Marta at the bottom of the great redwood staircase.

"Tell me of the king, Marta." He bowed in her presence as he liked to do.

"Time will tell, Elisiah," she said softly. "I've done all I can. However, I'm afraid it doesn't look good."

"Please care for Nateer for me," Elisiah said. "I have too much to do to prepare for their attack…"

Marta cut him off. "Not now, Elisiah. First you must see the queen. She doesn't know what has happened, as I sent Chalna to keep her busy in the garden. They are there now." She looked in the direction of the waterfall. "Go to her. I'm sorry you have to be the one to tell her, but you are his dearest friend, and I think she would want to hear it from you."

Elisiah bowed his head, knowing she was right. "Thank you for reminding me of my duties. I will go to her now. Please have some men standing by to help me. She will not take this well."

With that, Elisiah headed to the back of the garden near the waterfall, where the queen was tending the garden with Chalna. They were talking about the prince as Elisiah arrived. He stood in silence, watching them until they saw him.

"Elisiah." Nateer was the first to notice him. She looked at him as he stood in silence and she noticed his body was shaking. She stood slowly, her knees weak, as she knew something was wrong.

"Your Majesty." Elisiah felt weak. His eyes were welling up and his voice was wracked with pain. "There has been an incident."

Nateer started to tear up as she felt Chalna's hands holding her shoulders. "Hikaru?"

"He has been injured, Nateer. Marta is with him now." His voice quivered.

The queen ran into Elisiah's arms and started to cry. She wiped her eyes as she uncontrollably wept. Chalna joined in the hug and rubbed Nateer's back, trying to comfort her.

"How badly is he hurt?" Nateer struggled to talk.

"He is resting in your chambers. Marta has done all she could, and only time will tell," He revealed.

"Take me to him," she commanded.

Elisiah helped to hold her up, as she felt faint, and the three walked together, slowly but steadily, toward the opposite end of the garden where four men were waiting to help. Two of them took over holding the queen as they ascended the stairs and made their way to the chambers of the king and queen.

Opening the door to the chambers, Nateer saw Hikaru laying motionless on the bed with a tube protruding from his chest. She pulled away from the men, and with all her remaining strength, she bolted for her husband and collapsed at his side, crying openly. Chalna was shocked at seeing the king in this condition and tears streamed down her cheeks. She stood shaking, unsure of what to do. Elisiah also wept as he walked over to the bed and looked at the king for the first time since the attack.

A few minutes later, Marta entered the room and approached the bed. She reached down and put her hand on Nateer's shoulder, giving her a gentle squeeze. She motioned Elisiah over to the door.

"I will care for the queen and king now," she reassured him. "You need to take care of the people. We all need you now. I'm sorry so much has been put on your shoulders."

"I only wish there was something I could do for the people who didn't make it into the caves," Elisiah confided.

"You've done everything possible to ensure the safety of as many people who could make it. Even if you could get everyone on the island into the caves, we wouldn't have enough room to keep them all." Marta was trying to ease Elisiah's mind. "We must now concentrate on the people we could save."

"There is going to be a lot of confusion and panic, and we need to keep them calm. The men will have a purpose defending the castle, and I ask that you organize the women and help Queen Nateer when she needs you," Elisiah asked. "I need time to think."

"I used to recommend the gazebo but now I like the patio outside the front doors," Marta said with a smile. "You know I will, Elisiah." Marta knew what she had to do. She turned to Chalna. "Stay with the queen," she requested. "She needs her friends and family right now, and until the prince returns, you're it." Marta smiled at Chalna and hugged her daughter tightly.

About six hours had passed since the attempted murder of King Nikodym, and Elisiah was still on the balcony. He was looking down at King Dolmar's ship, which heaved gently on the calm evening waters. Longboats from each ship were approaching from all directions, and the men on the king's ship were ready to receive them. He could see and hear the celebration going on far below on Dolmar's ship. He heard the large redwood doors open and close behind him but kept watching the ship and the activity surrounding it.

"Elisiah." Kataan's soothing voice carried in the calm evening. "The prince has returned... he's with his father."

Elisiah turned to the old man, who was standing with his hands clasped in front of him.

"Thank you, Kataan," Elisiah returned softly. "I will go and see him after he has seen his father."

"Perhaps you should go to him now, while he is with his father," Kataan added. "They will both need a lot of help in the coming days, and you will need to share in their responsibilities."

"I don't think I can face the king right now after what I let happen." Elisiah was bordering on self-pity.

Kataan looked deep into Elisiah's eyes, and his face was hard and cold, something Elisiah had never seen before. "Do not annoy me with your self-incrimination. You have a duty to your king and his people. Stand up strong and show him that fear is not one of the worries he needs to add to his growing list. The young prince is not ready to assume the role he may be thrust into, and you are his best hope. Bury your self-doubts right now and carry on. You have never withered in doubt before now, and now the strength of your character will be tested as never before."

Elisiah knew Kataan was right in his assessment and perhaps it was what he needed all along. "Okay, Kataan, I'll go to them now."

King Dolmar and Commander Batris stood across the table the Trolan people had given Dolmar and surveyed the maps of the island provided by Batris's men.

"Gather the men of the island and put them to work. I want a proper deck built here first. If these people are good at building, let them build," the king sneered.

"I'll have Colig draw up the plans, Your Majesty. Shall I have the woman dispersed among the men?" Batris was cordial.

"Reward them already? Gather the women and put them to work. The men can be rewarded when they've done something. I'm surprised at you, Commander." Dolmar looked coldly at Batris.

"The men have been at sea a long time, Your Majesty. I merely meant to entice them, give them something to work for." Batris was slowly backing down.

"If any of your men need enticement, send them to me. Now, I want you to keep as many of these people alive as possible. Kill only enough to make an example. I don't want my armies building docks or logging forests; that is for my new subjects. Tomorrow at dawn you will start rounding up the men. Find out the name of the person who now speaks for these people and bring him to me. Perhaps he will be more reasonable than the last one." Dolmar stood tall as he dictated his orders to Batris.

Batris did not show his displeasure with the way the king was treating him, but he wondered why he was speaking to him that way.

"I also have new orders for you." The king stepped around the table and looked out toward the island. "Commander Colig will come to my ship to serve as my personal guard. I have decided to promote Tragar to second-in-command aboard your ship. You will inform Commander Colig immediately. Commander Tragar will join your ship after dinner."

Batris was shocked but kept his composure. "Your Majesty, may I know why you have chosen my ship to send Tragar?"

"It was his wish to serve under you. I see no reason why not ... after all, he did discover the island." Dolmar narrowed his eyes as he waited for the commander's reaction.

"As you wish." Batris smiled as his face tightened.

"Let's go for dinner, shall we?" Dolmar lightened the moment. "Tomorrow will bring great wealth for both of us."

CHAPTER 12

As Elisiah walked through the doors to the royal chambers, Prince Lavar and Queen Nateer knelt by the king's side. The queen's head was against her son's chest, and tears rolled down her cheeks.

Elisiah knelt beside the queen. "Oh, Nateer, I'm so sorry"

The queen looked sympathetically at her old friend. "He's gone, Elisiah."

Stunned, Elisiah looked up at the king for the first time. Tears welled up in his eyes as the reality of her words set in. He looked at Lavar, whose face was blank and cold, then back to the king.

No, it can't be." Elisiah started to shake. "How could I have not seen this coming?"

"There was nothing you could have done. You were only doing as Hikaru requested," Nateer said softly through her tears.

"The question is, what do we do now?" the prince asked quietly.

"We protect our people. Somehow we must drive these savages from our land." Elisiah's eyes tightened as he spat out the words.

"I think I know how," the prince whispered, barely audible.

"What's that?" Elisiah asked.

"I think I know how to get rid of them," the prince said a little louder. "The reason I returned was to tell you of what we have discovered at the end of the tunnel we explored."

The queen cut him short. "Tell us about this a bit later, my son. I must talk to you both about something of great importance."

Nateer took the hands of both men and looked each in the eye. "Now that Hikaru has been taken from me… I have no wish to rule a kingdom through a war. I'm afraid I wouldn't even know how. I was proud and honoured to be the wife of King Hikaru Nikodym, but my role is to serve the king and to be his wife. It was the king's role to lead his people."

"Please, Nateer, the people need to see your strength, they need to believe in you," Elisiah said. "Your presence will hold the kingdom together and prevent panic, especially when they attack. I beg you to reconsider, Nateer." Elisiah bowed his head to her.

The queen put her hand on Elisiah's shoulder and looked at Lavar.

"He's right, Mother, you must help us by leading your people, and I have a way to do it. I am not ready to lead a kingdom to war either. I have not earned the respect of everyone a man needs to be a leader. Perhaps one day I will have earned that respect, but now is not the time for the kingdom to change hands." Lavar smiled at his mother and squeezed her hand slightly.

"Alright," Nateer spoke softly. "I will think about it tonight, and we will discuss it further tomorrow. Now, before we go any farther, I think there is someone waiting to see you."

Lavar lowered his eyes and blushed, as he also wanted to see Chalna.

"She's waiting for you in the garden." Nateer nodded in the direction of the door.

Lavar rose to his feet. He placed his left hand on Elisiah's shoulder and his right hand on his father. "We will talk about our findings after dinner, if you don't mind," Lavar said.

"As you wish." Elisiah bowed to Lavar.

"I'll see you at dinner, Lavar," Nateer added as he walked out the door.

"He seems to have taken his father's death rather well, hasn't he?" Elisiah asked the queen.

"I don't think it has hit him just yet," Nateer speculated.

"Perhaps not. And you, my queen, how can I help you?"

"I need to be alone for a while, Elisiah. Marta will be here shortly to check on Hikaru." She lowered her head as she spoke. "I will inform her of the funeral arrangements when I see her."

"I must return to the men working at the entrance of the cave. If you need anything from me, please don't hesitate to ask," Elisiah said.

"There is one thing you can do for me," the queen requested. "Spend the time to mourn our loss. Don't get caught up in defending the people without taking the time to grieve." Nateer smiled at Elisiah as he rose and stood over her and the dead king.

"I will, my queen ... I will." He looked over at the king again before leaving to see the men.

Chalna waited in the gazebo with her head down, plucking the petals off a flower to pass the time.

Lavar could see Chalna was lost in thought as he approached. He picked a bouquet and stealthily made his way to the back of the gazebo. He reached over the rail to place the flowers in Chalna's eyesight. She dropped the flower she was torturing and turned to Lavar in surprise.

"I've been waiting for you," she said with a touch of sarcasm.

"Just waiting?" Lavar asked. "Haven't you been counting the days until my return?" he mused.

She looked at the flowers Lavar had picked for her and buried her nose in them to appreciate the mixed scents as she formulated her response. "Are you going to stand there all day or are you going to come and sit with me?" she asked coyly.

Without a word, Lavar made his way around to the steps at the front of the gazebo. He looked up from the bottom step and gazed into her light-green eyes.

She held out her arms to the prince, who stepped up and hugged her tightly. He ran his fingers through her long black hair, and they embraced in a passionate kiss. Chalna led the prince to the seat on the gazebo where they would be better hidden from view.

"I'm sorry to hear about your father. I hope he recovers soon," Chalna added sympathetically.

With a look of sorrow, the tears started to flow from the prince's eyes. He wiped them again and again to try to hide the fact that his emotions were running rampant. "He passed away about an hour ago," he choked out as his throat started to swell.

Chalna's eyes started to flow. Momentarily stunned, she sat back and held Lavar's head close to her chest. Together they cried in silence. Chalna rocked back and forth, stroking his hair. "What will become of us without the king to guide us?" she asked through her tears.

"We must be strong and fight back with every ounce of energy in our beings," the prince returned. "They must pay for what they have done. I just don't understand how they can be so cruel and callous."

"I've heard stories from some of the men and women who have sought refuge in the castle, but I couldn't really believe it could all be true," Chalna responded.

Lavar lifted his head from her chest and looked onto her eyes. "It's true, Chalna. I've personally seen their arrogance and ferocity. I have to meet with Elisiah and help plan our defense. I need you to be strong for me and help my mother. Your mother is going to be extremely busy, and unfortunately we are going to have to grow up a lot quicker that expected."

Chalna wiped the tears from her eyes and nodded to Lavar. "I will do everything I can." She smiled slightly and ran her fingers through Lavar's hair one more time.

The young prince also drew a slight smile and reached for both of Chalna's hands. He drew her closer and they embraced again.

"Go," she said bravely. "You have work to do."

Marta closed the door of the royal chambers after she entered and awaited the acknowledgment of the queen before proceeding. Nateer was still knelt by Hikaru's side holding his hand. She looked up through tear-riddled eyes.

"Please come closer," Nateer asked.

Approaching the queen with her head hung low, Marta approached carrying the burial robe of kings.

"I saw Elisiah in the hall," she confided quietly. "I came to help you prepare."

"Thank you, Marta. You've always been so good to me," Nateer replied, smiling at the old woman.

A loud rap on the door interrupted them.

"Come in," Nateer called out.

The heavy door swung open to reveal Chalna holding a plate of food. She approached the two women and curtsied in their presence. "I thought you might be hungry," she said apologetically.

"Oh, my dear, you're so thoughtful." The queen was pleasant even in her grieving state. "Please stay for a while. I want to talk to you about Lavar."

The sound of the prince's name brought a smile to Chalna's face. "I am at your disposal, my queen," the young lady vowed.

"I'm worried about the prince," the queen said. "He loved his father very much, and I'm afraid his emotions might overpower his common sense. He will need support from his friends and family to grieve his loss. He will also need direction to help defend the kingdom that will someday be his."

"He's a fine young man, Nateer," Marta interceded. "I feel he may be stronger than you think."

Chalna looked up at the queen. "The prince also loves his mother very much. So much that he has asked me to be with you and attend to your needs, and I have told him I would."

"I'm sorry so much pressure has been put on your young mind. Please be assured that I have Marta to help me. Lavar only has his male friends to comfort him, but they are no match for the love of a woman." The queen put her hand on Chalna's shoulder then drew her closer and hugged her tightly.

The morning sun was bright and hot, even in the early morning hours.

King Dolmar lifted his pounding head from his pillow as the sun coming in warmed his face and hurt his eyes. As he rose to a sitting position, he realized he was still wearing the same clothes as the day before. With his eyes closed, he licked at the dryness inside his mouth. He rubbed his hands on his weathered face and pressed his fingers around his eye sockets. His mouth stretched wide as a yawn overtook him. Opening his eyes slightly, he held his hand up to shield the light. He ran his tongue around the inside of his mouth again and looked around for something to quench his thirst. He lifted his arms over his head and stretched hard as another yawn overtook him. As he stood up, a rush of nausea forced him to sit back down on the edge of the bed. His head pounded as if his brain had expanded larger than his cranium. All the joints on all his bones pulsed with pain as he laid back down to let the nausea pass. Lifting his head to adjust his pillow, he spotted a flask on the table but was unable to convince his body to retrieve it.

"Perfect," he said to himself. "First day as the ruler of a new country and I can't get my old carcass out of bed."

The dryness in his mouth was now nagging him to try again for the flask on the table. Pushing off the bed and steadying himself on an end table, Dolmar rose to his feet once again. He tried to take a few deep breaths, but the rush of oxygen made his sinuses hurt. His pounding brain would not allow his eyes to focus properly. He unsteadily made his way over to the table, and he needed both hands to keep himself upright when he reached it. He hung his head down with his eyes closed, which made him more unsteady. Finally, he braved opening his eyes again and reached for the flask.

Misjudging the distance, his hand grazed the handle and dumped the contents across the table. The flask rolled off the table and crashed on the floor. Enraged by his miscalculation, he kicked at the chair and upended the table. He smashed his heel down on the remnants of the flask and kicked again, only to skin his shin on the leg of the overturned table. In frustration, he screamed out for the guard and sat down on the chair in the middle of the room.

As the guard entered the room, Dolmar had his head in his hands and his elbows on his knees.

"Get me some water."

Prince Lavar, Elisiah, Kataan, Barook and Bastian were all sitting on the balcony watching the mass forces of their adversaries heading for their shores. The sheer number of men approaching was unlike anything they had seen before. Within a few minutes the harbour was littered with small craft, which looked like a swarm overtaking them.

Elisiah broke the silence. "So it starts."

"How long can the men protect the entrance of the cave?" Kataan asked Elisiah.

"As long as we have to," Elisiah replied.

"I will lead Barook and Bastian into the caves to solve a small engineering problem while you hold them off. We also need to keep filling in the tunnels in case they get through our initial defences." The prince was unsure if he should be making the decisions but he realized they were his to make. "How many people were we able to save?"

"Around two thousand," Kataan surmised. "Mostly women and children. We have between four or five hundred men cutting stone to fill the tunnels and about the same defending the castle and packing the stones."

"I need about fifty men to complete the work in the centre of the volcano before we can safely move the women and children," Bastian said.

"Take as many men as you need to build the lift system," Elisiah said. "We must disperse the people in some manner or it will be hard to organize and feed them."

"Okay, gentlemen, I think we all know what we need to do, so let's get to it." The prince seemed enthusiastic to start.

The attack on the island was well underway when King Dolmar made his way to the bridge of his ship. Waiting for him was Captain Maxum and Commander Colig, who was observing how Batris was implementing his plan of action against the Trolan.

"Good morning, Your Majesty," Colig said as the king approached.

"Don't patronize me, Colig, I don't take it well," the king shot back coldly. "Proceed with your report." Dolmar reached out to steady himself on the rail as his head protested his movements.

"Commander Batris has deployed five thousand men to begin the invasion. Three ships have been sent to deploy another two thousand men to the northern tip of the island. The men's orders are to capture the enemy and confine them until further orders. Updates are to be reported to Commander Batris every four hours." Commander Colig bowed to the king as he delivered his report.

"I want a base camp set up near the shore immediately. Make sure it's comfortable. I'm tired of sitting on this tub." The king's voice was as unsteady as his legs but his meaning was clear.

"Immediately, Your Majesty," Commander Colig replied, still unsure of his position. He looked around momentarily then bowed to the king and backed away. Once he was out of earshot, he spoke quietly to himself. How am I supposed to find something more comfortable than this?

Captain Maxum stood with King Dolmar. "I am going to enjoy the sight of war again, your majesty."

"I am promised it will be a short war, so we shouldn't be here long." Dolmar replied.

Looking over at the Revenge, Colig decided to delegate the responsibility to the man who had replaced him as second-in-command of the king's fleet. "Prepare the longboat," he yelled out. "It's time to test our new commander," he said under his breath.

In ten regiments of five hundred men, they set out down the road-ways, gathering anyone they came across. With little opposition, they separated the men from the women and children. The men were chained together in groups as large as fifty. After they were inspected, they were separated into groups according to age and strength. The women were similarly separated, with the twelve-to twenty-year-olds taken away to a different camp. The older men were taken to work the mines or farms, depending on their particular specialties, and the younger men were taken to start stripping the forests of the giant redwood trees.

From his vantage point on the Royal Descent, Dolmar watched as the invasion progressed. Now into its sixth day, Dolmar waited for the island kingdom to fall under the siege; something he had been promised would happen quickly. He could see the forests falling and the massive trees being piled high in preparation for the building of a proper dock in the bay, but he did not yet have a proper place to live, and no attempt had been made to attack the castle. He had been watching Colig closely for the first six days his new captain of the guard had been on board. His predecessor had been left behind to keep the peace with his neighbouring country. Although he was somewhat bored with the small, terroristic wars his men were engaged in, at least he had a comfortable castle from which to monitor the campaign.

Dolmar was not a man that trusted many people, and Colig was no exception, but he did have a certain demeanor that Dolmar admired. He could see Beil's trademark training in Colig and he knew what he could expect from him. For now, Dolmar would sit back and wait a bit longer.

Commander Batris also watched the progress of the invasion from the bridge of the Revenge. Although the past days had been full of reports and strategy planning, Batris was ever aware of the king's presence. Commander Tragar was working out well in place of Commander Colig, but Batris felt uneasy with his new first officer. First off, he was not a trained military officer. Ever since his arrival with the king, Batris did not trust him, nor could he shake the feeling that something was going on behind his back.

Now that the island had been secured, it was time to attack the castle.

Batris examined the castle, as he had every day since his arrival. With the scout searching the area for another entrance, Commander Tragar prepared the archers for a little demonstration. Lining up fifty old and crippled men around the base of the only known entrance to the castle, Tragar summoned a hundred archers in a semi-circle in front of their enemies. Tragar signalled for the trumpeters to attract the attention of the castle occupants.

With the trumpets blaring, Commander Batris watched the fortress balcony appear to fill with curious onlookers. Once he was satisfied the demonstration would be seen by the Trolan leaders, he signalled Tragar to begin. Tragar sneered as he lowered his eyes from Batris and looked up at the balcony. His sneer turned to a smile as he raised his right arm. With that, the archers drew their bows and aimed their weapons. Tragar held his arm up for a painfully long time to emphasize his point, then finally he chopped through the air, releasing the deadly barrage. In a heap, the old men fell silently to the ground.

From the balcony, Prince Lavar and Elisiah lowered their heads, and a stream of tears flowed down the cheeks of the young man. Elisiah put his arm around Lavar and pulled him close.

"Nothing could be done to prevent this," Elisiah said, trying to comfort the prince.

"We have to do something, Elisiah," the prince shot back. "We can't just leave them out there to be slaughtered."

Elisiah ran his hand across Lavar's shoulders and squared himself to the young prince. His eyes hardened as he tightened his grip shoulders. "Our first concern is the people we have already saved. Once we have the ability to house and feed these people, we can worry about saving the others."

Lavar twisted away from Elisiah as his own eyes hardened. "My duty is to all the people." He glared at Elisiah in a way that made the hairs on the back of Elisiah's neck stand up. "Can't you see what they are doing? We have to fight back; we can't just stand here and watch this. If you want to be a coward, then go and help the women cook."

Elisiah was stunned at the behaviour and hurt by the Prince's words. "What weapons would you chose to fight such a force?" Elisiah asked calmly.

"We'll make weapons," Lavar shot back angrily. "Or we will take theirs. Either way, they are going to pay for killing my father."

"Your father knew we could not fight them with conventional weapons." Elisiah's voice rose to equal Lavar's. "These people were born to fight. They have been at war for a hundred years and they know how to fight. Look at their weapons and look at ours. Do you plan to kill them with farming equipment?"

Lavar was enraged that Elisiah had spoken to him in this manner. He grabbed Elisiah and threw him to the ground. Before Elisiah could get up, the prince was on him and buried his fist into his chest, knocking the wind out of him. Two men grabbed Lavar and pulled him off before he could administer more damage, and they took him aside.

Painfully, Elisiah rose to his feet and signalled for the men to release the prince.

"Don't you tell me that my father was afraid to fight!" Lavar screamed. "My father wasn't afraid of any man." He kicked the ground and slammed his fist into the shoulder of one of the men who had pulled him off. "And I will kill any man who says he was!" The tears welled up as he stormed back and forth in front of Elisiah.

Holding his chest as he caught his breath, Elisiah saw at a side of Lavar he had never seen. "You're right, Lavar," he started slowly. "Your father wasn't afraid of any man, but your father ruled with his mind, not just his heart. He knew we had to exploit weakness in our enemies and use the weight of their own offence against them. If you want revenge, you won't get it by standing in front of them. You have to outsmart them."

"When, Elisiah? When are we going to outsmart them?" Lavar asked sarcastically.

Elisiah put out his hands to Lavar. "We have already started. We've started to frustrate them, and they are making mistakes. When the opportunity arises, we must be ready."

Lavar stood with his hands on his hips and stared into the eyes of his father's best friend.

"I've already lost one of you, and I refuse to lose another. You're not the only one with a heavy heart, who has lost someone special. I'm just sorry you have to grow up so fast," Elisiah was stern, yet sympathetic.

"You were my father's best friend. He loved you and trusted you as his own family. If that was good enough for him, then who am I to discount your wisdom?" Lavar's voice was calm yet unsteady. "And I'm so sorry."

"They are predictable and therefore we must not be. We have to finish working in the caves before they figure out how to get up here. I'm going to need your help." Elisiah's calm demeanor was soothing to the angry young prince. "And forget it; I understand."

Deep inside the mountain, Barook and Elisiah led an enterprising building endeavour. The lift at the base of the cliff was starting to take shape, and more and more supplies were being transported to the mountain's core.

Bastian's crew had bored a hole through the sixty-foot-high wall and were in the process of widening it while the lift system was being tested and securely fastened to the cliff face. Barook figured it would be another two weeks before the entire system would be ready to operate.

The floor of the cave was riddled with makeshift tents on both sides of the creek. Along the wall opposite the lift system, more permanent structures were being built to feed the masses of people that would soon be arriving.

Barin had completed his survey of the cave as well as finding another exit. The trails the animals had followed led to a lush valley that was inaccessible from any other part of the island. The valley was fed by a river originating from a permanent snow pack high above on the ridge of the mountain. A stunning waterfall enchanted the mountainside and culminated in a large lake at the bottom.

Barin and Jessard had surmised a lack of predator animals had produced a rich bounty of wildlife that teemed around the lake. There was enough timber to build the necessary shelters as well as a water reservoir and irrigation flumes.

Commander Batris stood in front of the cave entrance to the castle. The entrance was now completely filled in with huge rocks and gravel. He stared at the sheer cliff intensely, looking for another opening or an inspiring solution to his dilemma. He watched the Trolan as they prepared their defence high above.

Like insects, he thought. Industrious little ants that I will squash.

"Commander Tragar," he said dryly.

Tragar approached Batris apprehensively. He knew of Commander Batris's disdain for him and proceeded with caution. He faced Batris and saluted as he bowed his head slightly. Although he showed respect, he didn't lower his eyes from his peer.

"What reaction did we get from our little demonstration?" Batris asked.

Tragar looked over at the prisoners who were carting away the dead bodies. He clasped his hands behind his back and stood at ease.

"The usual," he started. "Tears and anguish. They do seem unusually passive, though. None of the hysterics or screaming one would assume. They're almost resigned to die."

"They are buying time," Batris stated. "Something is happening inside the castle, and the prisoners are trying to give them time to do it."

"What do you mean?" Tragar eked out before he could stop himself. He looked over at the undaunted commander and added, "The prisoners are building a dock in the inner harbour, as well as renovating a command post for the king. We have them widening the roads and harvesting the forests…" Tragar suddenly realized how easy all that had been.

"They have done everything to divert us from that castle," Batris said, thinking out loud. "The only time we tried to force them, they accepted death rather than empty that cave. Every time we try ourselves, we get bombarded from above. We need a way to shelter our men from the rocks. I want a movable shelter built from those massive trees. I want it large enough and strong enough to withstand the barrage. We will move it as close to the entrance as we can and build onto it from there. We can use the rocks they bombard us with to build up the sides to form a large tunnel, and we can empty the cave from there."

Tragar stood for a second, trying to draw a mental picture of the commander's request.

"Have the prisoners build it and move it into position," Batris added.

"Commander, we will need to round up more young men, and they are very hard to find. Since we started to round them up, we have found more and more old people and less middle-aged and younger. We know they must be out there, but we simply haven't been able to find them," Tragar apologized.

"Send out more patrols. They have to be hiding somewhere. In the meantime, have your men help ... whoever can be spared. Keep in mind, I want that dock finished and the king wants his command post." Batris looked over at Tragar and smiled sarcastically. "Welcome to the King's Navy."

Tragar ignored the comment and excused himself.

For the past few weeks, the king, along with Captain Maxum, had questioned and taunted Colig. They would devise scenarios and query Colig on strategies. Then they would question Colig's strategies and test his gall. They had even tried intimidation, but Colig was well skilled in temperament. In this short period of time, Dolmar was gaining respect for Colig and realized what an asset he would become.

Dolmar spent most of his time on the Royal Descent but would venture to the island occasionally. The heavy security was usually enough to discourage travel, although he did like to keep an eye on the progress of his command post. Although the decor was lavish, it was not the castle he wanted. He knew very well the procedures of war, and he would have to be patient a bit longer.

Queen Nateer spent most of her time in her room. She sat stately in a padded wooden chair near the window. With her hands clasped on her lap, she watched over the island in silence. The tears flowed freely down her once-rosy cheeks. Her complexion was pale, and her black hair no longer shone in the light. She thought back to when she was a young girl and used to climb to this very spot and looked over the harbour. The serenity of the calm winds carried the songs of the native birds. The leaves rustled lightly in the background, and the sun glowed off the people's faces. The view was magnificent and always inspired awe every time she saw it. But that was all gone now.

The harbour below was being transformed into a huge port in which the enemy intended to dock their immense ships. The hillside was now barren of the massive trees. She could now see the house that once belonged to Marta and Kataan. She knew the renovations that were nearing completion were forced upon her people through ruthless torture in open displays She saw her people being whipped and beaten as they worked on the dock. Now they were being forced to build something new.

She raised her cuff to dab at her flowing tears.

Elisiah also watched the construction of the new structure. Whatever it was, it was going to be big. He also watched the merciless beatings bestowed upon the victims below, the unfortunate souls they could not save. He tried to keep the others in the castle from witnessing the carnage, but it was difficult. He also knew the queen was watching constantly, and he was concerned. He had graciously requested an audience, but she had refused him thus far. He knew she was grieving the loss of her life partner as well as grieving her people's despair. She was hurt right now and needed some time to heal.

Elisiah inhaled deeply and refocussed on the action below. He looked over the cliff towering over the entrance of the cave. At this point, the bombardment had proven effective, but he was sure this new structure must have something to do with disrupting his offence.

As of now, about a half-mile of the tunnel had been filled in. They needed a backup plan; he was pretty sure these people were not going to give up easily and were not going to stop until they had achieved their goal.

Lavar had spent his time between the caves and Elisiah and wanted so badly to see Chalna. He and Elisiah had both realized the need to organize the people working in the caves and agreed that Elisiah would best be served to the defense of the castle.

Any time he had a spare moment, Lavar's thoughts would turn to Chalna and his mother. He would become depressed when he thought about his father for too long, so he tried to limit his thoughts to happier times. He heard his mother would only see Marta and Chalna and thought he should go and see her. He missed her deeply and felt badly for not spending enough time with her in her time of need.

He heard very little about Chalna and she was the person he missed the most. He always smiled when he thought about her; he would stare blankly and grit his teeth behind a devilish grin. When he snapped himself back to reality, he often found his hands sweating.

Lavar was impressed at how calm and organized the people were. All were uprooted, many had lost their children or family and others had lost everything. Still, the people had purpose and looked out for each other. He couldn't help but notice that Marta was the person that really ran the whole operation down here and was relieved that he had such strong support from all the elders. They all realized they had a much better chance of survival if they stuck together and helped out wherever they were needed.

The men working in the caves needed to be fed in shifts, which was a tremendous undertaking considering the men were a long way from the cooking facilities. Even under all this pressure, the people had come together well.

Deep inside the mountain, Barin was preparing to join Jessard and Barook to return to the castle. The inside of the cave and the valley beyond were now ready to accept the transfer of many of the survivors.

The men and women that were working on the lift were now working on building shelters in the valley beyond the cave. At the base of the cliff, deep inside the mountain, the three men arrived together. As they entered the lift, each man surveyed their handiwork. Barook smiled as he looked over the lift with its counter-weight system. The lift would ascend the one hundred and forty feet to the tunnel entrance in about thirty seconds and could hold thirty people.

Barin was thinking about the valley beyond the cave and Jessard was thinking about the potential of the different minerals they had discovered here.

"It will be nice to see Lavar and Elisiah again," Barin said.

"That's Prince Lavar," Barook reminded him, "And soon to be King Lavar."

Barin just smiled at Barook.

"I wonder how the people in the castle are making out?" Jessard added.

"We will know soon, my friend." Barin looked at Jessard, still smiling.

As the lift reached the entrance to the tunnel, the men lit a torch. The tunnel was much easier to follow now that the renovations had been completed. A rope had been secured the entire length of the tunnel, and torches and provisions were placed strategically along the path in anticipation of the crowds to come. The tunnel had also been widened in places, and rope bridges were built over the chasms. Although it was still slow-going, it was a much safer passage. The original five-day trip was now down to just over a half day.

King Dolmar took a deep breath of the salt air. With his hands on his hips and his chest stuck out, he stared at the castle. The morning light seemed to make the majestic black castle glow. He could also see the progress of the huge structure Commander Batris was constructing. The massive redwood trees looked impervious to the rocks the Trolan were dropping. He was interested to see how this would play out.

Along the shore, the dock was also nearing completion. Three impressive piers protruded from the main dock. The first of these piers was complete, with Commander Batris's ship Revenge attached. Dolmar preferred to anchor farther out where he had a better vantage point.

Today Dolmar planned a trip ashore to visit the residence being renovated for him. He was impressed on his previous visits, but he would not show his pleasure to his men. He merely talked of the small castle as being adequate.

He smirked as he surveyed the transformed landscape. Although the slaves had removed thousands of trees, the distant hills were still covered in what seemed like an endless supply of building material. Once the other two piers were complete, he would begin shipping the wood to different parts of his empire. The more he looked at the timber, the more he wondered what else could be exploited on the island. He turned and looked back up at the castle high above.

From the lower deck, Colig climbed the stairs to the bow of the Royal Descent where King Dolmar stood.

"Your Majesty." He bowed, regardless of the fact he was behind the king.

Dolmar merely waved his fingers for Colig to approach.

"When shall I have the guards ready for your departure?" Colig asked as he stopped beside the king.

"Change of plans, Commander." Dolmar looked briefly at Colig before returning his gaze to the castle. "Today I wish to go hunting."

Colig showed no expression over the sudden change of plans. "How far into the island do you wish to travel, My Lord?"

"As far as I need to, Commander," the king replied. "Round up some of the younger slaves. They should make good sport."

Colig smiled and bowed his head slightly, keeping his eyes firmly on the king. "Male or female, My Lord?"

Dolmar's eyes tightened as he revisited the last hunt in his mind. "Female," he said calmly. "Pick a few good ones and you can have one when I'm done."

"Yes, My Lord." Colig smiled. "I will have them ready in an hour. Would you like a tracker, or do you prefer to track them yourself?"

"No, I think I would like to track them myself. Prepare my horse and twenty guards. I don't want the peasants to feel I am vulnerable while I am out hunting." Dolmar was thinking aloud. "An hour will be fine. Dismissed, Commander."

Irid Tragar stood at the base of the cliff that marked the entrance to the caves. He watched as the titanic structure began to take shape. No one was as pleased as he at the progress being made by the slaves. He knew very well that Batris was carefully watching every move he made. He also knew Batris would not hesitate to crush him politically if the opportunity arose. Although he knew the pressure from Batris, he also seethed at the thought of the glory for his work going to a man that despised him.

The structure before him was now sixty feet long and fifteen feet high. The width at the bottom was twenty feet. The massive redwoods had proven impervious to bombardment because the enemy was not able to launch large enough stones at them.

The entire structure rested on logs that acted as rollers. As a section was completed, the structure would be moved forward toward the cliff. As they moved closer to the cliff, the rubble would be moved down the tunnel and stacked against a part of the cliff that could not be protected from above.

At this point, the structure was a mere one hundred feet from the cave entrance. Within a week, the tunnel would be theirs.

The serenity of the situation faltered as Tragar noticed the approach of Commander Batris. Typically foul mood, he thought.

Batris walked toward Tragar with the arrogant confidence a man of his position could afford.

"Good afternoon, commander." Tragar tried to sound sincere. "To what do I owe the honour of your presence?"

Commander Batris glared at Tragar for a moment, trying to decide whether the comment was insolent or sincere.

"You are late with your progress report, Mister Tragar." Batris emphasized the mister to return the perceived insolence.

"My apologies, Commander," Tragar replied, biting his tongue. "As you can see, the structure is proceeding as projected."

Tragar rubbed his chin with his thumb and forefinger. "Perhaps another demonstration in discipline would speed up the progress," he suggested.

"If your progress report is late again, Mister Tragar, you will be the example in discipline," Batris snapped. "Do I make myself clear?"

"Very clear, Commander."

On the balcony outside the front doors of the castle, Elisiah was preparing for the second part of his plan to defend the people. He was going to flood the entrance tunnel as well as the caves under the castle after the Lakar soldiers started digging out the entrance and then divert the entire force of the underground rivers of boiling water down the tunnel, making passage impossible.

Initially, Elisiah decided to use the water in the storage bins to fill the caves and give them time to divert the river. The men who were taking shifts at the cliffs, cutting stones from the face and using them to bombard the attackers, were now digging out shafts in the mountain to change the course of a river. Relentlessly the men worked, with the thought of the women and children's very existence to strengthen them.

Once every five days, the men would travel back the length of the tunnel to the castle and their families. Although the visits were brief, they fueled everyone's spirits. The following day, the men would return to the tunnels or caves and carry on the desperate work.

Elisiah turned when he heard one of the large doors open behind him. To his pleasant surprise, Prince Lavar walked arm in arm with Chalna. The two shone when they were together, and Elisiah couldn't help but smile when he saw them. Somehow, seeing them took some of the pressure off his shoulders.

As the pair approached, he bowed graciously. He held his head down until the couple stopped in front of him.

"Your Majesty," he said, raising his eyes to meet those of the prince.

Lavar felt a bit embarrassed by the reverence shown to them by a man he loved almost as much as his own father. He realized the show was for the benefit of Chalna, but he could still feel his own cheeks flushing.

"Good morning, Elisiah," Lavar said. "I hope we're not disturbing you."

"No, your majesty, it's always a pleasure to see you and the beautiful Chalna."

Chalna closed her eyes and looked up, feeling the warm redness taking over her beautiful features. Her body trembled slightly being in the presence of a man she greatly admired. Trying to divert attention from herself, Chalna motioned over to the Royal Descent, which was moving closer to the harbour docks far below. "What do you think they are up too?" she asked no one in particular.

"I think their king has decided to pay us another visit," Elisiah answered.

The trio watched the Royal Descent dock and followed the party of men as they disembarked and assembled on the wharf. They watched as the band of ruffians dragged helpless female slaves down for inspection. The women, bound and gagged, were whipped with leather straps and kicked in the ankles if they didn't keep up.

From their perch high above the harbour, they witnessed the emergence of the enemy king. Chalna turned away, burying her face in the chest of the young prince. Lavar held Chalna tight in his arms. A single tear ran the length of his cheek as he and Elisiah stood silently, intensely focussed on the parade below. Both men struggled to keep their composure as the spectacle below unfolded.

Dolmar approached the young slaves slowly, surrounded by guards. He stopped at each of the young ladies being restrained by the guards and held upright. He fondled the ones he liked before tearing off their clothes and inspecting them further. After he had inspected all the whimpering women, he chose two. The unfortunate young ladies, naked and bound, were separated from the rest and brought before the king.

"Untie them," Dolmar ordered.

A young soldier standing behind the two produced a blade and sliced the bindings with little effort.

"Release them," Dolmar ordered again.

The soldier pushed the frightened young girls from behind to get them moving. Crying and confused, the girls screamed out in terror.

Shaking and stumbling, they tried to run but their fear impeded their attempt. The snap of a guard's whip started the girls running for the forest.

The king smiled and raised an eyebrow with a sigh. He turned to Colig, who was standing to his right.

"Ready my mount, Commander," he said quietly.

Colig turned to the soldier waiting on the bow of the Royal Descent and with the wave of his hand, a majestic animal was brought from the hull of the king's ship.

Lavar and Elisiah could barely make out the animal from the distance but had never seen anything like it. Lavar was the first to gaze upon the animal through the telescope.

As the beast approached, it pranced proudly and fluidly as if dancing for the king. The head of the beast thrashed back and forth, and its hooves pounded the ground furiously. Then, suddenly, as the king raised his giant hand to the beast, it stopped and lowered its head.

The king walked over to the animal, stroked its nose and reached behind its massive head to stroke the mane that ran down its neck. As the king fussed over the beautiful creature, two guards saddled its back in preparation for the ride.

The king looked toward the forest where the young ladies had run screaming and threw his body onto the beast. With reins in hand, a sharp heel to the ribs started the horse running in the direction of the game.

Lavar and Elisiah turned to each other and stared blankly for a moment.

"Your Majesty," Elisiah spoke quietly. "I have a plan."

CHAPTER 13

The early morning was cold, and a brisk wind threw fine grains of sand into the air. As Tragar waited for Commander Batris, he watched the slaves move the massive structure to its final resting place at the foot of the cave. He smiled, as he knew the end of the battle was at hand. He turned to look out at the Royal Descent, which had returned to its original position outside the harbour. His eyes tightened as he thought of how the king might reward him once the castle was taken.

Just a few more days, he thought. Just a few more days.

King Dolmar stood on the upper deck of his ship and stared again at the castle that had become his obsession. A fine mist surrounded the fortress and gave the impression it was floating on air. A bell ringing on deck signalled the arrival of Commander Batris. Silently, a longboat carrying the commander came alongside. Winch cables were secured, and a rope ladder was lowered.

The king turned and waited for his senior officer. Commander Batris approached and bowed respectfully. He waited for the king to acknowledge him.

"Tell me, Batris, how goes my war?" The king spoke easily. "Tell me of the great victory we are about to reap, and tell me when this victory will occur?"

"Your Grace," Batris started slowly, trying to analyze the king's seemingly jovial mood. "We have built a tunnel, which we have successfully moved into place at the entrance of the cave. The Trolan are no longer able to bombard us from above, and today we start to remove the debris they have used to try to block the tunnel. I believe they are defenseless, as they have shown no weapons and have only thrown rocks." He callously smiled.

"These defenseless people have kept me waiting for some time, Commander," Dolmar interrupted.

A silence followed. Commander Batris chose his words carefully. "The primitive nature of the inhabitants has made the task of training them more difficult than I originally anticipated. There is little that can stop us now. We have soldiers digging day and night."

"Soldiers?" the king questioned. "Why are the slaves not digging out the cave? That is not a job for soldiers."

"Once the tunnel was moved into place, the slaves refused to dig in the cave. I killed hundreds of them to set an example, but they refused to move. I can't kill them all," Batris said, defending his choice.

"Why not?" Dolmar asked. "They are all going to die anyway. You can't let them have any small victories, and not working while my soldiers dig is a victory for them. I can't have that." Dolmar was visibly annoyed. "If they don't work, kill them all. We can round up more. There can be no disobedience."

Batris was surprised, knowing how hard it was becoming to find more inhabitants, but he did not question his orders.

True to Batris's word, Dolmar could see the tons of rubble being carried from the cave and stacked around the massive tunnel built by the Trolan slaves. He saw the slaves burying the bodies of those killed by Batris in his efforts to get them back to work.

The morning light also brought an end to the bombardment from above. Elisiah had decided they had to concentrate all their efforts and resources on completing the shaft to the underground river. He watched the enemy soldiers removing the rock and knew it would be a race to finish before the Lakar soldiers.

He carefully monitored the water levels in the caves. Once the water level started to drop, they would have to break through to the river before the cave emptied.

"Elisiah." A familiar voice echoed through the tunnel. Barook approached from the dimly lit passage with books in his hands.

"It's good to see you again, my friend," Elisiah replied, holding out his right hand.

Barook shifted his books to shake Elisiah's hand. "I've been doing some calculations and I think we only have two or possibly three days before they break through."

"Yes, I agree." Elisiah smiled. "And now we will be ready for them."

"Are you sure this is going to work?" Barook asked hesitantly.

"I'm sure it's our only chance," Elisiah responded. "If we fail, we could all become slaves."

"Then we must not fail," Barook responded quietly. Shifting his books again, he gripped Elisiah's shoulder. "I'm proud of you, Elisiah. No one could have done more than you have." With that, Barook carried on down the tunnel.

Queen Nateer sat quietly looking out her bedroom window at the harbour. The death of her husband had almost consumed her with grief. It sapped her strength and made her frail and old. Time was slowly returning her strength but would not release its grip on her heart.

With a very faint knock, the door to the queen's chambers opened. Lavar entered and closed the door behind him. He smiled at his mother and tried not to notice her frail condition.

Nateer stood and turned to face her son. She forced a smile and stretched out her arms to him. "Oh, Lavar, you are all I have now," she said as she hugged him tightly.

Lavar embraced his mother tightly. Finally, he released her and looked into her eyes. "It's not true, you know."

"What's that, dear?" Nateer looked puzzled.

"I'm not all you have," he answered, smiling. "You have an entire kingdom that loves and respects you. You have people that have given their lives to protect you, and you have friends to comfort you. As much as you need your friends, they also need you."

"I'm afraid I don't have much left to give." Nateer looked down solemnly.

"You have to give back what the people have given you," Lavar returned. "The people need to see you. They need to know you are okay."

"I'm sorry, Lavar." Nateer smiled and stroked his hair. "The death of your father has been so hard on me. He was everything to me, all I've known since I was a little girl, and I would give up everything if I could just have him back."

Lavar wiped the stream of tears from his mother's cheek, tolerating those in his own eyes. His chest pounded, and a fire burned in his stomach. "I'll get even with them," he seethed

"No, no, Lavar." Nateer's gentle voice was soothing. "Revenge will only make you cold, and it won't bring your father back. Soon you will be the next ruler of this land, and you must look through clear eyes, not the blurred eyes of hatred. Your father was so very proud of you … please don't let everything he taught you be in vain."

Lavar smiled slightly and stroked his mother's hair. "I'll make you a deal. You come out of this room, and I promise I'll make you proud of me."

"I don't need to leave this room to be proud of my son," she replied. "But you have a deal."

Lavar stood and held out his hand. Nateer smiled and took the hand of her only child. Arm in arm, they walked to the door of the queen's chambers. As they reached the door, the floor beneath their feet began to tremble.

"What was that?" Nateer was startled.

"That, Mother," Lavar said with a smile, "was Elisiah."

Everything was ready. The day had arrived. Thousands of soldiers waited on the dock and at the mouth of the long tunnel.

The king stood on the deck of the Royal Descent and admired the formation of his troops. With the ship anchored about five hundred metres outside the harbour, he could see everything clearly. He looked up at the castle and sneered. Finally, the treasure he sought was within his reach.

It was also a proud moment for Commander Batris, who knew he would be well rewarded once his soldiers marched into the castle and delivered the treasure to the king. He knew the peasants would soon be surrendering to the might of his troops. He stood on the dock at the head of the line of soldiers, ready to signal the invasion.

The calm that surrounded him suddenly changed. A low rumbling sound hummed in the background. The rumbling intensified and grew to a thunderous roar.

From his ship, Dolmar could see the ground shaking. Furiously, rock and mud blew out of the end of the tunnel and obliterated most of the army assembled there. The remaining survivors scattered and tried to run to escape the avalanche approaching at over one hundred miles an hour. Water followed the rock and mud, and the avalanche had grown to encompass trees and anything in its path. The enormous structure the slaves had built now funnelled the torrent and increased its ferocity. It strained and creaked, waning under the pressure but being held temporarily in place by the tons of rocks the soldiers had packed around it.

With blinding fury, Dolmar watched the unprotected ships in the harbour become enveloped in a reign of terror from inside the mountain. The ships tied to the dock were splintered on impact. Relentlessly, the water poured from the entrance of the cave. The ships were pelted with rubble as a huge wave created by the avalanche tossed them like toys, flipping several and sending them to their depths.

As abruptly as it started, the deafening roar subsided and Dolmar was left to watch as the huge wave now approached the Royal Descent. Holding firmly to the rail, the king screamed at the wave in defiance. The ship lifted and heaved under the great pressure, tossing its contents around and smashing the helpless crew.

Dolmar screamed again at the wave, which had drenched him but could not relieve his grip on the rail. The ship continued to toss and sway in the aftermath as the water disrupted the tide. Dolmar screamed again as he inspected the carnage laid out in front of him. Five of his ships were gone completely and he could see no signs of survivors. The soldiers standing at alert only moments ago had now vanished. He scanned the harbour for the ship of Commander Batris but could not find it. He pounded his fist and screamed again, much longer this time.

He turned and glared at the castle. His eyes tightened as he clenched his teeth and squeezed his lips. His body temperature flared, as he was losing his mind in a furious hatred. Everything in front of him was inconceivable.

Standing on the balcony, Elisiah smiled as he also scanned the carnage. The great dock built by his enemies was badly damaged, possibly unsalvageable. The ships moored there were gone, as was half of the fleet. Steam now poured out of the tunnel as a river of boiling water occupied the cave. The army below was completely devastated. The few that did survive wandered aimlessly among the bodies of those who did not.

Prince Lavar approached from behind, arm in arm with his mother. The queen looked frail but her natural beauty shone through. She smiled at Elisiah as she looked into his eyes. She could see the warmth in his smile. Before speaking, she surveyed the damage with her son. Finally, she turned back to Elisiah. "It seems you have dealt them a mighty blow."

Elisiah returned her smile. "We have."

Lavar pointed to the slave encampment in the distance. "Elisiah." He summoned his friend. "Look at this." He pointed vigorously. "The camp wasn't damaged in the avalanche."

Elisiah strained to view the people who were no longer being guarded. Many had already fled into the forest, while others searched frantically for lost family members.

"Have mercy on their souls," Queen Nateer said softly, almost to herself.

"At least now they have a chance," Lavar added, "If they can find a safe refuge."

"I don't think this is over yet," Elisiah stated. "I think we stirred the pot and now we all have a chance." He scratched his head and rubbed his tired eyes. "Somehow we have to establish contact with them. We have to get down and back without being detected."

"How about a small party of men scaling down the cliffs? We can hoist them back up with ropes," Lavar suggested.

"We must move quickly while the enemy is in disarray. We may not get a second chance," Elisiah said.

"I'll go get Jonas. He and his friends are the best climbers on the island. If anyone can get there and back undetected, it's them," Lavar offered.

King Dolmar summoned the captains of the remaining fleet.

Commander Colig had a smug look on his face. Fate had worked favourably for him, as he was now in line to take over command. Those who were his oppressors had conveniently disappeared. He smiled as he thought about the wisdom of Dolmar to reassign him and thus save his life. Now he was sure the king would give him his just reward.

The long table King Dolmar had received as a gift from the people of Trolan now served as the main fixture in the king's makeshift war room. The five remaining captains sat around the table waiting for the king and reliving the disaster that befell them. Each man was shocked at the events which had transpired and discussed the damage to their respective ships.

Colig stood by the door, listening and waiting for the king. He surveyed the room and the men inside. Staring at each man individually, he tried to decide which ship he would be given by the king. Which man would pay the ultimate price for the kingdom and surrender his ship to the new high commander, Commander Colig? He liked the sound of that. Now his skill as a warrior would come out from behind the shadow of Commander Batris. Batris would no longer take credit for his brilliance. Now he would show the king who the real leader of the fleet should be.

The door beside him flew open. Slowly and methodically, King Dolmar entered the room. The men around the table fell silent. Dolmar stopped at the head of the table and leaned over, placing his hands on the wooden surface. He looked silently into the eyes of each man. When he was done, he righted himself and turned back to look at Colig.

"Gentlemen," Dolmar started quietly. "What happened to my magnificent fleet?" He turned back to face the men as he motioned for Colig to come and join them. "Where is Commander Batris?" he asked.

None of the men dared say anything unless they were spoken to directly. Dolmar looked at Colig. "Well?"

"Commander Batris was at the front of the line with the troops when the onslaught destroyed them all. He is dead," Colig stated without emotion.

Dolmar lowered his head and shook it slightly. "Damn it. He was a valued general." Dolmar looked at Captain Sordain. "What condition is your ship in?"

Sordain hesitated for a second. "She can be made seaworthy in a few days, Your Majesty." He bowed his head respectfully, not taking his eyes off the king. "Most of the damage was confined to the holds. One of the masts was splintered but repair crews are working as we speak."

"When your ship is ready, go and bring me Commander Beil." The king spoke slowly. "The rest of you, I want my army rebuilt. Repair that harbour and clear the debris. Use as many slaves as you can round up. I'm tired of showing mercy to these people. No one defies the king of Lakar and lives to tell about it. Now, clear the room."

Each man rose and saluted the king as he exited the room. Captain Maxum remained.

Colig sat stunned at the table. Dolmar showed uncustomary patience when he walked over and sat down beside Colig. "You seem somewhat surprised, Commander," Dolmar said.

"Your Grace, I thought I was in line to take over command of the fleet," Colig replied in shock.

"Beil, Batris and Tragar all came to me with this wonderful vision of a great castle in an unknown land. Batris and Tragar are now dead, and that leaves Beil. I am fully confident in your abilities, Commander, and the time will come when you will bring great glory to the empire. Right now, I need my most tested tactician to deliver these farmers to my feet, that I may crush the life from them with the soles of my boots," Dolmar explained. "Take charge of the cleanup and be patient. Find the body of Commander Batris and hang it from a pole in the harbour. I want everyone to know what happens to those who fail and disappoint me."

"As you wish, Your Majesty."

"Your majesty," Maxum spoke. "It would be my honour to bring these people to their knees, for your glory."

"You are needed here, as the captain of my ship." Dolmar replied. "Right now, I need Beil. Besides, you are retired. You have always been a great soldier, but this is a time for younger men."

CHAPTER 14

The sun beat down on his bruised and battered body. Sharp pain emanated from his buried legs. His arms moved freely but his back screamed in pain. He could feel the blood rolling down his face and his vision was blurred.

Tragar had been standing beside the tunnel when the nightmare started. His body was mercilessly thrown two hundred yards and slammed into the rocks that had been piled at the base of the cliff. Now he could feel himself falling in and out of consciousness. He talked to himself to keep awake while trying uselessly to free his legs. He wasn't sure, but he thought he could hear voices approaching. He tried his best to summon his loudest voice. "Help me," he cried out. "I'm over here."

Now the approaching footsteps were unmistakable. Standing with the sun directly behind him, the would-be rescuer looked down at the broken man.

"What have we here?" the man asked calmly. "An enemy soldier, and of command rank. What do you think we should do with him?"

"Slit his throat and leave him to die," came the angry reply.

"Now, now," the first voice replied. "Is that what we have been taught to do? Unbury him and tend to his wounds. I think perhaps Elisiah would want to talk to this man."

"You mean we are going to drag him all the way back to the castle?" the second spoke up.

"That is what we are going to do. He will be the first to see the castle; after all, that's why they are here. After interrogation, he will die."

All the focus had been removed from the castle as the Lakar soldiers forced the few slaves they could find to clear the debris. The bodies of the Lakar soldiers were lined up row upon row as they were retrieved. Colig watched as two soldiers approached, dragging the lifeless body of Commander Batris behind them.

The body was mangled almost beyond recognition but there was no mistaking the man's features. The two soldiers dropped the body at the feet of Commander Colig and saluted.

"The king wants an example made of this man," Colig growled. "Tie his body to a large pole and have it erected where it can be seen by the king." Colig kicked the face of the fallen commander and smiled. "Take him away."

From the bridge of the Royal Descent, King Dolmar fumed at the defeat his army had taken. He saw the body of Batris hanging from the pole in the harbour and spit in his direction. "You fool," he seethed, "You have caused me this embarrassment and you will not escape my wrath in death. I swear I will hunt down and kill every member of your family." His hatred burned inside of him and consumed his every thought.

Dolmar paced the deck continuously as he played the last few days in his mind. News of this embarrassment must not reach the outside world. If his enemies knew his army had been devastated, the wars against him would escalate to the point where he may not be able to handle all the countries he had conquered. He knew his armies were stretched thin and used fear to control the slaves, and he knew how fragile the situation was.

He looked over at the piles of dead soldiers on the island. Again, he became enraged with blind hatred. Revenge, he thought. I will have revenge.

The following day brought the return of the climbers from the valley below. The captive they brought back was barely alive now, but they afforded him no special treatment.

Prince Lavar and Elisiah were entertaining Chalna and Queen Nateer when the party arrived. Until now, there had been no room for celebration, but this victory had afforded them the time. The front doors opened to the balcony and the climbers brought the unconscious body of the Lakar soldier and laid it at the feet of Prince Lavar.

Elisiah was the first to recognize him as being with Commander Batris. Chalna and Queen Nateer both stood silently over the man. "Clean him up and tend to his wounds," the queen ordered solemnly. "Make sure he is well guarded and call me when he is strong enough to talk."

"Mother," the prince said, "Why show mercy to an enemy that has proven so ruthless to our people?"

"Your mother is right," Elisiah interrupted. "No good will come from killing this man." Elisiah put his hand on the shoulder of the young prince. "Perhaps we can learn more about our enemy by talking to him."

Prince Lavar could see nothing but revenge. He wanted to kill this man with his bare hands. "He killed my father."

"Their king killed your father," Elisiah corrected. "These men only follow orders."

Rage was growing in the young prince. "You make sure I don't see his face again," he warned. The prince looked at the climbers, Jonas in particular. "Get him out of here," he yelled. To his surprise, Chalna followed the men to the castle.

"Where are you going?" he asked in a challenging tone.

"To see to the needs of our enemy," she calmly shot back, "And what are you going to do?"

Lavar's eyes widened and burned. He thought of a quick, sarcastic response but held his tongue. His fight was not with the woman he loved, but with his own emotions.

Before closing the door, Chalna stopped and looked into the eyes of the prince. She smiled and closed the door behind her.

Lavar looked at Nateer. "What's the matter with her?"

"She is a strong-willed young lady," Nateer replied. "Some days that will bite you and other days it will save you. Try to remember, Lavar, you may rule over them, but you do not control their thoughts. That is what separates us from our enemies."

The next few weeks passed with little fanfare. The building in the newly discovered valley through the caves was going well. People were being fed, and the survivors were in good spirits. The news of the battle had spread quickly, and Elisiah was a hero to all who knew him. The men who had worked so hard now had a chance to rest. Although they had achieved a victory, the enemy still clung to their shores and showed little signs of defeat.

The victory had also given the islanders the much-needed time to plan the burial of King Nikodym. Until now, all their efforts were on defense, but now they could make funeral arrangements. Kataan took the lead in the planning, as he considered the king as his own son. The funeral would have to be quick, as they would not have much time, but it would help everyone find a bit of peace and solace. He would confirm plans with the queen and Elisiah, and the funeral would take place in a few days.

Dolmar still stalked the deck of his ship with a passionate rage. Every day he would take the time to spit in the direction of the rotting corpse of Batris. Now he waited for the man he knew would bring him victory. Once Commander Beil arrived, he would kill a hundred slaves for every soldier he watched be buried. Beil would be here shortly, and then the tides of war would change.

He looked in the direction of the city, where his temporary accommodations were no longer being worked on, and it infuriated him even more. If he had to stay on this tub much longer, he would lose his mind. Nothing was going his way, and that was not acceptable. Soon he would be in the place he should have been by now. He was unaccustomed to patience. Now he had it thrust upon him and he did not like it.

Chalna approached the door to the room that held the prisoner. Every day for weeks she had attended to the wounds of the unconscious soldier. Her routine included changing the dressings and sponge-bathing his limp body. He had regained consciousness several times but was usually delirious when he did. Sometimes he would cry out for his wife and child, and other times he would just cry.

Chalna used these opportunities to try to feed the man and get him to drink a high-protein mixture she had made especially for him. She wondered who would be a wife to such a man. She thought she must be a slave, but if she was, why did he call out for her so? She had many questions but few answers.

She took a damp cloth and wiped down the face and chest of the man. She was amazed at how large he was and how toned his muscles were. Slowly, the man's eyes opened. This time he was not delirious, and he stared directly at her. Chalna took her eyes off him for a second and he lunged for her throat. He grabbed her with his massive left hand and ripped the locket from around her neck.

"Where did you get this?" he growled, holding firm to her throat.

Chalna was choking under his power when one of the guards rushed into the room. He drew his sword and placed the blade against the throat of the enemy. Tragar released his grip on Chalna's throat but held the locket firm. Chalna gasped for breath, coughing and wheezing.

"I got it from my mother," she spat out between coughs.

"Where is your mother now?" His voice was almost calm now.

"My mother died many years ago, when I was very young. I hardly knew her, and this is all I have left to remember her."

"Who is your father?" Tragar continued.

"I don't know. I never knew him," she replied. "May I have my locket back?"

Without hesitation, Tragar returned the locket.

"Were you born on this island?" he asked with the blade of the guard still touching his own throat. Now that the man had calmed down, Chalna asked the guard to back off and return to his post.

"No, I don't know where I was born. My adopted parents found my mother and myself cast ashore. It was assumed we came from an island nearby." She calmly divulged.

"There is no island nearby," Tragar offered.

A long silence followed as Chalna reattached her locket.

The soldier grew passive and quiet. His eyes welled up, and a tear flowed down his cheek. "Your mother's name was Chalna," he said softly through the tears. "And your name is Chalna," he continued after a moment.

Chalna's own eyes started to water as she clasped her locket.

"And my name is Irid Tragar," the still-solemn voice revealed, "And you are my daughter."

Chalna turned away in astonishment. Could he have seen the inscription on the back of the locket, she wondered. No, he had ripped it from her neck but did not have time to inspect it. How could he know her mother's name? What was happening?

She ran from the room crying and shielded her eyes from the guard. The man's eyes tightened as he ran to Tragar and raised the blade of his sword in the direction of Tragar's throat again. He held it up long enough to make his point.

Tragar put his finger on the blade and slowly pushed it aside.

"Play with the heart of that lady and you will surely perish," the guard promised.

"I lost her once," Tragar confided. "I lost my wife fifteen years ago. Your blade may draw blood, but you cannot kill a man who is already dead." Tragar sat up, the blade of the guard now only inches from his throat. "I don't know what game you are playing, or how you found out about my family and planted this mole, but if you do not kill me now, I will find out."

The guard retracted the blade slightly. "If you die, it will be at the hands of Prince Lavar. If you live, it will be at his mercy."

"I wish to speak to this Prince Lavar." Tragar wiped the last tear from his cheek. "Let him judge my life. But I warn you, I will only talk if Chalna is there."

"The prince would rather kill you than talk to you," The guard said coldly.

"If you think I will be your prisoner, then I welcome death," Tragar replied.

The guard smirked at Tragar as he turned and walked out the door, locking it behind him.

Tragar lowered his head into his hands. Once again, the tears returned as memories flooded his mind. Could it be true? Could this be his daughter? Could he ever be close to her if she was? There was too much to think about, and his body was still screaming in pain. He needed sleep, and he needed to think.

The morning brought the return of the Infamy. The vessel moored alongside the Royal Descent on the outside of the sheltered bay. A long plank was drawn between the ships and the dignitaries on the Infamy prepared to disembark. The soldiers on the opposite ship were now ready to receive them. Commander Biel was impeccably attired in his best dress uniform.

King Dolmar was equally grand on board the Royal Descent as he waited for the man whom he considered closest to a friend.

Two of Beil's personal guards preceded him across the plank and stood at the other end facing each other. Beil slowly walked the distance of the wooden runway and then between his personal guards, who were also impeccably dressed. When he was fifteen feet from the king, he stopped and waited for instructions.

Dolmar smiled slightly for the first time in months and extended his right hand to Beil. Commander Beil started to remove his cape, which was customary in the presence of royalty.

"Commander," Dolmar began. "You need not remove your cape. Come forward and greet me."

Beil slowly walked toward Dolmar and dropped to one knee. He took the outstretched hand of the king and kissed the back. He then released the hand and returned to attention, his eyes focussed on the king.

Dolmar looked toward the harbour. "Walk with me, Commander." Beil walked alongside Dolmar to the bow of the ship. "Tell me what you see," Dolmar asked in a deep monotone voice.

Beil surveyed the harbour, still littered with floating shards of wood. He gazed at the dock that was being rebuilt and the mounds of dirt that held the bodies of Lakar soldiers. His eyes followed the path of destruction to the massive tunnel that led to the caves. Steam poured out like a cloud. He looked up the cliffs to the castle, which now looked impervious to invasion.

"When I heard of this disaster, I begged only for your safety, Your Majesty," Beil began. "I felt responsible, as I was not here to protect you. I felt grief for the men who had died, not having the chance to fight our enemies. Most of all, I felt regret that the man I trained failed you so miserably."

"Spare me the sentiments, Commander," Dolmar interrupted. "Where is Captain Sordain?" he asked, looking back to the Infamy.

Beil looked down for a second and back to the king. "Captain Sordain is dead," he replied coldly.

Dolmar raised one eyebrow. "How did he die, Commander?"

"At my hand, Your Majesty," Beil confessed. "The evening the ship arrived in my harbour, the crew began to recount the tale of this tragedy. Within a day, the word of the defeat had spread to not only our men but also to our enemies. The fact that we could be defeated was now common knowledge and spreading. This insolence could not go unpunished. I could not punish the whole crew, so I decided to make an example of their captain."

Beil turned and looked at the centre mast of the Infamy. Just below the crow's nest hung the body of Sordain. "I wanted to make sure we didn't have a repeat of the crew's mistake."

"I never liked him," Dolmar confessed. "He was too soft."

Dolmar pointed to the body of Batris. "I also wanted to make sure we don't have a repeat of the mistakes made by the previous commander."

Beil looked at the rotting corpse. "He was a good soldier," he said quietly.

"Look over all the maps we have of this rock," Dolmar said. "I want that castle, and I want it soon."

"Who has taken over command for Batris?" Beil asked.

"I have," Dolmar stated matter-of-factly. "And now the commission falls upon you, Commander. You bring me that castle and I will grant you any wish."

Beil smiled as he reached into his pocket to retrieve his firestone. Rubbing it between his fingers, he looked back at Dolmar. "I wish to be the man who rebuilds your great armies. I have grown weary of babysitting slaves and peasants. I want the glory of war to pulse through my veins again. And I want to serve this empire until my dying breath."

"So be it," Dolmar agreed. "Every man should occupy the position that suits him best."

Lavar walked the path to the gazebo. Sitting quietly sobbing with her head in her hands was the girl that had stolen his heart. He approached her quietly and put his hands on her shoulders. He gently massaged and kneaded her shoulders and neck and stroked her hair. Although he loved her intensely, he was unsure how to comfort her.

"I heard you had a conversation with our prisoner," Lavar said softly.

"He told me he was my father." She sobbed.

"It has to be a trick," Lavar returned, still stroking her hair. "Probably part of their training to get inside of our heads."

"He knew my mother's name." Chalna raised her head from her hands. "He knew my name."

"I swear I will find out what is happening," Lavar promised. "I will interrogate him personally," he added.

Chalna put her hand up to her shoulder and placed it over Lavar's.

"Elisiah has tried to talk to him, but he refuses to talk to anyone but me, with you at my side," Lavar confessed. "It's hard to believe Elisiah couldn't get anything out of him."

"Then it seems we must try." Chalna wiped a tear from her eye as she patted Lavar's hand.

Silently, the pair rose and faced each other. The love Lavar felt was overwhelming, and he hugged Chalna for several minutes.

Chalna's tears flowed freely again, and Lavar felt hurt by his inability to protect her from her feelings. He took her hand and together they walked the path through the garden and up the stairs to the room where the prisoner was held.

When they entered the room, Tragar was seated at the window, which offered a view of the harbour. He turned to face them but did not speak. When he looked at Chalna still weeping, his heart was heavy, and a tear escaped his eyes.

Chalna and Lavar sat across from Tragar with a guard between them.

"My name is Prince Lavar, and I am the son of the ruling family on Trolan," he started. "And you have met Chalna."

The sound of her name brought another tear down the cheek of the immense man. "My name is Irid Tragar," he replied solemnly.

"What is your rank?" the prince asked.

"I have no rank," Tragar responded, looking at the pendant around Chalna's neck. Chalna noticed his gaze and removed it, clasping it in her hand. She asked, "Why do you keep looking at this?"

"Have you ever seen anything like it before?" Tragar asked

Lavar and Chalna looked at each other quizzically, for indeed they had not.

Tragar stood and looked out the window. "I was a merchant seaman several months ago when a storm wreaked havoc on my ship and set us adrift until we reached your shores. When I returned to port, it was my duty to report the presence of this uncharted island. The king gave me this commission as a reward, but I am no soldier."

"Tell me about this locket," Chalna said.

Tragar still looked out the window, afraid to face them and show the emotion he felt. "The locket was acquired in a land called Alkar. I had it made by one of the finest jewelers in the land. I gave it to my wife before I went off to purchase land in a country called Mayak. Once everything was ready, I sent for my wife and daughter. They never arrived."

Chalna was visibly shaken as she listened to the story. "How can I believe this tale you tell?" she asked.

Tragar turned and looked at Chalna. "Your radiant beauty rivals only that of your mother's," he said. "And she was the most beautiful woman my eyes ever looked upon. The day we were married, I vowed that I would always love her, and I always have. My life ended the day she disappeared with my daughter. I persecuted myself for years not knowing what happened to her … and you. You look so much like her that I am having trouble…"

Tragar stopped to clear his throat. "I worked my way up the chain of command until I had my own ship. For the next ten years I searched every port I entered, looking and hoping. Although I had become old and bitter, I never stopped loving her, and my heart would not let me be a complete man again."

The room fell silent, except for the sobs of Chalna. The sight of his love weeping brought uncontrollable emotion from Lavar, and his eyes welled up. Chalna rose, walked toward Tragar and placed the locket in his hand. Tragar rolled it in his fingers, looking at it with tears in his eyes.

"No," he said. "You keep it."

He tapped his chest above his heart. "Your mother is in here."

With unbridled emotion, Chalna threw her hands around the waist of her hesitant prisoner and hugged him. Tragar held his hands to his side as he looked at Lavar. Slowly, he closed his arms around her and reciprocated her hug.

Beil had studied the maps and particularly the geography of the island. He knew the island was largely soft volcanic rock, which he felt he could manipulate. Observation told him the castle could not be protected from the balcony. He knew the existing entrance through the caves was impenetrable because of the boiling water that now flowed through it. The steam that poured out also rained down boiling condensation.

He planned to bore holes into the unprotected rock face. The holes would be fifteen feet deep. Next, they would recess logs into the holes, which would protrude fifteen feet outside the cliffs. Upon these logs, he would build a road to the balcony of the castle. His plan was daring, yet time-consuming. He would have to get permission from the king, or he would have to come up with a new plan.

A knock on the door brought an invitation for dinner aboard the Royal Descent. Beil gathered his maps and prepared for his meeting with the king.

"A road to the front door of the castle?" Dolmar was surprised at the ambitious plan. "How long do you feel it will take to complete this road?"

"If we can climb forty feet per day, the first stage should be complete in twenty days if we consider an angle of fifteen degrees. The length of the first stage would be twelve hundred feet. Stage one would be on land and built on scaffolding anchored to the face of the cliff for extra strength. It will ascend four hundred feet and join the second stage. The second stage consists of crews boring holes in the face fifteen feet apart. Here we go out over the ocean a further eight hundred feet to put us on the east side of the castle, where we can't be attacked. Providing the men boring the holes can stay ahead of the crews building the road, we should complete stage two in another forty days. Stage three, another sixty days, bringing the total to one hundred and twenty days," Beil boasted.

"One hundred and twenty days." Dolmar was impressed. "One hundred and twenty days." "Alright then, one hundred and twenty days, but not one day longer, understand?"

"Yes, Your Majesty. I have ways to make the men work harder when I have a deadline to meet," Beil replied.

"Come, Commander," Dolmar offered. "Eat and drink. Your one hundred and twenty days don't start until tomorrow."

Elisiah and Lavar started the morning as they did most mornings—looking over the harbour and their enemies. Somehow, this morning was different. The enemy had a renewed energy and purpose. Work on the dock had almost stopped, and the lumber was being moved to the base of the mountain. A small army of men had gathered, including men equipped to scale the cliffs.

Three of the remaining five ships were also setting out to sea.

"Do you think they are leaving?" Lavar asked.

"I think they are going to get reinforcements," Elisiah replied. "They are madder than ever now. I'm sure they are preparing another surprise for us, and it looks like we may not be as fortunate as we were last time."

"What do you mean by that?" Lavar wondered.

"Barook and I talked about this earlier. The mountain is mainly volcanic rock, which is very soft, as rock goes. If they are up to what I think they are, we won't have a defense against them." Elisiah pondered.

"I'm not sure what you are getting at." Lavar was puzzled.

"Barook had devised a lift system to run from the balcony to the base of the mountain. He had planned to run it down in twelve separate lifts, each ascending two hundred feet to platforms secured to the rock face. We could transport hundreds of people in a short period of time. If they are planning something like that, we have no way of attacking them," Elisiah confided. "I don't know what else they could be doing down there."

"They are building a road," Barook stated matter-of-factly as he joined the two men.

"What makes you so sure?" Lavar asked.

"I've been watching them and what they are doing," Barook said. "If they follow the base of the cliff to the water, we can't attack them from above any longer."

"I was just discussing that with the prince," Elisiah replied.

"A road?" Lavar scratched at his ear.

"The first few days as the scaffolding was being built, it was difficult to figure out what they were up to. In the next few days they have built almost two hundred feet of road and scaffolding," Barook estimated.

"How long will it take to get up this high?" Lavar asked.

"I would think their plan will hit a stumbling block when they reach the water," Barook thought aloud. "However, time will tell. As Elisiah stated, the rock is soft, and a tunnel could be dug at a good rate; probably fifteen feet per day."

"How long?" Elisiah repeated, interrupting Barook before he started to do a long calculation in his head.

"Probably six months," Barook spoke slowly, raising an eyebrow.

"Then we have that long to finish moving into the valley," the prince stated.

"Prince Lavar," Elisiah said. "Barook and I have devised a defense to protect us from further attack, and we would like to discuss with you."

"Then I think you should also discuss your plans with my mother," Lavar said. "After all, she is the queen."

Elisiah smiled back at Lavar and replied, "I do believe you are correct, Prince Lavar."

Beil stood on the deck of the Infamy and watched the work progress. Erecting the framework for the road was more time consuming than he originally planned. The climbers however, had exceeded his expectations and within two weeks had marked out all of the route for stage two of his plan. They had started to attach small platforms at strategic locations along the route. With these platforms in place, the slaves could begin to bore holes into the mountain.

Commander Colig approached and awaited instructions. His eyes burned a hole through Beil as he stared at the back of the man who had taken his rightful position. He despised Beil and every decision he made. He hoped silently Beil's plan would also fail.

"Commander Colig," Beil sneered. "Come closer, I want to look at you when I talk to you."

Colig approached and bowed his head in a shallow show of respect. "How can I be of assistance?" he asked as if the words burned his tongue.

"I'm not happy with the progress of the initial stage of my plan. What seems to be the holdup?" Beil demanded.

"We've lost half of the fleet," Colig said. "Most of the slaves escaped, and most of the ships have just completed repairs. I have every available man working on your plan, Commander. I don't know what else we can do."

"I want to double the work shifts. I want our men and the slaves working on that road day and night. I have a schedule to keep, as well as a promise to a friend," Beil replied. He stared at Colig for a minute. "You think you have what it takes to be a leader, don't you?"

Colig thought for a second before he spoke. He looked around to see that they were alone. "Yes," he replied. "I do think I am capable of leading these men, as depleted as they are. However, the king has decided otherwise. I follow orders, Commander Beil. My personal thoughts are not part of my professional career."

Beil looked into Colig's eyes and smiled. "Well versed, I see. What I demand of you is not easy, Commander. If you complete the tasks I have laid out for you, you shall be well rewarded. The level of command you now enjoy is very difficult to achieve. Don't fail now, Colig. I think you can be a great asset to me, and I trust you realize the opposite is true."

"I know you have a history of completing your tasks, Commander," Colig replied. "And your success in battle has given you great honour and prestige. I cannot say I will always be happy to follow your orders, but I will always complete my tasks. I look forward to benefiting from your experience."

Queen Nateer entered the room gracefully, followed by two valets who attended to her needs. One of the men pulled out a chair at the end of the table. Prince Lavar stood at the table to her right and took her hand in his. Beside Lavar were Chalna and Barook. Across the table stood Elisiah and Irid Tragar, with guards at each shoulder.

Nateer motioned for the men to sit as she did the same. Each person bowed to the queen as they sat. She gazed upon Tragar for a moment. "How is our guest?" she began.

"Thanks to the gentle hand of Chalna, I have fully recovered from my injuries," Tragar returned humbly. "And how is Your Grace?"

"Injured," Nateer confided, looking down for a second. "I fear my heart will never heal. Your king has taken everything from me except my people."

"Please believe me when I say that I am truly sorry for the grief I have brought you. I can't say I'm sorry for discovering your island, as it has resurrected my life, a life I thought was over," Tragar said as he looked over at Chalna.

The queen looked at Tragar and slowly spit out the words, "Please believe me when I say I don't give a damn about your life. I care only about the lives of the people I love, and you are not one of them. Your only purpose here is to tell us what you know. Elisiah thinks you can help us, so you will live for now. If I feel you are not useful, you will be returned to the bottom of the cliff without a rope, do you understand?"

Tragar smiled at the hollow threat and bowed to Nateer.

"Excuse me, Your Majesty," Elisiah began. "I believe we need to discuss what we are going to do about our friends. It would seem they are more determined than ever."

"Your Majesty," Tragar interrupted. "May I speak?"

"No, you may not," Lavar shot back as he stood and glared at Tragar.

"Wait, Lavar." Nateer put her hand on her son's. "Let's hear what he has to say. After all, that is why he is here."

Lavar slowly returned to his seat, still glaring at Tragar.

"Your Majesty," Tragar started again. "King Dolmar has brought his most experienced warrior to bring this island to its knees." Tragar looked over at Chalna. "However, time is not on his side. The king is frustrated and that makes him dangerous, not only to you but also to his own men."

Elisiah looked at Lavar and Barook as Tragar paused for a moment.

"The room you afforded me has a wonderful view of the harbour, and I have been watching the activity going on," Tragar said.

"Get to the point," Lavar shot across the room.

Tragar smiled again. "If you would allow it, I would like to show you the harbour so I can explain."

"Why would you want to help us?" an angry Lavar asked.

"Look over the harbour and you will know the answer to that question," Tragar returned.

"All right." Nateer started to stand before the valet could reach her. "Let's go to the balcony and reveal the mystery." The entourage stood as the queen did.

"This better be good," Lavar warned as they headed for the balcony.

They went down the stairs and onto the front balcony, the guards watching their prisoner intently. Tragar led the way with an unshakable confidence. He placed his left foot on the ledge of the balcony, almost daring the guards to follow him.

The valets placed a throne-like chair for the queen about ten feet from the edge of the balcony where Tragar stood. Queen Nateer ignored the chair but did not approach Tragar closely. Tragar turned back to address Nateer and Chalna. He almost ignored Lavar, Elisiah and the guards.

"Your Grace," Tragar began. "What do you see before you?"

"Defeat." Lavar stepped in front of his mother. "Your defeat and that of your mighty king." Lavar spat on Tragar.

Tragar looked through Lavar as if he did not exist and waited for an answer.

Unsure of what Tragar was looking for, Queen Nateer put her hand on Lavar's shoulder.

Tragar smiled slightly. "Do you see the ship in the harbour?" He pointed to the ship Beil had arrived on.

Nateer, unamused by Tragar's questioning, sighed slightly, trying not to show her impatience.

Tragar did not wait for a reply. "That ship belongs to Beil. He is the most ruthless of all. He has been the overlord of the largest of the king's provinces. He has exploited more people and more lands than any of his rivals."

Tragar pointed to the rotten corpse tied to a stake near the dock. "That is the body of Commander Batris, and that is what happens to people who fail the king."

Tragar now took his foot off the ledge and looked at Lavar. "You asked why I would want to help?" He looked back at the corpses. "I am already dead," he stated as he looked into Lavar's eyes. "We have a much different way of life. We take prisoners to do our bidding, but we do not become prisoners. Even if I escaped and returned to Dolmar's forces, I would be debriefed and then I would disappear."

Tragar looked at the silent crowd and then at Chalna. "If I am to have a life, it would not be in the company of anyone I have known in the past. Before I die, I would like to know more about the people who saved the life of the lady that wears that necklace."

Chalna clutched the necklace but did not speak.

"You mean to tell me that if one of your men is captured, you would kill him rather than have him serve again?" Queen Nateer asked.

"Our soldiers are expected to fight to the death; therefore, there should be no way of being captured. Being captured is a sign of cowardice, and that is not tolerated," Tragar returned.

"What kind of king would kill his own people?" Lavar asked.

"The kind that would kill your father in cold blood," Tragar reminded the prince.

Elisiah saw the rise in Lavar and wisely stepped between the two men. "How many ships does Dolmar have at his disposal?"

Tragar continued to stare down Lavar before turning his attention to Elisiah. "He has ten fleets of ten war ships. He also has around a thousand ships at his disposal for various tasks."

"Over one hundred ships and we have faced ten of them…" Elisiah thought out loud.

"You need not worry," Tragar offered. "Dolmar is powerful but he is greedy. That is his weakness. In my humble opinion, he can ill afford to call on reinforcements."

"Why?" Lavar seethed.

"Dolmar rules over many lands, perhaps too many. His rule has never known peace. He and his armies are constantly at war; it's like an adrenaline rush. For the past few years, Dolmar has been forced to reduce his offensive campaigns. His armies are stretched thin trying to maintain his power. He has found to conquer is easy, but to control is much more difficult." Tragar turned back to the harbour. "I can see by the body count he is getting frustrated."

Elisiah walked over to Tragar and looked at the harbour with him. "What do you think we should do?" he wondered.

"There is nothing you can do. Your fate is in the hands of time," Tragar replied.

"Perhaps we will have more time than you think." Elisiah smiled.

CHAPTER 15

Dolmar was quickly tiring of his daily routine. He paced the deck obsessively and relentlessly. Occasionally he would stop and curse the castle and the people in it. Too much time was passing, and he still did not have his prize.

Twenty days had now gone by. Beil was becoming more aggressive toward his overworked men. His ferocity would have led to the deaths of hundreds of slaves if he thought he could spare them. As it was, there were now only hundreds where there were thousands a few weeks ago.

He was falling behind schedule; he knew it and Dolmar knew it. He thought about his options. Failure was not among them. His dinners with the king were becoming less enjoyable, as it was getting harder to defend the imminent threat of failure. He knew he had two choices: he could ask the king for additional ships, or he could call in a few favours and procure some ships full of slaves from Alkar.

A knock on the cabin door brought the successor to Jordain, and new captain of the Infamy. Beil looked down on his subordinate with a hint of disdain in order to impose his authority. "I want you to return to Alkar with this message." Beil handed an envelope to Captain Malik Gar. "I am requesting three ships loaded with slaves. I want you to help procure the slaves and transport them back here. I want your ship stripped down to reduce weight and take only a minimal crew. You must be back here within forty days."

"Yes, Commander," Gar replied respectfully. He had a great respect for a man considered a living legend. This was the first time he had met Beil personally, and he wanted to make a good impression. He stood silently and waited to be dismissed.

Beil rolled his firestone amongst his fingers. Its warm glow helped. "This mission is of extreme importance," Beil said. "This obsession of the kings is becoming quite perilous for me, and I don't like that feeling. I need manpower, and soon. If you are back within forty days, I will increase your rank. That is all."

Captain Gar saluted and retreated to the cabin door. The adrenaline flowing through his body was almost uncontainable. Outside the door, he breathed deeply for what seemed like the first time since he entered. Now he would get to show what the son of a slave could do.

In the early morning light, Captain Gar piloted his ship past the Royal Descent. On the bridge, King Dolmar stood with Commander Beil. All eyes were upon him. Although he could not see them, he knew the people in the castle were also watching. All his life he had waited for his chance. Although he respected his predecessor, he had known Jordain wouldn't last.

His personal agenda had come to fruition even quicker than he had planned, but he was ready. He was going to be Beil's favourite when this campaign ended.

High on the cliff above Gar, his intuition was correct. Lavar, Elisiah, Barook and Bastian all watched as once again a ship left the harbour.

"Reinforcements?" Barook asked.

"Not according to our guest," Lavar spat out sarcastically.

"Your Majesty," Elisiah said seriously. "Tragar did not kill your father, and he is no longer our enemy. Why must you hate him so?"

"He brought the man who did kill my father." Lavar glared at Elisiah. "He brought this upon our people."

Bastian and Barook excused themselves as they realized this conversation was going to continue. Elisiah waited for them to retreat before gesturing for Lavar to sit. Lavar rolled his eyes but succumbed to Elisiah's wishes.

"You're afraid he is going to take her from you," Elisiah stated bluntly.

Lavar was a bit offended. "He has some kind of control over her; I can see it in her eyes."

"Both of them had been waiting for this for a long time." Elisiah's voice had a soothing tone. "Have you stopped to think about what Chalna is feeling? Have you considered the range of emotions she must be going through?"

Lavar lowered his eyes, feeling just a little smaller.

"I didn't think so." Elisiah waited for a moment to let that thought sink in. "Tragar has had a hole in his heart for nearly twenty years. Time will not heal the heart exposed to true love. That is the spell he holds over her. It is also the spell you hold over her."

Lavar looked back to Elisiah. "How can you defend a man you don't know?"

"You heard it yourself, he was never a soldier. He was a merchant who searched relentlessly for the lives he thought he had lost. He hasn't harmed anyone." Elisiah maintained a level tone.

Lavar squinted at Elisiah and disdainfully shook his head.

"It's not a competition, young prince," Elisiah continued. "There is room in her heart for her father and her mate. Don't let your blind jealousy or rage push away the love you are destined for. Don't force her to choose. She needs your support, not your disapproval. Don't tell her you love her, show her. She needs to know how much you are willing to sacrifice to be with her. I don't think your anger is too much to ask, do you?"

The tension in Lavar lightened. What would Elisiah know about love? he thought.

"Take her for a walk in the garden," Elisiah suggested. "Take her some flowers and read her some of that poetry you're so big on. Ask her how she feels then go talk to her father."

As the men talked, the skies darkened. The warm sun that had been so prevalent over the past few months was fading. Elisiah and Lavar could feel the faint droplets of moisture.

"Finally," Elisiah said.

"Yes, it's quite late this year," Lavar said.

The men smirked at each other and relief came over them. "Let's see how the work progresses when the cliffs are slippery," Lavar said, almost giddy, as he knew this was just the start of two months of rain.

The crew of the Royal Descent also noticed the change in weather. With uncanny ferocity, the sea began to swell, and the wind began to sing. It was not a song the men on the remaining ships wanted to hear. With precision, the men began to batten down the ship and prepare for a battle with nature. The once calm and peaceful harbour now offered little protection as the waves funneled through the tributaries surrounding the island.

King Dolmar stood braced at the window in his quarters. "Another freak storm?" he wondered.

"Tragar's storm lasted nine days," Beil informed the king.

"I don't want to be on this tub nine more days in good weather. I should have stayed on the island and ridden my horse in the rain," Dolmar returned.

"Nine days of this will really slow down progress on the cliffs," Beil thought aloud.

"Still ninety-nine days by my calendar, Commander. Think you will make it?" Dolmar asked.

"Sometimes cleaning up someone else's mess has its pitfalls, Your Grace." Beil shrugged.

"Don't worry, Beil. Have faith; you're too good a warrior to fail." Dolmar smiled.

Beil realized he had never had to test his friendship with the king and wondered how good a friend he was. "In just over a month we should have another twelve hundred slaves to work on the mountain," Beil boasted.

"That's a lot of slaves, Commander. You'll have about five hundred men to guard almost three thousand slaves." Dolmar seemed concerned.

"Yes," Beil countered. "This is going to be a bit tricky, but the slaves are well aware of our disciplinary measures. Rarely do we have problems, and besides, where would they go?"

Dolmar chuckled. He knew very well that Beil was a master of maintaining control. The ship rolled with the waves and the pressure of the wind. At times, Dolmar and Beil had difficulty maintaining their balance.

"I hate storms," Dolmar mused. "It makes it difficult to drink." He laughed at his own joke, as did Beil.

"I'm sure tomorrow will bring a better day." Beil smiled. "I plan to visit the worksite tomorrow. You know, a little moral support." They laughed again.

"We will go together, my friend," Dolmar offered. "I want to get my feet on solid ground again. I don't think I've gone hunting for weeks. What do you think, Beil, you think we have time to go hunting?"

"Only if the day doesn't count against me." Beil shrewdly asked for another day.

Dolmar smiled at Beil and shook his finger at him. "You're sly. Very well, if it's a good hunt, I will give you another day for each seven days of rain."

Rarely had the fall rains been so eagerly anticipated. Elisiah, Barook and Bastian all knew the storms would reek havoc on any dock built in the harbour. Now King Dolmar was going to find out why the islanders had never built one. Out on the balcony, Nateer, Lavar, Chalna, Elisiah, Irid and Barook all stood watching as the surf pounded the once-placid shoreline.

Irid was puzzled by the unexpected jubilation over a storm.

"It isn't just a storm, Irid," Barook explained. "Every fall the winds come from the southwest and bring these cold, wet storms that generally last until the beginning of winter—around two months, give or take a few weeks."

"Two months of this?" Irid was surprised. "How can you handle it? It's practically dark at midday."

"We use this time to rest and prepare for the coming year. It's a time of reflection. We take time to appreciate our lives and our families and be with our friends," Barook said.

"Sounds dull," Irid groaned.

"We've always had so much to be grateful for. We work hard for ten months a year, and rest for two. The time off is essential for harmony. We have gatherings and ceremonies … this is when the young men and woman get married," Elisiah added as he looked over at Lavar.

Irid could only think of how boring it must be to spend so much time doing nothing. Then he thought about how he could spend this time to get to know his daughter. When she was near him, he watched her intently, noticing the subtleties that reminded him of his beloved wife. After a short daydream, he noticed Lavar was standing silently to his left. The two men watched Chalna as she glided across the balcony, graciously conversing with various village elders.

"She really is your daughter, isn't she?" Lavar broke the silence between the two.

"Yes, she is," Irid replied.

"I'm not afraid of you," Lavar said, summoning all his courage.

Irid reacted with a huge smile and a quiet chuckle. "Did you think I was trying to intimidate you?"

"You do intimidate me," Lavar confessed. "But I'm still not afraid of you."

Still chuckling, Irid added, "You have guile." He placed his large hand on Lavar's shoulder. "I admire guile."

"Maybe you're not what I thought you would be," Lavar revealed. "All we've seen from your people is incomprehensible violence."

Irid was quiet for a moment.

"There is no doubt that King Dolmar is prepared to exact any measure to ensure order is maintained. However, we were not always this way. Dolmar's father brought fifty years of wars upon us, and his son has learned well how to rule. My father was a farmer. When I was five years old, the government came and took my brother and forced him to join the war effort. He died two years later. My father was able to pay a fee to keep me out of the war effort."

Lavar had mixed emotions about Tragar's confession. All he knew for sure was he would have to interact with Tragar if he wanted Chalna, and Chalna was all he dreamed about.

Tragar was not lost to the knowledge that Chalna was in love with this young man standing beside him. "Every day, every one of us is tested, and every day we make choices. I am choosing to go forward, to prove to everyone that even if you go through hell on earth, you can still choose to be respected."

Lavar felt overwhelmed. A year ago, he knew nothing of this madness, and now he was sinking into a pool of self-pity. He was mad. Mad, mad, mad. How could this be happening to him, and what did he do to bring this on? In an instant, his emotions overwhelmed him, and he looked down, turning away from Tragar to hide a tear that ran down his cheek.

Tragar did not smile. He blinked repeatedly and stood solemnly, trying to digest the sight of the young man openly showing his emotion. He tried to think back to a time when he was an emotional young man. He patted Lavar's shoulder a couple of times and added a slight squeeze. The only emotion he had ever seen from the young man was anger, and he felt unsettled.

After a harrowing trip through the harbour, Dolmar was now comfortable in the house once occupied by Kataan and Marta. The renovated home sat on a hill, which still gave him a clear view of the harbour and up the cliff to the castle. He watched as his ship tossed in the turbulent swirl that the harbour had become. The debris from his once powerful fleet now smashed relentlessly against the deteriorating dock. The wind blew the rain horizontally across the landscape. A constant mist had formed around the base of the cliff where the slaves tried to work through unbearable conditions. The once pliable rock walls were now slippery and sharp. The logs were now heavier, and the ropes were more difficult to handle. The death toll continued to climb as the mountain exacted its revenge.

Dolmar still paced silently across the room, looking out the windows constantly. None of the four remaining ships were able to launch a boat for a week as the storm continued to intensify. If this continued much longer, the ships would have to head out to open sea to find a safer shelter.

If this happened, he and his men would be very vulnerable to an uprising. He felt uneasy. For the first time in his reign, he felt threatened with failure. For the first time he wondered if he really needed to fight a war against mother nature to win another land. Was the fight worth the prize? A lot of firsts for a man who had never really been tested.

Beil also looked out the window of the house he now occupied, from a much closer position near the construction site. Work had slowed considerably since the rain had begun. The slaves were wearing down and he knew more slaves were five weeks away. He couldn't send his men to round up more, as most were stuck on the ships being tossed around in the harbour.

The morale of his own men was fading under the constant barrage of bone-chilling rain. Although the men were housed in dry barracks, their armour was not easily adapted to these conditions. The roads were now deep, muddy and slippery ruts. Waterfalls were forming on the very cliffs they were trying to bore into. Beil knew he was not going to complete his mission if the incessant rain did not subside. The thought of failure drained the blood from his face and made his knees feel weak. He knew he would have to confront King Dolmar with his dilemma and decided to see him sooner than later.

He rolled the firestone in his hand and between his fingers. Adrenaline and anxiety filled his body. It was time for him to test his friendship with the king.

Lavar sat in the gazebo, head down, with a single purple rose he had freshly harvested from the garden and a small silk cloth. Eyes closed, he listened to the water fall down the wall behind him. He concentrated on the sound and on the birds in the distance. He felt surreal in the moment.

Opening his eyes, he gazed at the lady who had stolen his heart. The very sight of her changed the beating in his chest and the rhythm of his breathing. His mind drained of all thought, and he hesitantly blurted out, "I love you."

It was all he could think of, and it surprised him.

Chalna's eyes widened; she was caught off guard by what she thought she had heard. She walked closer and knelt down so she was eye to eye with Lavar.

"What did you say?" she asked quietly.

This time without hesitation, he placed the rose into Chalna's hand and looked deep into her green eyes. "I love you."

She threw her arms around Lavar's chest and hugged him tightly to hide the tears filling her eyes. She squeezed her eyes shut, which forced a tear down her olive cheek. She pulled back and looked into his bright blue eyes.

"What brought that up?" she asked with childlike coyness.

"Your father," Lavar replied softly. "I watch how he looks at you and how he talks about you. His voice has a quiver and is much lower in tone. His entire body relaxes, and he just doesn't look as big and strong anymore, and I can see that he loves you."

He brought her hand up between them and showed her the rose. "A purple rose … that means I loved you from the first time I saw you. I know that because I feel the same way your father does, and I always have."

Chalna could no longer contain her tears, and her body started to tremble. "Until now, I could only hope you felt the same way I do, and I love you too," she replied quietly. Lavar took the small silk cloth and dabbed the tears under Chalna's eyes and down her cheek. He smiled, and holding her steady, he kissed her lips, tenderly at first and then passionately.

As Beil entered the castle once owned by Kataan, he was met by two slave girls. One knelt and cleaned the mud off his boots. The other took his overcoat and offered him a warm, damp cloth and a dry towel. He washed his face first and then held the cloth on his eyes for a moment longer. He dropped the cloth on the floor and snatched the towel from the girl's hand. He dried his hands as he kept his eyes on the girl, who looked only at the floor. He dropped the towel and wiped the soles of his clean boots.

Two of Dolmar's guards waited to accompany Beil to the library. With a gesture of his hand, the guards led the way. One spread the doors open and led Beil into the room. "King Dolmar will join you momentarily," the guard stated as he retreated into the hall, closing the doors behind him.

Beil turned slowly in the room and admired the grand selection of artifacts that complemented the rows of books on spectacular redwood shelves. One painting that particularly interested him was of a valley as it was before a damn was built. It was a formidable canyon, which was now a huge reservoir for water and irrigation. He could tell the painting was very old. It was large and placed in the centre of the far wall over the fireplace. The colours showed late-summer scenery, looking up from the bottom of the canyon. He found it mesmerizing. He walked slowly past the bookshelves, reading the odd title. Then, stopping in front of the fireplace, he again gazed upon the painting.

Where is this canyon? he wondered. He knew of the dam but did not know where it was on the island. He turned when he heard the library doors swing open. He lowered his head slightly, keeping his eyes on the king as he approached.

Dolmar stopped a few feet from Beil. He looked over his old friend for a second. "What are we going to do with this weather?" Dolmar began. He gestured toward the window that overlooked the harbour.

As they approached the window, they could hear the rain pounding against the glass. Looking over the harbour, Beil said, "It has become difficult to continue construction on the cliffs."

"Our struggle is far more involved than just the cliffs, Commander," Dolmar confided. "This little conquest has proven to be expensive in far more than time and money." Dolmar looked at Beil. "We have ships in the harbour that are barely able to stay afloat." Dolmar shook his head in disbelief. "This damn rain makes all of our hard work useless. We can't even move the lumber we had harvested off the island."

Beil remained silent, waiting to see what the king had to say.

"We must find a new harbour for our ships," Dolmar said. "They are getting pounded. We need to re-evaluate our plan here, my friend."

"The only safe harbour on this island at this time is on the other side," Beil said.

"Too far away," Dolmar replied.

"The road from here is narrow and winding. It would be difficult to travel with provisions," Beil added.

"Options?" Dolmar queried.

"Nothing I can see offhand," Beil replied. "I recommend sending the fleet to find the nearest safe harbour and send a landing party back to report."

"Let's look at the maps." Dolmar led Beil over to the table to a collection of maps that once belonged to Kataan. He fingered through a few and pulled out one that showed the southern quarter of the island. The cliffs around the castle were sheer and impenetrable with the pounding surf, but on the main island past the cliffs was a fishing village with a protected, deep-water port. "Here." Dolmar pointed. "If we can land and secure this harbour, we could only be three or four days away."

Beil looked silently at the king. He looked down at the map, pulled the firestone from his pocket instinctively, and rolled it in his fingers.

"Tell me, Commander, what is really on your mind?" Dolmar asked. "What do you think we should do?"

"We need to abandon the castle right now and concentrate on regaining control of the situation." Beil spoke quietly yet confidently.

"Explain?" Dolmar asked.

"In our haste to take the castle, we have neglected the rest of the island. We know almost nothing about it other than what we see on the maps, and we have explored much less than half on our own. We really only control the harbour and about a twenty-mile radius around it. Right now, half our men are being tossed around in the harbour and the rest are being worked to death. We are low on slaves and they are being killed on the cliffs, unable to work in this rain." Beil stopped and let his thoughts sink in for a moment. He looked at the painting over the fireplace.

He looked back at Dolmar and then to the maps on the table. "I think we should take the men from the cliffs and build a road to the nearest safe harbour. We should send the army to secure the town and prepare for the ships' arrival. The sooner we secure a port, the better our chances of surviving the weather. We need the men that are on those ships." He had devised a plan he hoped the king would agree to.

Dolmar traced a route to the town on the far side of the island with his finger. He tapped the map a couple of times. He looked at Beil and motioned for him to join him in walking back to the window. They looked over the cliffs and up to the castle.

"You're not going anywhere," Dolmar grumbled at his nemesis. "Alright, Commander, let's refocus on this problem," he conceded.

"We should replenish our supply of slaves as well," Beil added.

"Do as you feel necessary, Commander," Dolmar said.

"About that map…" Beil said. "Did you notice the small island?"

"What are you referring to?" Dolmar asked, returning to the table.

"There is only an outline showing no real definition. The only detail is around the castle and the harbour valley. The rest isn't filled in, as if it hasn't been explored. I wonder why that is."

Dolmar looked through the other maps but could not find any concerning the small island. All the other maps of the main island were well detailed.

"You may need these maps, Beil," the king offered.

As Beil took one of the maps from Dolmar, the king held it tight and looked into his eyes. "You have a reprieve until this weather passes, but make no mistake, Beil, I want that castle."

"Yes, Your Grace," Beil replied, bowing to the king.

The morning rain pounded the castle, which brought smiles to the faces of most of its occupants. Today when Elisiah looked out, something was different. The sound was different, and the ships were no longer being tossed about in the harbour. He realized he could no longer hear the sound of construction on the cliffs either. He could see small boats landing on the beaches that offered some semblance of safety past the tattered pier. He surmised they were the last of the invading force on the island. What were they up to? Where are the ships? he wondered.

Everything was eerily quiet. As he surveyed the harbour, he was joined by Lavar, who was now realizing what Elisiah had noticed moments earlier. He took the time to look over the landscape. "Are they gone?" he finally asked.

"I don't know," Elisiah replied. "I can see they are still in the city."

"What about the ships?" Lavar asked.

"I think they have finally realized the futility of trying to advance in this weather," Elisiah surmised. They must have gone to a safer harbour, probably the fishing village. That is the nearest safe, deep-water harbour. They must be low on provisions."

"The fishing village?" Lavar responded.

"I would think so," Elisiah guessed.

"Can we warn them?" Lavar asked.

"We must try," Elisiah agreed. "They won't have much chance against four ships full of half-starved soldiers."

"Half-starved animals, you mean," Lavar said, showing his disdain for the enemy.

"Perhaps, young prince," Elisiah conceded. "Come, we must assemble the council to discuss the latest turn of events."

It had been four days since the order to set sail had come down from Commander Beil. Now the deep-water port was in view. The intensity of the storm had only increased since they left the chaos of the previous harbour.

Maneuvering through the tons of debris was hazardous enough but rounding the small island had brought a change in currents and nearly threw two of the ships into the rocky shore. One of them was hung up temporarily on a hidden reef until a rogue wave dislodged the fledgling ship, sending it shoreward and precariously close to the rocks. Only the reinforced hull saved the crew from certain death.

Now this sheltered cove was a welcome relief. Although the rain still pounded and the wind still howled, the men were able to secure the ships and set out for provisions. The village seemed abandoned, and no one came out to greet the strangers. There were no ships anchored, not even the smallest rowboat.

As dusk set in, the village took on an eerie look and feel. The Lakar soldiers were on high alert as they entered the vacant buildings, searching them one by one. Many had been burned to the ground and some were still smoldering, half burned. Few remained untouched or undamaged. The ominous sound of the creaking doors sent chills down the backs of the men assigned to open them.

One of the rooms of an undamaged house showed the inhabitants had left in haste. Pots were left on the stoves, fireplaces unattended. Some of the tables had full cups and half-eaten dinners. Unheard and unseen, the inhabitants had all disappeared into the night.

On the bridge of his ship, Commander Colig stood cross-armed, staring at the smoldering village at the end of the dock. Only the torches of his own men lit up the streets.

The rain seemed to lighten up as they rocked against the dock they were anchored to. With most ships still anchored outside the safety of the dock, the rough weather was a welcome reprieve from where they had been a few days ago. The winds still licked up, swirling around the horn that protected the harbour. Although the seas were much more stable, the wind still tossed the ships and tested their anchors.

Colig thought about how long he should stay anchored to the dock, as his ship was much heavier than the fishing boats that previously occupied the space. Once the occupation was complete, he would set up a base camp and prepare for the arrival of the king.

With the arrival of the ships, the people from the fishing village had no resistance when finding refuge in the surrounding villages many miles away. Thousands of displaced people made a pilgrimage to the palace and north to unoccupied cities. They had a torturous journey through the mud on the rain-soaked roads. The women and children had to walk, as the beasts of burden toiled with their belongings.

Every one of them knew of the hardship that lay ahead, as the roads were rarely travelled at this time of year. Slides and washouts would be a daily occurrence and staving off pneumonia would be close to impossible. Undaunted, they pressed on. Ahead of them lay the most perilous part of the journey, as the village was on the other side of a steep and jagged pass through the mountains.

At the site of the castle, the work had almost come to a complete halt. From the balcony, the council could see the house of Kataan was still occupied by Dolmar.

"Elisiah," Lavar wondered. "How many men do you think are down there guarding him?"

"Probably his most trusted and battle-trained men," Elisiah replied.

"Do you think we should take this opportunity to attack?" Lavar asked.

"Although it sounds tempting, we are not soldiers," Elisiah countered. "I feel we would have little chance against them."

"I know who is a soldier," Lavar said softly.

"I still don't know if I trust him," Elisiah said as he stared down at Kataan's former home.

"Shouldn't we at least talk to him?" Lavar asked.

Dolmar and Beil looked up at the castle with distain. The wind and rain had been a constant companion for almost a month, and Dolmar's patience was wearing thin. He could not ride his beloved horse as the roads were almost impassable with the thick mud. He ached to go hunting and was beginning to hate this island.

Work on the cliffs had stopped, as most of the slaves had escaped with the poor supervision. The soldiers were exhausted and spent most of their time foraging for food. Dolmar had only a handful of guards protecting him, and Beil had a skeleton crew guarding the Royal Descent as she floundered in the frightful waters of the harbour. No one could even board the ship, as the longboats they did launch were swamped and the men lost. Anger burned in Dolmar's eyes.

Beil found the firestone was rolling in his fingers more often than ever before, and the red that glowed inside was more intense.

The two stood, silently staring. Beil was no longer comfortable in the presence of the king as he knew how volatile Dolmar could be.

Commander Colig was now fully entrenched in the secured fishing village. The houses were meager, but he had transformed a warehouse to be a suitable abode for the king. His next task would be to build a road back through the forest to the city of Kataan.

All the remaining ships had skeleton crews while the men were hard at work cutting down the massive trees to use as a road to bridge the deep mud on the existing road. The task was daunting, as the city was many miles away and the pace of the work was painfully slow. Without the slaves that Colig was told would be readily available, every item on his agenda took on a whole new dimension. He knew the consequences of failure, so he pushed his men even harder.

Disgruntled, the hungry and exhausted men pressed on. At least they had a trail to follow. The rain continued to pour down upon them, and soon they began to fall to sickness. The harder Colig pushed them, the fewer were able to complete a day's work. Colig questioned the viability of this mission. In all his years of service, he had never faced this much adversity.

"I am not a soldier," Tragar replied. "I am a merchant sailor. Do you think you would have captured a soldier so easily? He would have killed himself rather than be taken prisoner."

"You said you wanted to help so you could live," Lavar shot back.

"I do want to live." Tragar turned to look more closely at the prince. "That is why you don't attack an army with fisherman and farmers." He smirked.

"Look outside," the prince demanded.

The two of them looked over the near-empty harbour. The king's ship was tossed like a toy in a tub of water. The saturated mountainside, now barren of trees, began to move ever so slowly.

"There is no one there but the tyrant trying to kill us," Lavar fumed. "Let's get him now while he is vulnerable."

"Fisherman and farmers," Tragar repeated, a little louder.

"If we can't defeat him with might, then we must defeat him with cunning," Elisiah spoke up as he approached. "We have knowledge he does not possess." Elisiah positioned himself between the two men, sensing the tension in the prince.

Tragar's interest was piqued, as he also considered himself a thinking man.

"We need a diversion, maybe two, and then attack when they can't defend," Elisiah surmised. "I can think of one immediate advantage. The hills above the city move daily. If we could speed that up, it would provide one distraction."

"They are desperate for slaves," Tragar added. "We could display the islanders to them and draw them out into a trap."

"We need to isolate the king," Lavar said.

Elisiah smiled. "Gentlemen, I think we have a plan."

Chalna and Queen Nateer sat in the gazebo enjoying the garden. The birds sang and flew high above. The soothing sound of the waterfall and the quiet surroundings were mesmerizing. They had spent much more time together lately as Nateer struggled to get over the death of her husband. Both women missed the attention of their men. They found solace in knowing how important a task Lavar faced with the men who stood with him. All the men facing this adversity did so with dignity and pride.

"The last time I was here Lavar gave me a single purple rose." Chalna smiled.

"He loves you, dear," Nateer said. "I've never seen him light up like he does when he is around you."

"I wish he could be with me now so I could help him," Chalna thought aloud.

"I know he wishes the same, dear, but they all need to be without distraction if we are able to survive these invaders," Nateer said. "I know this may sound odd, but can we go out to the balcony and stand in the rain?"

"You know what? That sounds like a great idea." Chalna laughed. "Let's go."

The two ladies rose and walked briskly to the front doors of the castle. The guards held the doors against the intense wind. The ladies, each with the arm of a guard, leaned forward and headed into the wind. The rain beat down upon them, drenching their gowns in minutes. Chalna threw her arms out at her sides and pulled her head back. She closed her eyes and opened her mouth, listening to the splash of the water as it filled her mouth. She spat the water out and laughed.

The queen, more dignified, opened her mouth to let a little rain filter in and spat it out in the same manner as Chalna. They laughed and embraced and swung around in circles, enjoying the storm.

"I can't remember when I've had this much fun." The queen chuckled.

"It's good to see you smile again, Your Highness." Chalna said, smiling too.

In the council chambers of the castle, Elisiah, Lavar and Tragar had assembled with a cast of farmers, loggers, miners and fisherman to discuss the initial plans. After a few minutes of introductions, the meeting was called to order.

"Our plan is simple but requires the input of all of you," Elisiah said. "Timing will be crucial. We need to divide the remaining army to defeat them. Separate them, spread them out and get them out of formation to confuse them."

Looking at the head of mining operations, a Mr. Remanus, Elisiah motioned for the man to come forward. "We need the mountain behind Kataan city to fall, a landslide to make them nervous. If it's large enough, we can take out most of the city and isolate the king." Elisiah smiled.

"I can do that." Remanus also smiled. "With that mountain as water-logged as it is, I'm surprised it hasn't come down already."

"Mr. Toulu, as a logger, I think you could plan a nasty surprise for our foreign guests." Elisiah looked at a big burly man with a double-bladed axe in his hand. "I have a special plan for you and your men."

"We are going to need to get them to the canyon below the dam. It's narrow and steep on both sides. Easy pickings," Toulu replied.

"Mr. Blakenship. As a fisherman, you are used to the rough seas, and I will need you to attack the remaining ship in the harbour. Yours will be a most dangerous task. Can we count on you?" Elisiah asked.

The man stood to face Elisiah. "We will do what must be done. I will personally lead the attack."

"That leaves the rest of us," Elisiah continued. "We have a most peril-ous task ... to bring them out into our trap."

One thin, short-statured man, emaciated and an obvious escaped slave, stood, shaking and holding up his hand hesitantly. "If we blow the dam, it would wash the city into the harbour," he stated.

"We need the dam intact. It took twenty years to build and it is crucial to our crops in the spring," Lavar said.

"We can kill them in one swoop," the man insisted, still trembling.

Lavar motioned for the man to approach. As he did, Lavar took the man's head in his hands and pressed their foreheads together. "Your words will not go unheard," Lavar promised. "But we need that dam. If we have to, I promise you, it will happen."

A tear flowed down the cheek of the former slave. "Peace be with us," was all he said.

"How long before this incessant rain and wind pass?" Tragar asked.

"Thirty to forty days," Elisiah responded.

"I suggest we wait three more weeks before we attack," Tragar said confidently.

"Why so long?" Lavar asked.

"The soldiers have landed and secured the fishing village, correct?" Tragar began.

A moan and nodding of the heads in agreement confirmed his point.

"They are currently building a road to Kataan city and their resources are pressed to the limit. I say let them build. The more roads they build that are impervious to the weather, the better for you."

Another more upbeat mumble permeated through the crowd.

"The longer the king has to endure these conditions, the more agitated he will become. Agitation leads to mistakes." Tragar smiled.

Again, the crowd nodded in approval.

"If I was in his position, I would have sent for reinforcements, which I believe the ship that left two weeks ago was sent to do. At forty to fifty days roundtrip, they should arrive in three weeks. We need to attack before they arrive. The king's first advisor is a man named Beil. He is particularly dangerous, and we must also separate them. I have a plan for that, and I will take care of them personally," Tragar promised.

"We will have to get high enough on the mountain to stabilize it for a couple weeks. Then we can set explosive charges deep into shafts to create a huge slide," Remanus added. "We got this."

Standing up and looking over the crowd, a fisherman, weathered and dirty, addressed the silent room. "We will sink that ship," he stated emphatically. "We are going to get those bastards for what they have done to us."

A slow clap led to a large applause.

Beneath the cliffs of the unguarded castle, pilgrims had started to congregate. Unsheltered and vulnerable, they massed, unaware that the people they needed for support were unable to comply. For these unfortunate souls, they would provide the much-needed distraction the plan relied on. The resolve of the perpetrators of this plan would be able to save as many as possible. As the assembly was dismissed, the leaders of each group dispersed to relay their tasks to the men now charged with carrying out their responsibilities.

Colig now despised the island. He couldn't take the weather, he hated everyone near him, and he was frustrated with the knowledge that the road he was building may not be completed in time to save his neck.

All the ships that were supposed to be safe in the harbour were still isolated and being tossed about. They were totally ineffective as a display of force. He felt like a useless pawn in a much bigger game. Feeling his own mortality, his anxiety rose as he felt the situation fall away from him.

He was starting to realize the weight of command as the circumstances around his tenure become more perilous. He watched the futility of his efforts as a reflection of his career if he did not succeed. The pressure mounted as time passed.

Beil stood alone on the balcony of a house not far from King Dolmar. He no longer visited the king without an invitation and cringed when summoned to do so.

Another week had passed, and the weather had not let up. Starting to feel his own mortality, Beil also felt vulnerable and soft. Never before had these feelings entered his psyche. He was unsure of his next move and watched the days slowly pass and his initial deadline approach.

The time had come. It had been two weeks, and the time to attack was here. The plan started with the peasants. The villagers were to proceed into the forest, toward the city of Kataan. Quietly, they set up positions to draw the guards away. Now they sat and waited.

Tragar brought his part of the plan to the forefront. As the evening set in, the fisherman sent specially designed fishing rafts to the Royal Descent, pulled by brave oarsmen. Although a few were lost, the effort started to pay off when they locked on to the still magnificent ship. The men splashed oil on the hull from all sides and set it on fire. The men on board were caught completely off guard and started jumping overboard into the raging water.

Beil, standing and watching, was incensed and began to move toward the shore. He screamed at the depleted legion of guards. Sanity seemed to have left him as he watched the king's ship start to burn. Unaware of how helpless he really was, he swore at the burning ship and the men who had caused it. Intensely upset, he roared at the wind and rain. In the back of his mind, he heard the yelling voices of his men.

Now with the full moon glowing brightly through the rainclouds, the mountain above the city began to rumble. Deep yet quiet explosions preceded the earth-shaking rumble from high above them.

Dolmar felt the shaking and ran to the front of the house and out to the yard. Behind him he felt the gust of wind that came before the impending slide. Slowly at first, the face of the mountain began to move. As it descended, it increased speed until it started to swallow everything in its path in a scramble to the city and the ocean below.

Being high on a hill to the east of the city afforded a reprieve from the assault of mud and debris, but it still flowed through a series of channels surrounding the house. Although Dolmar was safe, he realized immediately that many of his men were not. The slide decimated much of the city below. A torrential flow of mud and rock engulfed everything in its path. All of the barracks were destroyed, and the landslide now entered the harbour, which was already contaminated with the debris from before.

Dolmar watched, mesmerized, as the slow-motion destruction played out in front of him. He could see his ship burning in the harbour below, until the mountain of mud caused a tsunami wave to hit the floundering vessel broadside and swamped the once impressive vessel. Only four guards remained at his side when the rumbling finally subsided.

Several minutes had passed since the slide started and the air was choked with debris particles. The light of the moon was gone in the aftermath, and the darkness was still inundated with the wind and rain.

After the air started to clear and the light slowly returned, the people began to move toward the destroyed city. Suddenly they began to scream at and taunt the surviving soldiers. Dancing in a frenzy in front of their foe, they defied their enemy to attack. In response, the disoriented soldiers left formation to pursue the inhabitants.

The wild dancing yielded to a screaming retreat made to draw the soldiers into the forest. The villagers scattered in every direction, drawing the soldiers out farther from their base. Now deep into the forest and unable to see clearly, the soldiers became confused. They could not discern friend from foe and became disoriented and unorganized. Realizing their peril, the soldiers started to return to the city.

Without warning, the roadways came under attack from swinging logs. Men were broken by the sudden attack and scrambled for the road-side. Once off the road, the men encountered deep trenches with spikes aimed at their ankles.

Now the arrows rained down from the darkness and forced the sol-diers to take cover and try to hold their ground. They screamed in pain under the relentless assault of the farmers and fisherman. Blood flowed in the deep trenches of the roadway. The returning forces of the poorly armed inhabitants overwhelmed the wounded and disabled soldiers they encountered, taking no prisoners.

Tragar and a group of hand-chosen men headed for the house of Kataan. Swords drawn, they crept silently toward the hill the house rested on. Unopposed, Tragar approached the house and stood in front of the reinforced door. Smiling back at his crew of fisherman, he ordered the obliteration of the door. As thirty men surrounded the building, a group of ten, armed with a battering ram, opened it.

The dimly lit room displayed King Dolmar, surrounded by four guards. In total silence, Tragar approached the king. The king stood defi-antly, invoking an aggressive response from the four guards around him.

Tragar stood unamused, looking at the man across from him. Although tall and powerful in stature, the king now seemed very much like any other man.

Dolmar was stoic, staring at a man that was familiar to him. Neither spoke. With reserved respect, Tragar addressed the king. "Your Grace," he started. "Your presence is no longer appreciated on these lands." He bowed as he had been taught to do.

Dolmar stood stone-faced toward his adversary. Silent and unintimi-dated, he stared deep into Tragar's eyes.

Although his blood pressure was up and the adrenaline coursed through his veins, Tragar summoned all his courage. Shaking within, he looked back at the man who was once his king. "Your majesty," Tragar began after a moment's silence. "You must come with us. Please, offer no more resistance."

Dolmar closed his eyes twice, only for a second, and ordered his men to stand down. He and his men lowered their swords to the floor. Each of the four soldiers remained on one knee. Tragar and his fisherman crossed the room, past the kneeling guards and up to the king. He stood proud as a statue, seemingly oblivious to his situation.

Tragar took another deep breath. "Your Majesty, please. I have no wish to place you in irons."

Dolmar looked down and gave the slightest nod.

"Place the men in irons," Tragar ordered. "Get the king a warm coat; we have a long way to go."

The king did not move quickly when pressed by his captures, but Tragar was not without respect for a man with the king's pedigree. With all the tension in the room, these two men seemed unattached.

"Move it now, men, we have a schedule to keep," Tragar said. He looked at Dolmar. "Your Majesty, if you please."

Heading back into the driving rain and mud-laden roads, the fishermen escorted their prisoners to the base of the cliffs. It would be hours before they got there, and it wasn't going to get any better throughout the night. In the distance they could hear the screams of the dying soldiers. Dolmar couldn't believe what he was seeing and hearing. His mighty arsenal was now gone.

Beil had survived the onslaught of the slide by running away from the moving earth toward the house occupied by the king. Most of the city, and especially the roadways, were destroyed. He could see the outline of the king's house, still standing, and he scrambled towards it. Every step was difficult, as his feet slid back with each forward attempt. He clawed with his hands and with each breath he strained to reach the house above him. The rain pounded down upon him and reinforced his resolve to reach the king.

He saw no soldiers as he pressed on. Finally reaching the house, he stood in the broken doorway. He surveyed the room but heard only the wind and rain. There were no lights and there was no sign of King Dolmar or his guards. He walked slowly through the room. Nothing was out of place, and he could see no sign of a struggle. Four swords and all the king's knives lay on the floor. He kicked at them and wondered what they were doing there. He knew his men would fight to the death, yet he saw no bodies. Everything seemed wrong.

Colig felt the earth tremble. He wondered what had just happened. All his men had stopped work when they felt the earth shake. It lasted almost five minutes, although it was not intense. He knew the shaking would have been much more intense at the epicenter.

Through the past three weeks, the road had progressed better than Colig had anticipated. As they proceeded, the men had come across many freshly downed trees beside the road, which they utilized to advance toward the city. The soldiers were grateful for the downed trees, so Commander Colig was not informed and the men looked more productive.

Colig's men were advancing at a rate of almost a mile a day, with almost a thousand working in shifts, day and night. He felt they would finish in a couple more weeks, in spite of the bad weather. His men made a mortar of mud and gravel to fill in between the tightly packed logs to make a smooth surface.

The road was now four feet above the original mud path. The men building the road used the carts left behind by the villagers to haul the gravel. Manpower was used, as no beasts of burden were left behind. The carts had to be repaired daily as they were well used.

The men with Tragar had finally reached the base of the cliff, where an entourage awaited their arrival. A series of lifts would take Tragar and Dolmar up the side of the sheer, towering mountain and eventually to the castle. Hundreds of men were prepared to power the lifts, which carried eight men at a time.

Dolmar looked up at the series of lifts and realized he had not been aware of their existence until now. Although he did not show it, he was impressed with the ingenuity of these peasants.

Tragar eased the king into the lift, silently watching him as the knew how dangerous the man could be. The king's guards were not treated with the same respect. They were kept separated from him and from each other, their hands and feet chained, and were unable to do anything more than walk. Heavy metal collars adorned their necks to prevent any attempt of escape.

The first lift rose approximately two hundred feet to a ledge. When pulled behind the rocks, the basket disappeared from view while another lift waited to ascend higher. Dolmar felt the prongs of a pitchfork pressing at his back. Still, he did not speak or acknowledge his captors.

On to the second lift, they ascended another two hundred feet to the third lift on a ledge that again hid the basket when pulled behind the rocks. Looking over the harbour from up here, Dolmar could get an overview of not only the devastation, but also the landscape from a whole new perspective.

Dolmar looked at Tragar and finally spoke. "How many of these lifts are there?" he inquired.

"Eight," Tragar revealed. "Each one rises about two hundred feet until we reach a landing. From there it is about a half-mile walk to the castle."

Dolmar again wondered why he hadn't seen this before. He realized he had not looked at this part of the cliff as it was basically hidden from the view of Kataan's house. Up and up the men rose, higher and higher, until they finally reached the top of the mountain.

Finally, Dolmar was able to see the full beauty of the magnificent castle, even from a half- mile away. As they approached it, he was in awe of its size up close. He stopped and stood for a few minutes and simply admired its black walls. Tragar allowed the king to stare for as long as he wanted.

Elisiah, Lavar, Bastian and Kataan were all at the rendezvous point to meet Tragar and his prisoners. Elisiah held Lavar back as they approached. Dolmar stopped steps away from the four men and quietly looked them up and down.

The four of them glared back at the prisoner king. Lavar wanted to hurt Dolmar as he had been hurt. Behind the men, the king's guards were escorted to Dolmar's side. Lavar pointed to each of them, one at a time. "Kill them, we don't need them anymore," he blurted out.

Elisiah and the rest of the group were surprised by the prince's outburst and stood there, momentarily stunned.

Tragar smiled a sheepish grin and grabbed the guard closest to him. He dragged the chained man by his shackled hands and threw him off the cliff. He watched as the man screamed until he hit the rocks below. Suddenly, the other three men realized their fate and tried to run. Each was immediately cut down by Tragar's men. One by one, Tragar personally tossed them off the cliff.

"Anything else, Your Majesty?" Tragar smiled, looking directly at Dolmar.

The king didn't flinch, accustomed to giving the orders. He would have killed them himself, as they had failed to protect him.

"Yes, bring that peasant along and chain him up," Lavar added. "Someone wants to see him."

In the darkness, they all headed for the castle silently, amazed at what had just happened.

"Your Majesty," Elisiah started. "We do not kill."

"Correction, Elisiah," Lavar retorted. "We did not kill." He looked back at Dolmar, who was walking proudly, hands clasped in irons.

"He did this and deserves to die for his crimes." Lavar was angry he couldn't exact revenge right now.

"That is not for us to decide," Elisiah said.

"You're right," Lavar said. "It's for my mother to decide, or he would be dead already,"

Elisiah looked at the prince. "I see your patience has run out."

Beil now came to the realization that the king had been taken prisoner. He sat in a chair looking up at the castle, wondering if that was where they had taken him and how they got him there.

He now had a dilemma. He had no soldiers to mount a rescue, and even if he did, should he? With Dolmar now gone, he could take over the army and seize power, becoming the new leader. He knew Colig was working his way back toward the city, and he had all the remaining soldiers on the island.

He noticed the rain was not as heavy today and the wind had died down. This was the first reprieve in months. Soaked and muddied, he went through the king's wardrobe and picked out some fresh clothes. As he dressed, he noticed how fine the fabric felt against his body. He could get used to this.

He lit lanterns and sat on the porch, overlooking the devastation as the night settled in. He was alone and hungry. He had never been alone unless he chose to be, usually on his ship in his cabin. He was exhausted and needed sleep. Nothing more could be done tonight, and the king's bed looked very comfortable.

The morning brought a halt to the rain and wind for the first time in months, and the sun beat down upon the island. A cool breeze came off the water and the rough seas had calmed. The full vision of the previous nights obliteration was now on full display. The debris that littered the harbour was now starting to wash up along the shoreline, and the bay started to clear. The morning tide also brought five new ships.

Beil stood on the deck of the house of Kataan and watched as longboats were launched from the vessels in the calm harbour. He surveyed the areas and decided to meet them at the shore, where the pier use to be.

As he made his way down through the heavy mud, he saw the mangled and torn bodies that were once his army. The fifteen-minute walk now took almost an hour. When he finally arrived, Commander Gar stood to greet him with a stoic look.

Gar bowed to Beil, who looked formidable in the king's apparel. He waited for his commander to speak.

"Forty days," Beil started. "I'm impressed. And with more ships than I asked for."

Gar smiled weakly. "Yes, Commander. I brought as many men and ships as could be spared. Some of the regions' governors were not happy to be relieved of so many slaves, but they dare not oppose the king's wishes." Gar looked at the lone figure of Commander Beil and asked, "Where is King Dolmar?"

"That is not your concern," Beil shot back sharply. "How many slaves did you bring back?"

"Eight hundred, Commander," Gar replied.

"Well, let's get them to work clearing this harbour," Batris ordered.

"What happened here?" Gar asked

"A miscalculation on our part," Beil conceded. "The rain caused the mountain to come down. Once we have cleared the harbour, I want to resume construction on the cliffs."

"Yes, Commander," Gar replied, looking at the mess around him. The mountain had significantly shrunk the size of the harbour, as a lot of the city had been washed down into it. He was overwhelmed at the scale of the destruction. "Where are we going to house the slaves?"

Beil smirked and looked around. There were few houses left standing, and most shops and warehouses were inundated with rock and mud. "I suppose that will have to be the first order of business," Beil responded. "I am going to have to re-evaluate how we are going to proceed. I want the slaves separated into three work forces. One will work on the cliffs, one on the harbour and one on clearing an area to house the slaves."

Gar was still looking around. "Where are all your men?" he asked quietly.

"We have lost many to the slide, but this knowledge cannot be shared. Commander Colig has almost a thousand men working their way back from the fishing village on the other side of the island and they should arrive shortly. We have to manage the slaves until he gets here. How many soldiers do you have?"

"Less than one hundred," Gar confided, realizing the peril they were in. "I'm not sure we can control that many slaves. Can I have your permission to leave most in the holds until Commander Colig arrives? We are so badly outnumbered the situation could get out of control if the slaves realize their advantage."

Beil knew Gar was correct in pointing this out and conceded to his request.

Colig was ecstatic the sun had finally graced the land. Finally, he and his men could dry out. He knew the village was only a few days' walk away and decided to take a trip there to report while his men continued with their task.

Colig and his men had been living and eating in rain-soaked tents for a month, and he was looking forward to seeing Beil and King Dolmar and having a fine meal with them. He salivated at the thought of eating something other than the slop they had been forced to survive on. Taking twenty soldiers with him and leaving the rest to work, he set out on foot for the city.

Although they were still muddy, the roadways were drying out and quickly started to harden, which made travel far easier than it had been for the longest time.

The morning also brought Elisiah, Lavar, Chalna, Tragar and Queen Nateer to the balcony for breakfast. The sea air was fresh, and everyone felt renewed. Everyone stood and waited for the queen to be seated before they sat or spoke.

Nateer looked at Tragar, who was seated next to Chalna. Prince Lavar was seated next to Chalna on the other side. "Lavar told me of your capture of your former king," she began. "Tell me, how did it make you feel, capturing such a tyrant?"

"I have no feelings to speak of, Your Grace. I was merely doing what I was asked to do." Tragar bowed respectfully.

"Don't be so modest, young man. I heard it was your plan, and you executed it to perfection," she replied.

Tragar smiled. It had been a long time since he was called a young man. "Again, Your Grace, I merely executed a small part of a much larger plan. We were fortunate everything went as well as it did."

"You've softened," Nateer said, sipping her morning tea.

The comment brought a quiet chuckle from the men.

"I beg your pardon?" Tragar was confused.

"You've softened," she repeated. "When you were first brought here, you were cold and hard. I didn't think you even had a heart."

"When I came here, I didn't know I would find my child," Tragar replied. "Perhaps my heart was buried so deep in my chest that I did not know it could resurface. I was not raised as your people were. I only knew cruelty and hardship my whole life." Tragar looked at his beloved daughter. "I am very pleased that Chalna was raised here, with a loving people, away from the life I knew. I am also pleased that you have shown me a new way, given me a new purpose. Everything I have done for the past twenty years was to find my wife and daughter; that was my purpose. But I don't think I am soft."

Tragar's remarks drew a chuckle from the seated guests. He looked at them, bewildered. He had not said anything funny.

"Your Majesty …" Elisiah began.

"Call me Nateer," she said.

"Your majesty," Elisiah continued, "With the passing of the monsoon season, we have lost our advantage over our invaders." He spread his arms out over the sea. "The morning tide has brought five new enemy ships, undoubtedly filled with soldiers to rebuild their armies."

"Not soldiers," Tragar interrupted. "Slaves. They do not have soldiers to spare, but they have many slaves. I'm sure they were brought here to relieve the soldiers of the daily tasks of rebuild so they can be soldiers again."

He looked around at the captive audience. "Dolmar has only been able to hold on to power through torture and murder. He has more lands than he can rule over, and his armies are stretched very thin." Everyone was quiet as Tragar spoke, so he continued. "One of his tactics is to release hardened criminals in the lands he has conquered and employ them in his armies. That is why they are so cruel. This is the first land where he could not employ this tactic, so he was already at a disadvantage."

He looked over the silent crowd and back to Nateer. "I think our advantage is the slaves. Right now, they have very few soldiers to guard them, and until Colig returns from the fishing village with his soldiers, they are vulnerable. If we can show the slaves that Dolmar can be defeated, I think they will join us in ending his oppressive rule, not just here, but everywhere."

The group looked amongst themselves and Lavar spoke up. "You sound like you have another plan."

"I have some tactical knowledge that can help with your plans," Tragar offered.

After finishing breakfast, all the guests walked to the edge of the balcony to look over the harbour. They could see men being taken from the ships to the shore, and the cleanup was underway. Elisiah was the first to notice how few slaves were actually working in the harbour, and they were under guard of only a handful of soldiers. He wondered why five ships had brought so few slaves.

"They can't bring all the slaves off the ship. They don't have enough soldiers, so they are not showing their hand," Tragar said, answering Elisiah's silent question. He walked over to the queen and got down on one knee in front of her. "Your Grace, may I ask a favour of you?"

Nateer gazed upon him. "You have earned our respect and our favour. What can I do for you?"

"Please, Your Grace, can you tell me where my wife is buried?"

"Chalna will be your guide. I think you and your daughter should make that journey together. You have my blessing and fortunately, your wife is buried high up on this mountain, not far from the castle."

With eight hundred new slaves, Beil was feeling better about his chances of fulfilling his mission. With only a few hundred working at a time, and working three shifts around the clock, tons of earth was being moved, and soon they would be able to rebuild the city. Carpenters built carts, and the slaves used them under the watchful eye of Commander Beil. He watched from the balcony of Kataan's house, where he had the best vantage point.

No one was allowed up to the house. As it passed to late afternoon, a commotion signalled the arrival of Commander Colig and his entourage of men. Beil had mixed emotions about seeing Colig's party, as he didn't want him snooping around, but he desperately needed the men from the other three ships. He was not overly impressed to see him, but he had to deal with the situation. He put on his boots and started to make his way down to greet Colig before he approached the house. Fortunately, Colig was first detained by Commander Gar, welcoming him back from his mission. The two embraced, as they had not seen each other in almost two months.

As Beil approached, they were well into a conversation about each other's exploits for the past months. They stopped to honour Biel's presence. As the sun shone down upon them, Beil was the first to offer his hand to Colig. "Commander," Beil said. "I assume from your appearance that the road to the fishing village is nearing completion."

"Yes, Commander," Colig replied. "My men should be breaking through the forest in a matter of days."

Beil looked over to the forest and tilted his eyes toward the sun. "I need you to return immediately to the fishing village and retrieve the king's ships," he said bluntly.

Colig was stunned. "I thought perhaps a nice meal with you and Captain Gar in the presence of the king would be a nice reward for our hard work."

"The king has taken ill and won't be joining us anytime soon. Nothing serious, but with the rampant sickness already around us, it is better to let him rest. I will be your liaison to the king and will relay his orders. For now, his orders are to retrieve his ships and men so we can continue our assault on the castle," Beil stated.

"Perhaps he can join me for a meal before he is to return?" Gar asked.

Beil smirked at the suggestion. "Alright then, aboard your ship tonight, but I want you gone in the morning. Leave enough men to complete the road, but I want those ships and men back as soon as possible. We have too many slaves without adequate supervision. I don't want a repeat of the escape during the storm. They must not know how vulnerable we are."

With that, Beil retreated to the house of Kataan, leaving the two men to share their thoughts.

Both men, disappointed, returned to the shoreline to board a longboat to head to the ship now resting in calm waters.

"What happened here?" Colig asked.

"I don't know. Commander Beil won't say anything to me and he is being very secretive about the king. I haven't seen him since I got back, and no one is allowed near the house." Gar scratched his head as he looked up at Kataan's former residence.

Although the meal aboard Gar's ship was not as extravagant as Colig was expecting, he was very gracious to his host. They spent the rest of the evening trying to figure out what had happened here.

In his third day of captivity, Dolmar was starting to get restless at his inability to control the situation. He paced relentlessly. He was not used to eating the food of a prisoner, and he was not impressed.

For two days he had no visitors or any interaction with anyone, even the guards. His food was silently slid through a compartment in the door on a piece of soggy paper. He ate with his hands, which he couldn't even wash.

As frustration set in, he thought about Beil and wondered if he had survived the slide. He knew if he had he would be planning a rescue, if he could. If only he could escape, he thought. As he made plans in his mind, he heard the lock on the door open.

He stood to face the men coming through the door. Elisiah, Tragar and four guards entered the room.

"You have an audience with the queen," Elisiah stated.

Dolmar looked around at his meager surrounding and offered both hands in front of him. One of the guards shackled his wrists and ankles as he stood silently staring at Tragar. Although Dolmar was now reduced to prisoner status, Tragar still felt slightly intimidated in his presence.

With the guards surrounding the king, they walked to the edge of the gazebo in the garden. Dolmar took in every detail as he walked. He noticed the stairs and the shimmering walls. He enjoyed the pathways in the garden and could hear the waterfall long before he could see it.

Inside the gazebo sat Queen Nateer. Very upright and proper, she looked up and down the man who had murdered her husband. Dolmar was still looking around and paid little attention to the queen, trying to intimidate her through his nonchalant attitude.

"Look at me," the queen ordered.

Dolmar continued to look around and finally looked at the queen on his own terms.

"You don't seem to understand your situation," Nateer continued.

"I understand you don't understand the gravity of your own situation." Dolmar scowled back at her.

One of the guards hammered Dolmar in the back, dropping him to his knees.

Looking up at Nateer, Dolmar smiled and slowly rose back to his feet.

"Now," she continued eloquently. "If you agree to end this campaign, we will return you to your people and you can leave in peace."

Dolmar openly chuckled. "This campaign will end when you surrender to me and I agree not to kill all of you."

Another hammer to the back dropped Dolmar to his knees again. This time he rose quickly and swung wildly at the guard who had dropped him. The guard was quick and avoided the swing, dropping the hammer into Dolmar's stomach and dropping him again.

"I suspected you were an untrainable savage," Nateer stated. "You will need to be put down."

Now Tragar was the one smiling.

"Take him back to his cage," the queen ordered. "Perhaps an empty belly will change his mind."

The guards bowed to the queen and picked up Dolmar by the elbows, dragging him until he stood and walked on his own. As the guards opened the door to the damp and dingy cell, Dolmar reached out and grabbed Tragar's arm.

"I will speak with you," Dolmar demanded.

Tragar looked at the guards. "Leave him in irons and wait outside the door." Then he looked over at Lavar, who nodded in approval. The two men entered and the guards closed the door and locked it behind them.

"I know you," Dolmar began. "Your face is familiar to me."

"I'm the one who discovered this island." Tragar was unimpressed that he had already been forgotten in the eyes of the king.

"You were the one who told Beil about this place and this castle," Dolmar continued. "Why are you helping these people?"

Tragar paced the room and looked straight into Dolmar's eyes. "The alternative was death," he replied without emotion. "If I returned after being captured, I would have been debriefed and executed. That is the procedure in your empire, is it not?"

"Perhaps I should rethink that," Dolmar replied.

"Too late now." Tragar grinned.

"Perhaps not, Tragar, is it?" Dolmar said quietly.

Tragar did not answer. He merely looked at the man in chains and enjoyed the fact that the mighty king was now at his feet.

"If you help me escape, I will make you governor of the island. You can live in this castle and rule without restraint from me. My gratitude will show no bounds," Dolmar said, pleading his case.

Tragar smiled and considered the king's offer. "All I expected when I told you and Beil about this island was a commission in your navy so I could continue the search for my family."

Dolmar looked around for a moment, trying to decide how to continue. "Then you shall have it."

"You left my fate in Beil's hands." Tragar was still smiling.

"Commander Beil is the man I leave in charge of these decisions," Dolmar confided. "One cannot rule an empire without the help and advice of those closest to him."

Tragar was not impressed. "Beil has his own agenda. He wanted to make sure I would disappear. He had control over Commander Batris, who despised the fact I was made second in command of his ship." Tragar's eyes tightened at the thought of Commander Batris and his disdain. "Your reward was more punishment than reward," Tragar thought aloud.

"You advanced in rank," the king shot back. "Did you really think you would get command of a navy ship when you were merely a merchant seaman?"

Tragar leered at Dolmar. "So what would make me think that you would now let me govern an island when I can't command a ship in the navy? I was the captain of the largest merchant vessel in your kingdom. That means something!"

Dolmar thought for a moment, straightened up, and looked at Tragar. "My fate is in your hands."

"That's where you are wrong," Tragar replied, smiling. "Your fate, as well as mine, is in the hands of a woman whose husband you murdered."

"Murdered." Dolmar laughed. "I merely expedited the control of the island peasants. Batris and Beil failed in their duties to complete the task."

"Explain it any way you want," Tragar said. "But she now controls your fate, and your men are not coming to your rescue. You were given a chance to leave in peace and chose to be defiant. That has sealed your fate. I do not intend to die saving your worthless life."

With that, Tragar rapped on the cell door.

"Tragar," the king screamed, "You will pay for your insolence."

Tragar turned to the king one last time. "I think not."

In the valley, high up on the other side of the mountain, thousands of people were now safe. They had completed building an entire village community. Now that the monsoon rains had stopped, fields were being tilled and planted and the people were beginning to prosper again. Although their hearts were with the people who could not be saved, they all helped those who could.

The town was a flurry of activity. Houses were being built for the people who were arriving daily. Bastian was a very important man, and Barook had a new purpose in his life. Bastian had moved his entire family here and led an army of carpenters in the quest for more housing.

Barook was instrumental in designing the town. He planned warehouses to store food and found new sources of coal had made work easier. They built a forge so iron did not need to be shipped from the northern part of the island. That journey had become more dangerous, as the enemy soldiers were again moving up the island in search of slaves.

Safety was now more important than ever before, as the new influx of slaves meant the soldiers were now beginning to scour the island again. As it always had, the island was providing for the inhabitants. They in turn were very respectful of mother nature and took only what they needed.

Looking over the valley, Barook felt bad for the displaced wildlife that were the original inhabitants. Many had provided meat for the men who had been brought to lay out and build the town. Barook grieved for their sacrifice and made sure enough space was left for the rest to flourish.

Commander Colig had completed his return to the fishing village and was preparing to board the Revenge to sail back to the port as Commander Beil had ordered. On the new, nearly completed road, travel was much quicker. By the time he made his return to port, his men would have completed the route.

His men now occupied the village and were a little too comfortable for his liking. They had become too complacent in his absence, and he would need to do something about it. He requested the presence of the division leaders on his ship. He was planning a feast to celebrate the completion of their latest task. He chose a large warehouse for the feast; large enough for the six hundred men under his command. Although his divisions had over eight hundred slaves, he did not plan on returning with all of them.

In an act of personal defiance, he would allow his men to torture and kill a hundred for sport. His men slaughtered the remaining animals for the feast, including deer, dogs, pigs, rabbits and any fowl they could hunt. The slaves preparing the feast were chained together so they could not escape, while his men partied. The slaves were in no condition to escape even if they wanted to, as many had not eaten in days. Food was scarce, and they could eat only what they could find.

A roaring fire was lit on the beach near the dock and the men drank what they could find, as the ship's cargo holds were nearly empty. The men ate and drank excessively, forgetting where they were for a while and making the most of Commander Colig's generosity. After they had their fill, Colig turned his attention to the slaves. He ordered one hundred slaves be brought out for the enjoyment of his men and he retired to the Revenge with one of the few remaining female slaves.

The soldiers went wild on the beach, taking turns beating the slaves mercilessly. Within an hour, all one hundred were dead. Unsatisfied, the drunken soldiers gathered more slaves, and in a frenzy, killed them as well. Long into the night, the soldiers tortured and killed the decrepit slaves.

Early the next morning, Commander Colig stood on the bridge of the Revenge and took in the carnage that was strewn across the landscape. Hundreds of bodies were heaped up in small piles, and many of his own men were passed out on the dock and beach.

Colig was infuriated. "Gather the division leaders," he demanded.

Beil also rose early, as the bright sun shone through the windows of Kataan's house. He stretched, and still naked, walked out onto the front porch. He could see the slaves were already hard at work clearing debris and working their way back toward the cliffs.

With his hands on his hips, he stared up at the castle and wondered about the fate of Dolmar. In the distance he could see an approaching soldier. He assumed it was one of Colig's men coming to report on the completion of the road.

He stood and waited, unconcerned about the state of his undress. The soldier stopped fifty feet away and waited for Beil to acknowledge him. Finally, Beil motioned for the man to approach. As he walked toward Biel, the soldier was careful not to notice the disrobed commander and looked at the ground as he walked.

"Report," Beil demanded.

"Commander. I bring news of the completion of the road from the fishing village to … here." The man still looked at the ground.

"How many soldiers do you have, and how many slaves?" Beil retorted.

"I have one hundred and fifty men and two hundred slaves. Commander Colig has six hundred soldiers and seven hundred slaves," the soldier replied.

"How long before Commander Colig returns?" Beil asked.

"He should return in two days now the seas have calmed." The man still looked down.

"Take your men to Commander Gar so he can reassign them to their new tasks. Have the slaves reintegrated with the others so we can get this mess cleaned up," Beil demanded.

"As you wish, Commander. Are there any other orders from the king I should relay to Commander Gar?" the man enquired.

"Not at this point," Beil replied. "I will send for Commander Gar, once Commander Colig returns."

With that, the soldier slapped his chest with his right hand and thrust it forward. He backed away without looking up.

With the division leaders gathered on the dock, Colig approached in a longboat. His men brought the longboat alongside the dock and he disembarked. He walked past the ten men who were charged with leading the soldiers under his command. He looked into the eyes of each, his hands clasped behind his back. He said nothing as he approached the first pile of dead slaves.

Fear now entered the men, as they knew Commander Colig was not happy. He looked back at the first man in line. He pointed at him and gestured for him to approach. As the man did, Colig scowled. "Start counting."

Shaken, the man was not sure what the commander wanted.

"The slaves," Colig offered. "Start counting."

The other nine men stood rigidly as the man counted the slaves in the first pile. Once he had reached one hundred, Colig stopped him.

"One hundred," he repeated. He looked at them all again. "One hundred."

The men dare not look at Colig's hard eyes. He looked down the beach at the rest of the dead slaves. "Continue counting."

The man continued to count the carcasses on the beach. After ten minutes, he returned. "One hundred and eighty-nine dead," he sheepishly reported.

"Follow me," Colig ordered the men, who were now surrounded by armed guards.

Approaching the raised road, Colig noticed more dead slaves scattered amongst the trees. "Continue counting."

By now, the hungover soldiers were starting to come out of their barracks. Slowly, the six hundred soldiers all appeared and wondered what was going on. Some even dragged dead slaves out of their barracks and tossed them onto the beach.

After three hours, the body count had reached three hundred and eighty-seven dead men and women. Colig was now seething. The ten men were paralyzed with fear and the effects of the evening alcohol screaming in their heads.

"One hundred," Colig began again. "I gave you one hundred slaves and your men killed three hundred and eighty-seven," he screamed.

Colig drew his sword and decapitated the nearest of his subordinates. A collective gasp ran through the soldiers, many barely awake. He glared at the other nine. "Today is your lucky day," Colig warned. "If I could replace you, you would all be dead."

Colig was gritting his teeth, he was so mad. "On second thought, I can replace you," He screamed. With all his remaining soldiers looking on in terror, he motioned for his personal guards to detain the leaders. One by one, he personally executed the nine men.

Having satisfied his own thirst for blood, Colig ordered most of the remaining soldiers back on the ships for their return to the city of Kataan. He ordered two hundred men to escort the slaves back along the newly built road.

Once everything had been organized, they abandoned the fishing village.

Elisiah and Queen Nateer spent the morning on the balcony overlooking the harbour, which was now bustling with activity.

"These people are incredibly single-minded in their approach to completing tasks," the Queen noticed.

"I'm amazed how effective they have been at clearing the harbour," Elisiah added.

"There are very few of our people left in slavery," Nateer said.

"Most escaped in the storms and are now safe with their families in the valley," Elisiah stated.

"I see they have finished the road from the fishing village," Nateer said.

"Very cordial of them to build a road for us," Elisiah mused.

Nateer was quiet for a moment, then asked, "How long do you think it will take them to get up here?"

"Up here?" Elisiah enquired. "According to Tragar, they will run out of time."

"Do you think they will try to rescue their king?" Nateer wondered.

Elisiah smiled. "Your Majesty, these people are not like yours. They live in fear of their king, and I do not think they are in a hurry to continue that regime."

"Do you think they will abandon him?" she asked. "If so, he will be of little use to us."

"Some of his men will seek the reward that would come with rescuing the king, but I suspect there are others who wish to replace him. When I look down to the house of Kataan, I can't see any urgency in getting the king back. They appear to be continuing without their king as if he were still there. Either way, they will have to show their hand soon," Elisiah surmised.

Lavar and Chalna approached them hand in hand, followed by a smiling Irid Tragar.

The queen was surprised. "Mr. Tragar, I don't think I've seen you smile like that before."

He bowed graciously. "My queen." He surprised everyone. Silence followed as they all looked at each other.

Tragar looked at the silent group. "What?"

They all chuckled.

"It seems your daughter has had a positive influence on you." The queen was smiling for the first time in a long time.

"It's a beautiful day, Your Grace, and I am in the company of two beautiful women," Tragar responded. Both ladies blushed.

Tragar put his large paw on Lavar's shoulder. "And this handsome young man will soon be a part of my family." Tragar grinned widely. Now it was Lavar who was blushing.

"Tell me, Prince Lavar," Tragar asked, looking at him. "When will this happen?" He was teasing the young man.

Lavar looked deep into Chalna's eyes and gently squeezed her hand. "Now is not the time," he said quietly. "I wish it was."

Chalna put her head against Lavar's shoulder and he stroked her hair.

"When is the last time you were that happy?" Nateer asked Irid.

"Twenty years, and now I have been happy since I first laid eyes on my daughter again." He stood in silence for a second. "Before that, it was twenty years ago, when I married Chalna's mother."

"Was she beautiful?" Chalna asked.

A tear started to form in Irid's eyes. "You are a perfect image of your mother. That is what makes it so very hard for me."

Looking at Tragar, Elisiah asked, "What do you think we should do now?" This brought everyone back to reality.

Irid turned to wipe his eye, not wanting to show vulnerability. "I think, with all due respect, that we should let them carry on."

Elisiah was surprised. "Why?"

"They are doing a great job of rebuilding the city and roadways, so why stop them?" Tragar smiled.

"That's a good point," Elisiah conceded.

"I won't stand for their brutal behaviour," the queen interrupted. "I don't care that those slaves are not our people. They have families, and I will not condone the behaviour of these beasts, even if it benefits us. We must end this."

The men looked at each other in silence.

Tragar was the first to speak. "Very well. Once Commander Colig returns to port, we will end this."

"How do you plan to do this?" Elisiah asked.

"In a way they will understand, I need to see Marta." was all he said.

For four more days Dolmar sat in his damp, dark cell. His only contact with the outside world was when the slot in the door opened, delivering his daily ration. He heard nothing at all. His internal rage was beginning to fade, and he was starting to come to terms with his captivity. So many things were going through his head. Not only his own situation, but all his kingdom, all his conquered countries, his armies and Beil. He thought about Beil a lot and wondered.

Beil stood on the porch as he had for the past week. The cleanup was proceeding well, and he had additional defences with the arrival of Colig's first soldiers.

Rounding the horn, Commander Colig led the four remaining ships and set anchor offshore. Beil knew he was running out of time, as sooner or later the other commanders and captains would find out about King Dolmar. He had to act quickly. He signalled for one of the guards and had him saddle the king's horse.

On the Revenge, Commander Colig was preparing a longboat for his meeting with Commander Beil in the former house of Kataan. He just wanted to get a glimpse of the king.

Commander Gar was also looking over the harbour and watched as Colig's boat reached the shore.

As he disembarked from the small craft, Colig could not see any welcoming committee. He expected at least a carriage to take him up to the house. He looked more closely at the damage that had been done to the city and realized where the shaking had come from earlier.

Before he could obtain a form of transportation, Colig saw Commander Beil arriving on the king's horse. He stood, puzzled, with his hands on his hips, as Beil stopped beside him. Beil looked down at Colig. "I need your seven hundred slaves to start working on the cliffs again."

"I don't have seven hundred slaves," Colig confessed. "I have three hundred and thirteen."

"Your own division leader told me you had seven hundred." Beil sat a little more upright in the saddle.

Colig felt small under the shadow of the enormous horse.

Beil was burning inside and wanted to kill someone. "And your soldiers?"

"Five hundred and ninety," Colig replied.

"Six hundred." Beil raised his voice. "You are supposed to have six hundred."

"We had an uprising," Colig lied.

"And almost four hundred slaves got killed?" Beil raised his voice a little more. Colig did not reply.

"Get your slaves unloaded and get them to work on the cliffs. Is that understood?" Beil belted out.

"Yes, Commander." Colig was even more confused at Beil's behavior.

"What happened to the ten soldiers?" Beil demanded.

"They were targeted in the uprising," Colig lied again. "They were the section leaders."

With that, Beil turned the mighty steed around and headed back toward the house.

Colig was left wondering what had just happened. Although he was unsure of Beil's behaviour, he wasn't going to disobey his direct orders. Before he returned to his ship, Colig decided to have a look around. He walked amongst the soldiers under the command of Gar. He talked to a few of the division leaders and it seemed Commander Beil was the only one seen giving orders. No one had seen the king since the landslide. He decided it was time to visit Captain Gar and the other ships' captains.

As the sun dropped over the mountains, the remaining eight ships' captains gathered aboard the Revenge. Colig wanted an evening meeting so Beil could not detect them arriving on his ship. Once everyone had arrived, they gathered in Colig's quarters.

Although he was not the senior officer there, Colig led the conversation. "I'm concerned about Commander Beil," he started. "Upon our return from building the road, I received a dressing down, rather than the usual meeting with the king." He looked at the others, who were unimpressed at this time.

"Beil arrived on the king's horse," he said. "Have any of you ever heard of the king allowing his horse to be ridden by anyone other than himself?"

They looked amongst themselves, shaking their heads.

"When is the last time any of you saw the king?" Colig asked.

"I haven't seen him since I returned," Captain Gar said.

The captain of the Royal Descent stood and waited for the men to stop mumbling. Captain Maxum was the most experienced of the captains. He had survived by swimming to the nearest ship. "My ship had been in the harbour for almost three months before it was destroyed. Every day I would converse with the king or one of his personal guards until a week ago, when the earth slid from the mountain." Maxum looked around. "I have not heard from him since. On the balcony of the king's house, I see only Commander Beil."

"What if something has happened to the king?" Gar asked. "Beil told me he was ill and needed rest."

"If something has happened to the king," Maxum said, tightening his eyes, "I will not follow Commander Beil." He looked around for a reaction but saw none.

"If we go as a unit, Beil will not be able to impose his will," Colig suggested. The others nodded in approval. "I suggest tomorrow morning, before we disperse the slaves, we should confront Commander Beil and get our orders directly from the king, if he still is the king."

"Agreed," Maxum said, followed by the rest of the men.

Another glorious morning blossomed before Lavar and Chalna as they watched the sun rise from the balcony. From here they saw the ships and crew start their daily routine, but today something was different. Only one boat from each ship was being launched, and none were slaves. Lavar realized they were the ships' captains by the way they were dressed and asked Chalna to quickly fetch Elisiah and her father while he watched.

Chalna ran for the castle doors. Within a few minutes she returned with the men. Lavar was at the edge, intently looking down at the harbour through the telescope.

"What is it you see?" Elisiah asked Lavar as they approached.

"Look." Lavar seemed confused.

"Eight boats, what of it?" Elisiah observed.

"Eight commanders," Lavar pointed out. "All going up to Kataan's house."

Elisiah smiled as he looked at Tragar. "To see the king, no doubt."

"No doubt," Tragar replied. "Please excuse me, I have a few things to do." Tragar now bowed to the prince, who was a bit taken aback.

The men watched with Chalna as Commander Beil exited the house of Kataan and headed to meet the eight men on the beach.

"How I would love to hear that conversation…" Lavar said quietly.

Within ten minutes, the eight captains were intercepted by Commander Biel and his personal guards. They were still a long way from the house and the king.

Maxum took the lead. "We have come to see the king," he demanded.

Beil smirked. "Get back to work," he ordered.

"Not until we see the king." Maxum was not intimidated.

"You will do as I have ordered." Beil spat out the words.

"The king gives orders around here, Commander, not you," Colig spoke up.

Beil was infuriated by having a subordinate speak to him in such a manner. "The king is ill and cannot be disturbed," he lied.

"We will see him now," Maxum demanded.

Beil drew his sword and pointed it into Maxum's chest. Colig looked over his shoulder at his men that had followed behind and nodded. Maxum's men had already drawn their bows and were pointing them at Commander Beil.

"Drop your sword, Commander," Maxum ordered.

Beil could see the poised soldiers and slowly lowered his weapon but did not drop it. As Maxum began to walk past Beil, he heard the defiant yell of the commander and dropped to his knees just in time to avoid a wild swing of the sword in Beil's hand.

Before he could stand, he heard the dull thud of an arrow piercing Beil's chest. Before Biel hit the ground, five more arrows were imbedded in him. Blood trickled from his mouth as he sank to his knees and dropped his sword on the ground.

Beil's personal guards did not move, under threat of the same.

Colig walked up to his adversary, who was still on his knees with his head down. He put his foot on Beil's shoulder and pushed him over. The rest of the men walked past him without looking down.

Maxum led the way to the house, followed by Colig and then Gar. Maxum was getting nervous as he got closer to the house. If the king was merely resting, he would pay for Beil's life with his own, and probably every one of the captains that had staged this little revolt.

He opened the door of the unguarded house. He could hear nothing as he entered. He stood with the other seven men as the guards searched the entire house.

"There is no one here," a guard reported. The news did not relieve the tension in the room.

Tragar and four of the queen's guards opened the cell of King Dolmar. The king squinted as the light entered the room for the first time in days.

"Get up," Tragar demanded. "We must hurry."

Dolmar was confused by the order.

"Hurry, if we are going to escape, we must do it now." Tragar was full of adrenaline. "Remove his chains," he ordered the guard.

Quickly, the guard removed the chains, which fell to the floor.

"Where are we going?" Dolmar asked, still confused.

"I decided I want this castle after all," Tragar replied. "We must hurry to the lifts. I have bribed the guards to let us go. We must take them with us as part of their loyalty."

Dolmar was now getting excited as the men ran for the lifts. Dolmar was having a hard time running, as he had not eaten in a couple days. He stumbled and fell repeatedly but was lifted by the guards and forced to run again.

When they reached the series of lifts, Dolmar was exhausted and his chest pounded. The guards pressed them into the first lift and began lowering them down.

Far below in the remnants of the city, the eight remaining captains bickered amongst themselves about what to do next. The walked quickly to the city centre and stood in the square, yelling and pointing. They all realized that the power was now open to the strongest of the leaders, and each wanted to be that man. So far, Maxum and Colig had been able to maintain order, due to the sheer number of men under their command.

Dolmar was excited to be reunited with Beil and the rest of his armies. As they descended in each lift, he began to feel more comfortable. But when they reached the last lift, the basket was nowhere in sight.

Tragar looked back up to the top of the cliff and waved his arms. Suddenly, a deafening roar started high above and an avalanche of boulders shot past them, some fifty feet away.

"What was that?" Dolmar pleaded. "And where is the last lift?"

"That was to get the attention of your men." Tragar smiled. The guards grabbed the king and restrained him.

In the city below, the avalanche brought an end to the quarreling and had the men focussed on the cliff, where they could see the silhouettes of a small group of men. Although it was a long distance, when observed through their magnifying glass, they knew it was their king by the clothing he was wearing.

They all started walking to the cliff and then broke into a trot to get there as quickly as possible.

Tragar stood high above, beside Dolmar, who was becoming impatient.

"What is the meaning of this?" the king roared.

"I intend to return you to your men." Tragar smiled slyly. "Once they have arrived, I will lower you down."

"Then why the guards?" Dolmar was livid.

"Just to make sure you keep your word to me," Tragar replied. "Once you have been returned, I will return to the castle and take my rightful place."

"You will get your reward once I am returned. I will keep my word." Dolmar eased up. The guards, in turn, released their grip on the king.

It took a full twenty minutes for the eight leaders and their legion of followers to reach the base of the cliff.

Looking down upon them and making sure he had their full attention, Tragar pulled a four-inch blade from inside his sleeve and plunged it into the chest of the shocked king.

"I believe this is your knife." Tragar smiled and pushed the king off the ledge. Dolmar screamed as he fell the two hundred feet to the army below. Tragar shook his head, as he stepped back into the lift and enjoyed the ascent back to the castle.

Maxum was the first to reach the mangled remains of the king. He knew of the anarchy that would follow once the death of the king reached the distant shores of his kingdom. Colig and Gar were the next to gaze upon the body. A long silence followed as each man dealt with the reality of the situation.

Colig was the first to speak. "I have a province to return to. I claim the province of Alkar. Beil will not be returning. There is nothing here for me," he concluded.

"I claim the throne," Maxum demanded. "Is there any man here who opposes me?"

The rest of the men stood blankly, each knowing they did not have the support of enough armies.

"We must surrender to the queen," Colig offered.

"I will not be led by these people," Gar interrupted. "And I will not surrender. I lead the fleet in the harbour, and I will decide what happens in this kingdom." He stepped well out of bounds.

"You will surrender your fleet to me, and you will follow my orders, or you will be relieved of command," Maxum ordered.

Gar stepped forward, moving closer to Maxum. "This kingdom will follow me."

Maxum shook his head and looked at Gar, who stood defiantly in front of him. He raised his hand over his head and chopped through the air. A single arrow ripped into the back of Gar's neck. He gurgled as he dropped to his knees and finally to the ground.

"You have been relieved of your command," Maxum said, ending the conflict. He looked around at the rest of the men. There was no further discussion.

"We will leave this land and re-establish our own kingdom," Maxum said. "Each of you will have your own land to govern, if you wish. You can remain in command of your ships and fleet if you want," he offered. "Follow me and you will retain your positions of power." He looked each man in the eyes. "If you do not, the kingdom will perish."

The men, still silent, considered their options. Colig looked to his men. "Bring the body of the king." Four of his soldiers gathered the crumpled body and returned to the shore, a half hour away.

Tragar had now returned to the castle and was met by Elisiah.

"Safe trip, Tragar?" he said.

"As planned." Tragar said. "Gather the royal family on the balcony this evening. They might enjoy what they are about to see."

Elisiah was curious about his comments but did as Tragar had asked. He turned and walked back to the doors. Tragar stayed and watched as the men in the city below constructed a large raft. They placed hay and kindling inside larger pieces of wood and assembled it on the raft. As night fell over the land, the body of the king was placed upon the pile of wood.

The body of Commander Beil was lashed to a long pole and hoisted up in the harbour, as he had done to so many of his own men, as well as his enemies.

The soldiers pushed the raft into the harbour and lit it on fire.

The royal family had all gathered on the balcony, along with Kataan and Marta and the rest of the elders. They stood in silence and watched the raft become a raging inferno as it drifted out to sea. After about forty-five minutes, the raft had burned completely and the soldiers began to disperse.

Tragar was the first to reach the balcony as the sun started to rise the next morning. He stood there alone until Prince Lavar finally came and stood beside him. Silently, the two looked over the empty harbour. They could see people on the beach below, but the ships were gone.

"Slaves," Tragar said.

"Not any longer," Prince Lavar revealed. "Let's go welcome them."

As the sun rose over the harbour, the trees swayed in the morning breeze.